The Therapist's Daughter

Megan Taylor

BLOODHOUND
— B O O K S —

Print ISBN: 978-1-917214-45-2

With love to my fabulous sister, Catherine, a very different Cat to the one in this book, and for Mum, again and always; hope you're still watching, xx

Part One

Chapter 1

Jill

6 August 2002

"Enough," Jill muttered. "For Christ's sake, *stop*."

She refused to put up with the racket from her daughter's room any longer. The ceiling was quivering, the whole house bristling, and with her head feeling just as invaded, she stalked out into the hall. But she'd barely mounted the stairs when the girls' infuriating whoops and laughter erupted into screams.

The noise was dazzling. It sheared the air like knives and Jill's first instinct was to cover her face. Instead, she broke into a run.

But though she flew up the steps two at a time, as soon as she hit the landing, everything apart from the screaming slowed to a sludgy dreamlike pace. The wallpaper's roses tumbled lazily past, the deep pile carpet tugged at her heels, and even when she made it, panting, to Caitlin's door, she felt like she wasn't keeping up, as if she'd left herself behind.

Another Jill remained holed up in the living room, still jabbing at the stereo and knocking back her Chardonnay, and still cursing Richard – *bloody Richard* – for abandoning her. He should have been home hours ago.

Except what was she thinking? Caitlin was behind that

door, part of those screams, and coming abruptly awake, Jill grasped hold of the handle and plunged inside, and the darkness was nearly as shocking as the sound. She longed to back away.

But Jill pushed on – what choice did she have? – and though her vision was struggling to adjust, the shadows weren't as solid as they'd first appeared. Here and there, they were punctured with tiny wavering stars and *candles*, she realised. At least the dark made some sort of sense.

Flames winked across the bookshelves and danced among the clutter on Caitlin's dressing table, the mirror doubling their shine. But the shadows were drifting with more than candle smoke and as the sweet earthy tang of marijuana hit the back of Jill's throat, her anger returned. Turning to the hazy girl shapes emerging from the bed, "*Caitlin*," she barked. "Stop this! You stop this noise right now."

But the screaming didn't stop. It didn't falter. It went on and on, raking through Jill's thoughts, and when she tried again – "Caitlin... Cat? My Kitty-Cat?" – her voice dropped to a hopeless whisper. And as she forced herself closer, it dawned on her that the bed held just Samantha and Alice, Caitlin's friends from school. Only they looked nothing like their usual good-girl selves.

Cowering together among the sheets, their faces were straining glimmering masks, their mouths black ragged holes, and as the screams kept tearing out of them, neither girl turned to Jill; they didn't even glance her way. They appeared concentrated, staring past the glowing dressing table to the window's alcove. In dread, Jill followed their gaze.

For a terrible icy moment, she expected to find the sash yanked open, the lace curtains billowing, and an intruder from a nightmare straddling the sill–

But the curtains drooped, limp as cobwebs, around a square of deeper dark. The night was contained, the window

4

sealed, the wall below it flickering gently. More candles clustered the alcove's corners and two more figures were huddled on the floor between them. Caitlin and her best friend.

The flames leapt and sputtered as Jill rushed over, but her daughter didn't turn to her either; it was like she didn't exist. The girls were hunched so close their shoulders merged, and it was impossible to tell if Caitlin was screaming. There was no separating her voice from the endless sound and Jill couldn't see her face.

The girls' heads hung together, a snarl of badly dyed black hair crawling over Caitlin's pallid blonde. They might have been praying, bowed down like that on their bended knees, except they were both reaching out to the inky floor – and were they holding hands?

Head ringing, Jill tried to swallow down a wave of disgust and focus on Caitlin, but the other girl, Livy McKinnell, refused to be wiped out. Caitlin was seventeen, but she looked delicate through the shadows, still Jill's doll-like little girl, whereas Livy – all hips and breasts, all overflowing flesh – was clearly something else.

Her fault, Jill thought. It was bound to be. *Whatever the hell this is–*

Then she tripped. She almost fell and as she wobbled, regaining her balance, an ashtray rolled away from her tottering feet. It spun towards the kneeling girls in a blur of spilling dog-ends, then bumped to a stop, striking the board set out between them.

Jill's outraged mouth dropped open – *the board, Richard's bloody Ouija board* – and "Christ," she groaned. Of course, she should have guessed her irresponsible husband was somehow accountable too. Bloody Richard and his bloody games.

When he gets home, Jill thought, and then *if he ever gets home...* And how pathetic, how ridiculous, the entire night was – why wouldn't the screaming stop?

"I told you to *stop*," she shouted, and Caitlin looked up at her at last.

But though Jill could see that her daughter's mouth was closed, her eyes were stretched so cartoon-wide that Jill felt a wild urge to laugh and perhaps that was the right response? The situation was patently absurd.

Except the girls on the bed were still screaming, barely pausing for breath, and no matter what she tried to tell herself, Jill was still afraid.

Through the shadows, Livy had also raised her head. She was staring at Jill with a different kind of intensity, both hands clamped over Caitlin's, and Jill was briefly spellbound by the candlelit tangle of their fingers and the thin glint of the upturned glass they were clasping as it slid on across the board.

"*Jesus Christ,*" she heard herself begin again and then a loud crack interrupted her. It undid everything. The darkness split and in the second before it settled, the entire room appeared to explode in jagged fragments. Even the screaming fell apart.

But still Jill's head went on jangling and it took her a few more frazzled seconds to understand. *It's just the Ouija glass.*

The glass the girls had been using as a pointer had shattered, and quite frankly, thank Christ for that. The madness seemed to be over, the screams dissolving into muffled splutters and gasps and childish hitching sobs.

But while Caitlin slouched over the board, her shoulders sagging, Livy had pulled away, her arms springing up as if released. And though Jill caught the mottled flesh of her palms, her hands glistening, cut open, it was the girl's shining gaze she returned to. The way that Livy was looking at Jill–

Her eyes were murderous.

Chapter 2

Caitlin

22 December 2017

"Home for Christmas?"

The woman's voice is light and level, but I almost jump out of my seat.

Since boarding, I'd been huddling by the window, my back turned to the carriage. I wanted to sleep but knew I wouldn't. Instead, I'd been paying close attention to the rain clinging to the glass. The delicate threads and silvery scratches, the countless, quivering, soft beads... I was doing my best to ignore the countryside beyond the drops. The bare black bars of winter trees.

But the woman – a smiling train guard, wearing too much thick beige lip gloss – makes everything rush back.

"What?" I snap.

Her smile doesn't falter. She nods at the suitcase jammed against my legs and the bags I've piled onto the seat beside mine. Gift wrap pokes between the handles, a barricade of cheery Santas and electric-blue reindeer. Not that I needed to have bothered fencing myself in; there weren't many passengers to start with, and now, judging from a quick glance around the carriage, I might well be the last one left. But towards the end of the line, the train was rarely busy, and I'm not exactly reassured.

"Going home?" she asks again.

My mouth goes dry. What the fuck am I supposed to say?

For several long seconds, we stare at one another, her smeared lips still smiling and shimmering, her head cocked slightly to one side. But then she's asking to check my ticket, and in relief, I break away, because I can do this bit, this normal, routine bit. I rummage through my packages for my purse.

But when I turn back, time sways with the carriage. Everything transforms. For a moment, the upholstery is garishly patterned, and the ceiling sallow. I smell cigarette smoke and the oversweet, honeyed perfume that my old classmates, Sam and Ali, used to wear. There's also the wet dog scent of sodden wool, and I remember my old, knitted school tights. That distinct itch against my thighs.

Stop, I think. *Stop it, Caitlin. You're a grown woman for fuck's sake.*

But for years I took this line most weekdays, rattling back and forth to my school in the city, and it's an effort to haul myself into the present. The teenager inside me is abruptly awake and she's restless, impatient to end this very same journey, to return to the village and catch up with Livy after dark.

While I'm shaking my head to clear it, the woman takes my ticket, scrawls on it with a biro, and calmly hands it back. Then she's sidling away with surprising grace, hips swinging with the aisle. I resist the urge to call her back. I've no idea what I want to say. Maybe an apology for my strangeness or my rudeness? Surely, I don't honestly intend to explain.

It's probably just that she's in her thirties, around my age – my real age – and I've screwed up the opportunity to have an adult conversation that might have reminded me of who I actually am.

Obviously, I say nothing, and within a minute, I'm snidely blaming the guard, specifically for her lip gloss. It belongs so completely in the fucking past.

And it's hopeless, even my thoughts are adolescent. A certain kind of adolescent, I correct myself; Scarlet never swears. Light-haired and light-hearted, my daughter's an entirely different creature to how I remember Sam and Ali, with their endless, snarky whispering, and of course, Livy was unique.

I cut the thought off before it can plunge me any deeper. My past has nothing to do with Scarlet, and though she turned thirteen three months ago, I've tried not to watch her too closely. So many mothers I know have made that mistake, overanalysing every miniscule change in their teenagers as if, at any moment, they might become demonically possessed.

But then, Scarlet's made it easy. It's impossible to imagine her growing secretive or sulky, let alone screaming and slamming doors. She isn't anything like the girl I used to be either; she's honest and open, still childishly unguarded. With her irrepressible giggles and optimism, she grounds me. My bright and funny steadying force.

Except right now, Scarlet's with her father, and since they're spending Christmas with his twenty-four-year-old girlfriend in Tenerife, I might well be on the verge of crazy even without this journey, the dizzying reality of *going back*.

Glancing at my crowded bags, I resist the urge to dig out my phone. I've already read Scarlet's last text repeatedly, and she'll be zipping through the sky by now, already far away. Besides, I'd also end up checking the time, and I don't want to see it. The minutes ticking me on.

But between the glittering raindrops, the woods are

dropping back, and I can't help acknowledging the familiar valley. The swirling dark river, gouging the land in two, is waiting up ahead. Soon the train will cross the bridge. It won't be long until I'm there.

I lift my gaze beyond the trees to the distant blurry hills. Towards their peaks, they're patchily pale. The leftover snow, gripping stubbornly on despite the rain, forms a bleak uneven covering like dirty gauze. *Hardly a winter wonderland*, I think, picturing the cards abandoned in my empty living room. All my friends' cheery messages left to gather dust.

These days, my friends are polite and dutiful. We meet in coffee shops or the occasional, well-lit, generic bar, where nothing ever gets too loud or messy. Still, they're generally a supportive group; they've even helped me out with work, Marissa offering me a few admin hours at her husband's gallery, and Clara begging me to help her out in the deli as if I'm the one doing her a favour and the money's just an afterthought.

Clara's been particularly considerate, superficially at least. When she discovered I'd be spending the entire festive period without Scarlet, she worried, although after I explained my plans, her concern turned to a simpler sympathy and perhaps a ripple of sly relief. Naturally, she'd have invited me otherwise, but clearly, I ought to be spending the time with my sick mother, especially if this Christmas might turn out to be her last.

In response, I'd murmured something vaguely affirmative, or maybe only nodded, briefly picturing it the way she would: me in dutiful nurse mode, sharing poignant, tear-pricked moments of reconnection and role reversal, tucking a frail old lady into bed.

But in all honesty, I can't believe Mum's truly ill, let alone dying. She's always been so resilient, so capable and careful, and utterly in charge. As she's aged, she's remained impeccably dressed and manicured, her hair a chic silver helmet, not a single lacquered strand allowed to wriggle out of place. It's hard to imagine she's relinquished any of that control. My mother isn't the reason I'm afraid of going home.

But there's no explaining that, not to anyone, especially not to my grown-up, latte-sipping friends. We'd need to plumb a whole new, deep, dark level of emotion, and friends – as I know better than anyone – aren't what they used to be.

I blink hard while the bridge's railings go blurring past, but as the woods press in once more, I remember to refocus on the rain. But though the drops keep shining bravely on, they smear with my wet eyes. There's no hope of containing anything, and it's hardly the first moment that it has struck me – maybe we only ever get one real best friend.

Livy, I catch myself thinking. *Livy, I'm coming back...*

Although it's utterly ridiculous, pathetic, after everything, to be conjuring up the tug of her as if she might be waiting still.

But my next thought's as inevitable as it's unstoppable. *Why?* I'm asking for the billionth time. *Livy, my Livy, why?*

And now I'm no longer simply thinking her name, it's filling my body, filling every vein, pushing up hot under my skin, and it doesn't matter that it's all so stupid and wrong. That it wasn't even my tragedy.

The carriage speaker crackles, and as the sound of the guard clearing her throat drifts overhead, I picture her casually licking her caramelised lips, preparing to intone her lines.

"We will shortly be arriving at Underton. Underton is our next stop."

And the village is an electric current zapping through me; it jumps me to my feet. I grope for the handles of my bags and case, my luggage battling against me as I heave out of my seat.

Through the rain, the verge is changing. Before giving way to the platform, roughly hacked branches and burnt-looking nettles float too close alongside the windows. I plunge clumsily down the aisle.

My bags hit every empty seat and I daren't glance up in case the guard is watching, but staring down at my expensive leather boots doesn't help either. They seem almost gleeful in the way they're hurrying me on, drawing me back, back to this place that I haven't seen since my late teens. When everything I knew ended, and Livy...

When so much was torn away.

The wheels groan as they slow, and though *her tragedy*, I go on telling myself – *not mine, not mine* – I'm far from ready as the train grinds to a halt and the doors slide open with a smooth conspiratorial hiss. There's no yanking at the window or fumbling with the latch outside. The station is right there.

But the gap between the train and the platform is as wide and deep as I remember, the drop ending in heaped wet gravel like mounds of tiny, shattered bones.

I fling my bags and case across, and then, resisting the temptation to shut my eyes, make the leap myself.

Still, I land as awkwardly as my things. Bright-blue reindeer and inane, grinning Santas spill out across the slippery concrete, and as I stagger upright, pain darts from my left knee.

Ignoring it, I scuttle about, fumbling to gather up my parcels, my hair and hands immediately soaked. There's nothing gentle or quivering about this rain. Each drop's a hard, stinging pellet, so cold it's almost ice.

The doors swish shut behind me, but I go on peeling my spilt things from the puddled platform, refusing to look up until I hear the engine's thrum deepen, then the crank and moan of wheels.

The train shudders as it leaves the station, shrinking towards more smudged hills and a gloomy waiting tunnel. But I can't stand to watch the last carriage disappear, and before it's swallowed by the black, I finally allow my eyes to close.

And in my own dark, I try to take charge of my breathing, inhaling long and deep. I recognise this air. Mulch and stagnant water, a ferrous aroma from the railway tracks, and the tomblike scent of stone.

But when I open my eyes, I'm staring down at just my sodden ticket. It's sticking to my palm, and I suppose I ought to laugh, seeing what the train guard's scribbled: a blurring smiley-face. But my jaw's too gritted and I'm too chilled, already wet through. Crumpling the ticket inside my fist, I look cautiously around.

No one else has disembarked here, but then, apart from Sam and Ali and me, hardly anyone ever did. But as I scan the empty platform, a shiver runs through me. I feel small and self-conscious, not only lonely, but exposed.

The slick skin on the nape of my neck has started crawling, and with the goosebumps rising and prickling, it's suddenly undeniable – a sense of being watched.

I take a step towards the poky shelter, but there isn't anyone skulking under its dripping eaves or behind its sagging rotted bench. And beyond the shelter, there's nothing except rusted railings, coiled with reddish bracken, and the darker lace of the crowding trees.

But, abruptly, *over there*, in a gap between the twisting branches–

For a fleeting moment, I think I see her. There's the shadow of a lifted arm, a tangle of dyed black hair, and then the pattern of branches reconvenes.

There's nobody here. Just oily-looking wood, rain-battered nettles, and the platform, with its glossy pools, stretching on and on. No one's watching me, no one's waiting. It was only a trick of the greying light, or of memory, or longing.

13

Her tragedy, the refrain returns, but it carries no weight, no substance at all, and I can't pretend that I wasn't still hoping, imagining. Trying to conjure back the girl who once destroyed everything–

Livy, my first love.

Chapter 3

Jill

7 August 2002

After leaving Richard at the police station, Jill felt hot and scattered. Although the roads were clear and the drive back from the next village so familiar she could have done it in her sleep, she had to concentrate. Her expensive shades weren't thick or dark enough and each time the car broke free of the overhanging trees, she found herself flinching at the windscreen's sudden blaze. The sun seared through the glass, straight onto her face, and she couldn't keep hold of her whirling thoughts. Her head was full of embers.

When the woods eventually gave way to her weaving driveway, she pulled over haphazardly, spraying an arc of gravel towards Richard's beloved Bentley, but she paid it no attention, leaping from her car and practically fleeing to the house. Keys clenched between her damp fingers as if in self-defence.

But once inside, with the front door pressed firmly closed, Jill turned to face the hallway slowly, taking a conscious moment to seek out the house's calm. She breathed in the precious cool and quiet, the light reduced to a harmless buttercup glow against the high pale walls.

Everything was shining politely. An amber sheen to the

staircase and its curving banisters, the Georgian side table and the parquet flooring boasting a darker chocolate gleam. Richard might have chosen the house, but it was Jill who'd cherished it, remaking it, and she knew it loved her in return. The soft gilt of the antique mirror was always kind, and when she gazed into it, she didn't look messy, she didn't look *scattered*, not even after she'd removed her shades.

An elegant well-preserved woman, Jill's complexion was still good, her face still pretty, and there wasn't the slightest hint of pink to her bright blue eyes. Despite the sweat she'd felt breaking through her smooth toned skin, the ivory silk of her blouse went on clinging in all the right places without a single stain or crease. She appeared just the same, if not better, than usual. There was no suggestion of any hidden burning thoughts. She didn't look like the kind of woman whose world could erupt in flames.

And Jill could hold on to all this – her steady gaze and her designer clothes, her quiet waiting house – for these things were clear and solid. Everything else was as slippery as a dream. *But, like all nightmares, it will pass...*

With a sigh, she dropped her keys into the blue glass bowl set next to the phone on the table. They landed with a satisfying chink against Caitlin's set, but Jill had already gathered that her daughter was still at home. She could tell from the way the air was sifting; Caitlin wasn't even up.

Rarely allowed a lie-in, she was probably luxuriating in the rumpled nest she'd have made from her bedclothes, unable to believe her luck. After the previous night's fiasco with the dope-smoking and the Ouija board, she'd have expected Jill to have woken her at the crack of dawn, and that was exactly what Jill had been intending. Then the police had called.

Jill took a reluctant step towards the staircase. Her daughter was the last person she wanted to face now and as much as she appreciated the house's calm, she knew it had its limits. She feared that whatever she said, however she said it, she would make all the wrong things seem too real.

She pressed her fingertips to her eyelids and then quickly snatched her hands away. She smoothed her blouse, tugged at her cuffs, and "Come on, Jilly," she muttered. "Time to get a grip."

Because she could do this, of course she could, and not just because she hadn't any choice. Wasn't she usually an expert in composure, able to detach, to cleanly compartmentalise, while others fell apart?

But as soon as her hand closed around the smooth warmth of the banister, the hallway jolted. The sunny walls fluttered and the air condensed. Yesterday's uncharacteristic panic made a fleeting return, reigniting her flickering thoughts, and for a moment, she no longer knew if it was day or night. She almost heard the screams.

But it was a different echo that froze her. As if she was hearing the news for the first time, it hit Jill that Theresa McKinnell had been murdered.

Stabbed more than twenty times.

"Her breasts and face got the worst of it."

At the police station, it wasn't the detective but the receptionist, Lynn, who'd described it, squeezing her large body up next to Jill while she hovered at the coffee machine. Although they had met at community meetings between the villages, Jill barely knew Lynn and yet there she was, releasing the details in a gushing whisper, her plump fingers abruptly claw-like, tugging at Jill's sleeve.

"*Butchered*," she hissed, her grey eyes glittering. She was all but licking her lips.

Jill leant away, trying to surreptitiously shake free her wrist, but Lynn's grasp only tightened. She wouldn't be deterred.

"And the way they found her," Lynn said, her face craning so close that Jill, assaulted by her pungent coffee-breath, changed her mind about a cup.

"Whoever killed her didn't even try to hide her," Lynn went on. "He left the front door gaping and they found her right there, in the hallway, lying just inside. Blood *everywhere*, pooled on the floor and splashed across the walls. And apparently nothing was taken, they don't think it was a messed-up burglary. Maybe an escaped prisoner, some crony who knew Theresa's ex? Or a random psycho? A serial killer in our midst..."

The next pause was long, but eager. Jill could feel it crawling, *clawing*, between them. She knew Lynn was expecting questions or exclamations, perhaps Jill's own half-baked amateur detective theories, but staring back at those eager, unblinking, tinfoil eyes, she couldn't find a single appropriate phrase, any sort of sane response.

But then Lynn's expression changed, her patchy face paling and emptying, and when she spoke again, her words were slower, infused with a disconcertingly childlike wonder.

"Things like this," she whispered, "just don't happen here..."

In contrast, Ward, the actual detective, or inspector, or whoever he was supposed to be, had been cold and brusque with Jill when she'd arrived. Obviously rushed in from the city, his tone was as evenly clipped as his salt-and-pepper beard, as bluntly cut as his off-the-peg slate-coloured suit. He had dismissed Jill from the outset, though she'd known Theresa and Livy for as long as Richard. In Underton, it was common knowledge how close the two families had become, but Ward clearly didn't care.

"No doubt one of the uniforms will be in touch later," he'd said, before coolly informing her that the only opinions he wanted at present were *professional*, his gaze skimming over her to Richard. Of course, it was her husband, the McKinnells' trusted therapist, who Ward most wanted to see.

Jill had graciously withdrawn to the coffee machine, though the tiresomely meaningful exchange of masculine glances had inwardly made her baulk. And when Lynn pounced, she had been trying to interpret the men's low murmurs that had started as soon as her back was turned.

"Jill... *Jill*. Darling..."

Richard, she realised, was calling her now, a sense of summons undermining the endearment as he strode over, and Ward was still looming behind him, peering pointedly at his watch.

But Jill's own tingling wrist was released at last. Head bowed, Lynn was turning and bustling off as if the whole lurid discussion had been Jill's idea and she couldn't wait to get away.

"I'll need to stay a while," Richard said, and Jill tried hard not to wince. He'd shifted to the placating, secretly self-important voice normally reserved for his neediest clients. "I doubt I'll be much longer, but you needn't bother waiting. You ought to be at home. Caitlin's there all by herself."

She nodded in response; *what an understanding, unquestioning wife, unflappable even now*. But watching the men retreat down a narrow corridor – more or less the same age and build, their shoes squeaking solemnly in sync – Jill's skin turned cold.

But what struck her more than the stark fact of Theresa's death, even with Lynn's grisly details, was how the most difficult things were always left down to her. Jill would have to tell their daughter that her best friend's mother had been killed.

She couldn't do it, not quite yet. *But soon,* she promised herself, *in another ten minutes, maybe twenty.* She gazed at the kitchen table, double-checking the carefully spread sheets of newspaper and the silverware set across it in military rows. *Half an hour at the most...* Jill liked to do a thorough job.

Not that it was entirely necessary. Most of the cutlery was gleaming, but Jill was running out of chores. She'd already scoured the kitchen till the white tiles and scrubbed sink dazzled. With its wide windows and patio doors, the room sucked in light. It was usually her favourite place, but with the rising heat, it had greenhouse potential, and this afternoon, the temperature was due to exceed thirty degrees.

Outside, the lawn was already blurring into the trees, everything shimmering an underwater green, and when Jill reached across the table, the air pushed back against her. She paused, with her hand outstretched.

It was hardly the first time she had felt the house stirring around her. A change to the atmosphere, too subtle to be a breeze. Jill cocked her head, imagining the walls exhaling. A gentle tide of wafting breaths.

As peculiar as the sensation was, it didn't normally worry her. It was probably to do with the house's age or alignment, some type of pressure thing. She'd only mentioned it once to Richard in passing. A mistake she wouldn't make again.

Jill should have known the subject would provide her husband with the perfect excuse to launch into one of his lengthy monologues, blathering on about "innate sensitivity" and "exteriorisations", and in the end, she'd had to cut him off. "For Christ's sake, Richard, *that's enough.*"

A definite instruction was the only way to drag her husband back when he entered full-blown lecture mode. It never took much for him to get carried away, and recently, his interest in what he called "the psychology of superstition" was bordering on obsessive. Richard seemed to think he was on the verge of some therapeutic breakthrough, but quite frankly, Jill had little faith in his ideas for the latest book.

Besides, she had her own reasons for keeping these sensations to herself. There were times when the house's waves felt comforting. It wasn't hard to interpret them as a kind of gathering sympathy, especially when Jill was feeling particularly alone.

Except this, she realised, was different.

The air had never seemed so crowded before, as if it was no longer simply rippling or softly expanding but packed with secret life. Jill's first thought was of invisible insects. She could almost feel them whirring past her face, ruffling her hair, but then the movement shifted, and *not wings*, she thought, *but hands.*

Desperate fingers scrabbling towards her, about to snatch hold of her–

The sudden panic took Jill back to Caitlin's room and the screaming, and *stop*, she willed, just as she'd done then. *Stop all this right now.*

Unlike the girls, the house obeyed immediately. Of course it did. Unlike the girls, it loved her.

And with the kitchen settling back around her, Jill allowed herself a small wry smile, even as she drew in a shaky breath and reached up nervously to pat her hair. But her hair was fine, not a pin out of place, and the air contained only the fridge's muted electrical purr and the garden's streaming greenish light.

Obviously, there wasn't anything in the room that didn't belong there. Unlike her husband, Jill wasn't susceptible to quasi-spiritual theories, and nor was she some dumb young girl attempting to conjure up lost souls. She was simply stressed, that was all, and no wonder. The pressure of last night, and this morning's dreadful news... Still, as much as Richard drove her mad, she realised some of his words had stuck. *Inevitably, you can't suppress your subconscious. It always finds a way.*

But for Christ's sake, what was wrong with her? Jill grabbed the bottle of polish and shook it vigorously because thinking about Richard wouldn't help anything. She wasn't one of his gullible clients, and anyway, what did he honestly understand about suppression? As far as Jill could tell, he did exactly what he pleased–

Stop it, she told herself. *Stop dwelling.* She had a job to do.

She expelled a bluish glob of polish onto her cloth, allowing its prickling, nostalgic scent to soothe her ragged nerves. When Jill was a child, she'd shine this very same cutlery at her grandmother's house – and it wasn't hard to guess what her husband might have to say about that. But Richard could believe whatever he wanted about regression and distraction techniques; at least the house was always clean.

After carefully wiping the intricate prongs of each fairy-sized cake fork, Jill moved on to the sugar spoons, unwilling to let up. But as she polished, her gaze slipped beyond the cutlery to the layered newspaper. Faded sheets from the local *Gazette*, where the stories were all about rerouted traffic and charity fêtes and unwanted dogs left to wander through the woods–

Things like this don't happen here.

Jill's shoulders stiffened. She tried to concentrate on the silverware, but the headlines kept drifting towards her, and with a start, she realised she'd let the damp cloth drop. She was clutching nothing but the sharp little antique paring knife, and not just holding it; she must have been squeezing it. Its sly honed blade was pressing into the meat of her palm, threatening to pierce right through.

Jill dropped the knife, her fingers leaping to her mouth. But the metallic taste made her recoil and she shut her eyes. Another big mistake.

Breasts and face... The thought was as unstoppable as the image that came rushing in alongside it. Theresa leaning close, her anxious smile diminished by her rounded girlish cheeks and generous cleavage. All that honey-coloured flesh.

Jill pushed back from the table, stumbling away from the papers and the polish and the knife's small winking glint.

But the images kept coming, and instead of Theresa's warm complexion, her familiar uncertain grin, Jill was picturing Theresa's mouth shocked open. Her eyes stretched wide and white–

And abruptly, Jill recalled Livy from the night before. The way the girl had looked at her after the glass had smashed, and now she was thinking helplessly about hands again. Livy's palms mottled with blood.

The girl's cuts hadn't been serious, but before Jill had driven Samantha and Alice home, Caitlin had led Livy to the bathroom to clean her up. They'd left the door ajar, and through the gap, Jill hadn't been able to help noticing how close they were standing. Caitlin attending to Livy's scratches with gentle strokes and murmurs, the basin between them swirling pink.

Jill had been so relieved when she'd returned around midnight to find Livy gone and Caitlin tucked up in bed alone.

But shouldn't she be feeling ashamed about that now? If she had allowed Livy to stay over, then the girl wouldn't have gone home to find her mother–

Butchered.

Self-consciously, Jill swallowed, but a taste like dirty

pennies went on clinging to her tongue, and turning to the enormous sink, she twisted the cold tap on, intending to splash her tainted mouth, but then more of Lynn's irrepressible words returned. *They found her right there, in the hallway...*

They, Lynn had said, not *she*.

Icy water blasted into the sink and staring down into its silvery gush, Jill's saliva became a brackish glue sticking to her gums. She gagged but couldn't spit. She'd assumed that Livy had discovered Theresa and called the police, but if not?

What had happened to Livy? Where was Livy now?

Absently, Jill turned off the tap, her gaze rising to the ceiling. Could Livy have sneaked back in while she'd been at the police station? Was the girl upstairs, right now, in Caitlin's bed? It wouldn't be the first time Jill had found them, and before she realised what she was doing, she was marching across the tiles, cursing herself for her cowardice. She should have gone to Caitlin straight away–

Then the front door banged. She pulled up short at the end of the table.

"Hello?" she called. "Hello?"

But there was no reply from the hall, the only sound a clumsy shuffling, and Jill stared at the doorway, half-expecting Theresa to materialise as she'd so often done. Shaking back her hair, or tugging at a bra-strap, her heavily made-up features breaking into that too wide, too eager smile.

And how could Jill still not fully grasp the reality of Theresa's death? *Stabbed more than twenty times...*

But what if it was Livy – what if Livy was just arriving now? Livy, a cruder version of her mother, always brazenly confident, entering every room breasts first, her chin held high. *Mrs Shaw, is Caitlin home?*

All over again, she pictured the girl's blood-streaked palms and shining eyes–

"Jill?"

Of course, it was only Richard, except as he slumped in the kitchen doorway, he hardly seemed like Richard at all. As well as the clotted catch to his voice, his whole posture looked off-kilter like something inside him had come loose. The man who'd stood shoulder to broad shoulder with the detective had vanished, and he'd taken off his tie, Jill noticed, staring at his sagging chest as if that was somehow the biggest shock. There were sweat stains on his shirt.

"Christ, Richard," Jill said, but she didn't sound like herself either. Through the pennies, she could taste the acid of genuine bile. Everything, basically, was nauseating, and it was more than what had happened – *blood everywhere* – it was the fact that Jill had ever known Theresa and Livy, that they'd come into her life, into her family. *Bringing their sickness into my home.*

"Jill," Richard said again, and he was still sounding broken and bewildered. As if nothing was his fault.

Jill's first instinct was to slap him. But though it was all too easy to imagine the gratifying clap, she forced her arms open. She leant into the damp shadows of his chest, and then made herself keep holding on even when his shoulders started to shudder.

"Richard," she said, "oh, Richard," and her words were firm now, louder than his sobs.

But it became too much when he grabbed her clumsily in return. Jill staggered backwards, away from his desperate clutching hands, and then realised that they weren't alone.

Caitlin was hovering in the hallway. Wrapped in a white dressing gown and caught between the slanting light, she looked insubstantial. A delicate little ghost.

"What's going on?" she asked. "What's happening?"

But before Jill could reply, Richard was pushing her aside, becoming another kind of man again. She could feel his mood changing, his quickening anger, and his questions, overriding Caitlin's, stunned Jill. They might have slipped from her own lips.

"Caitlin, is Livy here? Have you seen her? Have you spoken?"

Caitlin was shaking her head, her blonde hair sweeping her face, but Richard kept asking, lurching closer.

"Where is she then? You need to tell us. Where has Livy gone?"

He seemed about to seize their daughter's narrow shoulders, and Jill stepped hastily after him, but Caitlin ducked his grasp. She was staring past Richard, her small pale pink mouth hanging open. She was looking straight at Jill.

"I don't know," Caitlin mumbled. "Livy went home last night. You know that... I don't understand, I don't know. What..."

The air in the hall seemed to turn and flutter with her daughter's stuttering, and Jill wasn't sure if it was that, or Caitlin's young, frightened face, or her husband's strangeness, but somebody had to take control. And when she spoke, her words emerged with surprising ease.

"Theresa's dead," she said.

Chapter 4

Caitlin

22 December 2017

Screw you, Mum.

Like a lit fuse, the thought flickers through me. A flash of pure teenage rebellion about to explode inside my head.

My hand jumps to my mouth, though I haven't spoken the words aloud, but I do nothing else to keep the flare in check; it brings with it a relief. Obviously I should have known better than to have attempted to explain.

For what seems like the hundredth time, my gaze darts to the mantelpiece, skimming over the framed photo of my father, young and lean and laughing in a tuxedo, to the smugly ticking clock. It's nearly nine. For more than two hours, I've been trapped in Mum's living room, trying to justify the end of my marriage, with her sighs thickening the air.

"It's just such a shame," she says, "the damage to Scarlet. All that security... I don't know how you can sound so definite. You're giving up so much."

I bite my cheek against the urge to scream. Has she heard a single word I've said?

What other woman – what other *mother* – would respond like this to my tragic timeworn story of deceit and humiliation, how Phil, in his lies and growing coldness, allowed me to believe I was going crazy before finally admitting his affair? And even now, after he has openly left – right now, as he's swanning around a luxury hotel with his girlfriend and our daughter – Mum still refuses to believe there wasn't some way I could have made him stay. Everything is clearly my fault.

And, yes, she's registered each frantic word; I can see it in her frown. Though the lines cross-hatching her face have deepened with hurt and baffled disbelief, her confusion has nothing to do with age. Mum knows exactly what she's thinking and what she's projecting. I've seen that expression before.

Even her body exudes disappointment. Shrunken and sad-looking, she's hemmed in by floral cushions, engulfed inside a throne-like chair. Whenever she jerks towards me, she winces, disapproval running through the sharp angles of her bones.

"Your father and I," she begins.

And before I think it through, I'm standing, sweeping a hand across my face, then rubbing the pounding space between my eyes. I can't remember when I last felt this used up, this exhausted, and I'm an expert in insomnia. This day, almost the year's shortest, has gone on and on and on.

"Mum," I say, "it might be better if we talked more tomorrow," thinking *no way, absolutely no fucking way.* "I'm totally wiped out, and I'm sure you must be too."

I glance at the bed, set up against the living-room wall. Although the neat blue sheets perfectly complement the elegant forget-me-nots patterning the curtains, it still looks wrong, as weird as the shiny new walking frame beside Mum's chair.

I turn hurriedly to the tea things and start to tidy, but when I lift the tray, the crockery rattles as if it's my body that's grown untrustworthy, my hands shaky with age.

"Leave it," Mum says, "if you're feeling so *wiped out.*"

But somehow I steady my grip and ignoring the instinct to run, I pick my way carefully across the room. I don't allow the cups to clink and I don't glance back, though I'm aware of Mum craning towards me. Haughtily tilting her crumpled cheek for a goodnight kiss, or else frowning after me, still pretending to be confused.

I think of Dad, on the mantelpiece behind her, and despite myself, I quicken my pace, imagining his framed gaze joining hers. His dark eyes narrowed with amusement, but something wry underlying his frozen grin as if, in his own way, he's despairing of me too.

Screw you both.

The thought propels me down the hallway, past its dim closed doors, but when I reach the kitchen and hit the light switch, I'm thrown harshly back into myself. In the glare, the adult me makes a stark return, and with it comes a queasy wave of inadequacy. Looking around, I feel ashamed.

But it isn't the dissection of my fucked-up marriage that's getting to me now. It's the tiles and the cupboards and the cavernous sink. This once gleaming, pristine room.

That cliché, *the heart of the house*, as Mum used to say without a trace of irony, and in truth, it was always her place, her heart, far more than mine or Dad's. Her hopes and ideals reflected in the solid oak table and sparkling countertops, in the extensive collection of cleaning products stashed politely out of sight.

And at first glance, if you didn't know this house like I do, the kitchen might still appear spotless. But before I've taken three steps inside, I can feel the difference, and once I start counting the discrepancies, it's difficult to stop.

The floor hasn't been polished, and a couple of tiles catch the wool of my socks; they're finely webbed with cracks. There's a patch behind the taps where the grouting's grown grey and wormy, the sink is speckled with tea leaves, and there's no sign of the marble chopping block.

It makes me wonder about the rest of the house. The dining room and Dad's therapy room, hidden away behind their firmly shut doors, and upstairs, the study, and my parents' luxurious suite, which Mum has abandoned... Everything's probably still regularly aired, the antiques gift-wrapped in dustsheets, but what if it's all just been forgotten, left to slowly rot?

The kitchen's more than enough to deal with. Even the thin ring of crumbs around the toaster feels accusatory, and I realise how determinedly I've been downplaying the changes in Mum's appearance. Her obvious decline.

At first, I'd been shocked by her weight loss and the walking frame she was actually using when she met me at the door, but it wasn't long into her questioning that I chose to focus on other things.

Mum had taken the trouble to put on her pearls, and her hair, cut shorter than ever, was looking stylishly boyish and still glowing in its usual way. In the living room's benevolent lamplight, it was almost as distracting as her extravagant sighs, and perhaps I was simply adjusting. When I was growing up, she'd looked as young, if not younger, than my friends' mothers – nobody would have guessed she was several years older – but wasn't her face bound to betray her age at some point? Maybe, I tried to convince myself, there wasn't any need to worry after all.

But here, in the kitchen, where standards have so plainly slipped, I can't deny Mum's reality, the things that between her judgement and the general strangeness of arriving, I've refused to honestly see.

Mum's not just slim anymore; she's scrawny. Her nails remain perfectly filed, but her fingers have curled into brittle, twiggy, birdlike claws. Her wrists jut knobbly from her scarecrow arms, and despite her excessive cushions, there were several moments, as she swayed in her chair, when she appeared genuinely frail. Those sharp bones as light as glass.

I set down the tray with a careless clatter and draw in a ragged breath. I can smell the rain that's dried into my jeans, and my own tired skin, and too much of the room. There's a whiff of scorched metal, but not a hint of Mum's overpriced bergamot air-freshener or her just as beloved stringent bleach. The kitchen's most overpowering aroma is of cheap tomato soup.

And though Mum told me she has a girl coming in twice a day to help, as I go on looking, I'm dubious. I picture some slack-faced, monosyllabic teenager, evidently not up to the job.

Except there's no shifting the blame onto some random village girl. I've eaten nothing for hours except the dusty biscuits Mum unearthed, but the ache in my stomach's more than hunger. I should have come back long ago. I'm hollowed out with guilt.

I thought it was enough that Mum would visit us in London – Dad too, when he was still around – but since his death, she's made excuses, though none of them were to do with her health. She didn't admit to the falls and heart problems till a couple of months ago and the fact that the hospital's given up on the idea of operating was only mentioned, as if in passing, on the phone last week.

But why, Mum? Why didn't you tell me how tough things really are? I'd have been here before, no matter how hard. If you'd only let me know...

Although, being honest – and it seems that in returning, I can't be anything else – whenever Mum called I didn't ask properly. Aside from my reluctance to face this place, arranging a visit often seemed like yet another impossible wearying task.

My head already felt too crowded. My marriage was falling apart—

The kitchen closes in around me, walling off my protests before they can gather momentum, and each unsettling detail – the crumbs and the grout and the cracks in the tiles – begins to merge, blurring before my eyes.

Don't, I think, *I don't do tears,* but even that's another lie. It might have been true for a few years after I left Underton when the only way through was reinvention. But back then, I was young and determined. The minute I arrived at university, I chopped off my hair and packed up my grief. I never mentioned home.

The energy I put into that transformation seems astounding now. There was something ruthless in how I faked my smiles, emulating the most flippant girls in my Halls. I took on their chirpy music tastes and gym obsessions and downed their cherry vodka shots until I was just as popular, and not only with the girls. Boys definitely appreciated this new, uncomplicated Caitlin, and to my surprise, I liked them too. Before Phil, there was Jack and Liam and Tristan. For a while, on many levels, my metamorphosis appeared to work.

And later, young motherhood also helped in its own very different way. While it meant abandoning my English degree before my finals, obviously it was more than a distraction. All that bumbling exhaustion and worry, the overwhelming love...

But that was before Scarlet started growing up and Phil began to fade. Before I found myself forced back into my old spaces, feeling things too deeply again and struggling to maintain even the shakiest of façades. During the last few years, my tears have made a vengeful return. My marriage was such a lonely place.

Still, I'm no more alone than my sick, widowed mother. In

fact, she's probably sadder, ghosting around this big, old, empty house.

With a start, I realise I'm staring past the ancient table to the patio doors, where my reflection's gazing back at me, caught in the black panes. But if it wasn't for the small pale cloud of messy hair, I might not have recognised myself. This woman's all vague lines and shadows, a stranger made of gaps.

I wander over, but while the doubled room brightens around me, my face remains bleary, and when I reach out to touch it, my fingertips recoil at the chill inside the glass.

But suddenly my hands take charge. They're scrabbling for the key and grabbing at the handles, and it's only as the doors swing open that I register my thoughts.

Get away, Caitlin. Get away from here right now.

I plunge outside like I've been pushed, and if it wasn't for the cold, I might have kept going, running straight out into the night. Instead, I'm stuck. In the light from the kitchen, the patio's a tiny frozen island and I'm stupidly coatless and shoeless, the icy damp already gnawing through my socks, but I don't turn around. I can't go back yet. I lift my face to the stinging air. Beyond the patio, the darkness rushes in. At least the rain has stopped.

I take a hesitant step, but still can't see much of the lawn, just a few silvery patches where the grass is glittering with leftover rain or gathering frost, and the rest of the garden remains elusive. But as it dawns on me what I'm looking for, I force my shivering body on. I stumble out, towards the black.

The territory line between the garden and the woods was never a certain thing, and it takes a while for my vision to adjust enough to separate the inky spread of the forest from the starless sky above. But it's not those trees I'm interested in; I'm trying to untangle the nearest ones, searching for the tallest, oldest oak belonging to the garden. That once belonged to me.

Squinting, I cross the glimmering lawn, trailing breath in fleecy threads. The cold tastes sweet in a way that makes me think of well water and there's something well-like about the dark surrounding me too. A strange, soft echo to the noises beyond my puffing gasps, the creak of branches and furtive rustlings. I imagine insomniac birds and hunted rabbits, but when I come to a stop, the trees remain impenetrable, and nothing emerges from the invisible undergrowth. The night's too solid. It won't give me what I want.

But I refuse to believe that my treehouse might no longer exist, that it might have rotted away. After all, it's the place that continues to dominate my dreams. It can't have disappeared.

And of course, the treehouse was just as much Livy's as mine, and while I stand there, straining to unpick the sounds and shadows, it isn't hard to recall her husky voice. Like a rope slithering through the darkness. *Where are you, Cat? I'm waiting...*

A different kind of shiver ripples over me. I remember the old village rumours about spooks and bones and curses, but I can't pretend they have anything to do with the way my heart is beating, too large inside my chest. It's the same as I felt at the train station. There's the sense that I'm not alone out here. As if I'm being watched.

"Kitty!"

I jump – never mind that the voice is coming from the house behind me, and that it's obviously only Mum.

"*Kitty-Cat*, what the hell are you doing?"

She doesn't sound sick or frail; she doesn't even sound old. Her tone is shrill and demanding, and there's not a shred of affection in my childhood nickname. I turn around cautiously to face the windows' glare.

The kitchen's a vast gleaming aquarium, its details lost, and though Mum must be hunched over her frame, her silhouette looks oversized; she's merging blackly with the table. I can feel, rather than see, her impatient gaze, but for a moment, try as I might, I can't persuade my feet to move.

They're soaked numb, but it isn't just that. With the house looming over me, the thought returns, *get away, get away...* But there are too many voices, too many conflicting commands–

"Kitty!" my mother shrieks.

And abruptly released, I careen, skidding in my socks, across the slick grass to the shining patio. I slam clumsily inside.

"Sorry, Mum," I splutter. But though I'm fumbling to lock the doors, she isn't done.

"For Christ's sake, Caitlin," she says, and I can hear the sneer in her voice. "Have you no sense at all? Deliberately inviting the cold back in."

Chapter 5

Richard

8 August 2002

When Richard finally went upstairs to talk to his daughter, he had found her under her bedclothes, her face buried in the damp sheets. The crying was far from unexpected; Caitlin had been holed up in her room since late morning when Jill had forbidden her to leave the house. There was no way she'd be allowed to join the search for Livy no matter how earnestly she begged.

But when Richard first sat down, perching gingerly on the edge of the bed, his daughter's distress had seemed quiet, contained to a degree. Turning to face him, her tears were little more than a fine sheen softening her features, as light as summer rain.

That's my girl, he'd thought, gazing down at her pale glossed face. He was ready to explain and listen. Together, they would try to understand.

But he had barely begun to talk when everything shifted. Before Richard could grasp what was happening, Caitlin was twisting about in her covers and shouting over him, raking her fingers through her hair. She'd whipped herself up into a gale-force storm, and he couldn't make her stop.

"*It's not fair,*" she was wailing now, her mouth as sore-looking as her pink-rimmed eyes, her thin cheeks feverishly blotched.

"Why can't I wait at the hall," she asked, "while the others go out and look? When they find her, it will be me she'll want. It's *me* she needs. Why can't you get that? You're as bad as Mum – *why won't you understand?*"

Caitlin's voice was spiralling, high and helpless, and as Richard reached out to her, he recalled her toddler tantrums, how she would fling her small body to the floor, kicking and flailing and beating her paw-like fists. It had been tempting to laugh at her passion and fury then, but now... Richard's hand hung suspended in the air between them. He couldn't bridge the gap.

And it wasn't just the intensity of Caitlin's eruption; it was the way she looked so abruptly, so disturbingly, like her mother. Not as Jill ever appeared in her ordinary, day-to-day life. This was the most private Jill, the woman Richard had glimpsed on only a handful of occasions in all their nineteen years of marriage. A stranger who could rage so hard she seemed about to fly apart.

"Caitlin, you need to listen," he said, but though he was trying his best to sound controlled, the words cracked in his mouth.

There was something blocking his throat, something other than the threat of his own rigorously suppressed tears. Of course it wasn't just Jill who had her shadow side. In the speech Richard offered his new clients, he would try to explain it in basic terms. "We all have hidden selves," he'd say. "The parts of our personalities that we're afraid to see." And then, if he was in a playful mood, he might go on to misquote Emily Dickinson; "Each one of us is a haunted chamber, possessed by many ghosts."

Except this thing inside him felt remarkably corporeal. It threatened to cut off his airway along with his voice, but he refused to give in to its accompanying panic. So far, the sensation hadn't lasted longer than a minute or two, although when it had happened before, it started with his hands. His palms prickled and itched, drying to sandpaper, and it was only as the feeling spread, crawling up through his arms and into his chest, that it grew heavier and dirtier. Grainy layers of contamination rising inevitably towards his head.

But this afternoon, there was no warning. While his hand went on hanging there, numb and separate, the pressure had bypassed everything else, going straight for his throat and – *God* – his face... He needed to calm down.

Richard had been tolerating the experience to varying degrees since yesterday and however physical it might seem, he knew he could push through it. But even with his level of insight, he'd barely slept, and when he first felt overtaken at the police station, he nearly came as undone as the most deluded of his clients, the ones who regarded their internal voices as genuinely separate entities.

But dwelling on work was hardly beneficial right now and he certainly couldn't allow his thoughts to drag him back to the police. Besides, the feeling was already passing; he would soon be able to swallow. Rein his breathing in.

Like his nightmares, these bouts were just another anxiety symptom – totally understandable in the circumstances – and as disturbing as they were, there was no need to delve any deeper. In his current state, it was bound to be pointless anyway, as futile as trying out his therapy techniques on his red-faced angry child.

"She's your daughter," Jill had called after him when he'd climbed the stairs. *"Be her father."* As if he needed telling.

Richard managed to draw in a faltering breath, and relief

washed through him as he exhaled. There was nothing occupying his throat but tepid air and he was present once more, composed enough to try again.

"Caitlin," he murmured. "Princess..."

But she was glaring at his useless hand and then "What's fucking wrong with you?" she spluttered, and another toddler flashback accosted him as she yanked her entire trembling body away, plunging her face back into the pillows.

For several seconds, Richard didn't say anything. He couldn't *do* anything but stare down at his daughter's long blonde hair while it fanned and settled, covering her thin cotton T-shirt and the fragile arcs of her shoulder blades quivering underneath.

But despite her raking fingers, Caitlin's hair was shining in its usual way and the pillows helped. They muffled her crying, and without her face – that particular, unnerving face – perhaps Richard might still be capable of telling her what he'd come in here to say.

"My princess." His voice was clearer and his hand was his own again. He could reach out; he could touch her. He slowly stroked her head. "My little princess-cat..."

Her hair felt just as silky as it looked. Before she turned five, it had been even paler, glowing almost white. Old ladies used to stop him in the street to ruffle it. *Angel*, they said, never imagining the tantrums. Caitlin's outbursts had mainly happened at home, behind closed doors. They had been lucky in that way.

"There are things we need to discuss," Richard went on, and with his confidence returning, he decided to switch tactics.

He would talk to his daughter as if she was an adult, which in fact she nearly was. She would turn eighteen in a matter of days, although, Richard mused, she hardly realised that herself. Really, she was far too old to be grounded. What was actually stopping her from disobeying Jill and simply walking out the door?

Maybe there was something wilful about Caitlin's childishness. The idea was reassuring. That somewhere, behind the tears and yelling, a part of her was secretly grateful for having somebody to tell her what she could and couldn't do. That she still wanted parenting.

Leaning closer, Richard caught the cheerful citrus tang of her shampoo and there was even a kind of young freshness about the slightly sweaty scent of her unwashed sheets. There were times, despite her growing up, when his daughter still left him dazzled. Moments he experienced the same wonder he had felt during the earliest years of fatherhood when he was so frequently bowled over by her miraculous hair and soft new skin. All that reckless passion surging underneath.

Perhaps, Richard thought as he breathed his daughter in, *not everything's unsalvageable. Maybe she'll be spared at least.*

"Caitlin," he said. "Are you listening? I understand how tough this is, but there are some things you need to know. Things I'm going to explain."

He went on stroking her, smoothing her hair from the top of her scalp to its feathery tips drifting halfway down her spine. And though he could feel the odd tremor running through her, Caitlin's crying seemed to be subsiding and the motion was also soothing him, coaxing out the required words.

"The police called this morning," he said. "They aren't just looking for Livy because they're worried. They think... Ward thinks..."

But Richard trailed off, picturing Ward's neat greying beard and deft capable hands, so much more competent than his. At the police station, the man's grip on his shoulder had been light but persuasive, discreetly urging him on.

Would you mind taking a quick look at the body?

And recalling the detective's words, Richard felt engulfed again. His chest was full, and his throat, his head... He was being pushed brutally out of himself, helplessly wrenched back.

Breathe, he tried to tell himself, just as he told his clients. *Keep breathing. In... and out...*

But though he could see his chest rising and sinking, it felt as if someone else was mindlessly pulling his strings and yet for a few more seconds, he tried to keep hanging on. His gaze flitted from his daughter to the make-up piling her dressing table and then on to the inevitable scattered clothes and band posters, but the teenage trappings couldn't ground him. The room felt far less real than the poky office where the detective had taken him for "a private word" – but perhaps nothing would ever feel as real as that. The shock of Ward's request.

Would you mind taking a quick look at the body?

At the time, Richard was hit with such a dizzying sense of vertigo, it hadn't occurred to him that he might have had a choice. It was only now, as a thin insubstantial part of him went on hovering over his daughter, that he found himself wondering. *Why didn't I say no?*

But Richard's shock had already been overwhelming and alongside it, there was also the absurd urge to remain professional. Dumbly aware of what the detective and everyone else required of him, he followed Ward across the office in an obedient daze, trying to prepare himself. But he was expecting to be ushered down a long, twisting, silvery passageway lined with mysterious doors, before he realised, with a jolt, that this passageway was his own invention. It only existed in his mind and in the minds of some of his clients.

A world away from the station's scruffy corridors, it was the image he had been using since he started dabbling in hypnotherapy. While other practitioners offered visualisations of lifts or staircases, Richard preferred to think of a gentle tunnelling rather than a direct descent and he also liked the idea of a choice of different secret chambers. Emily Dickinson again.

But as unnerving as it was, conjuring up his passageway was a straightforward enough form of evasion. A means of protecting himself, Richard reasoned, from the truth awaiting him beyond Ward's office door.

Except when Richard thought of that, the room he pictured was just as fake. An icy space hung with bizarre medical implements and dominated by ominous drawers like oversized filing cabinets, it was entirely constructed from crime-show clichés.

And there weren't any other rooms waiting for Richard. No scary drawers. They didn't even leave the office. Before they reached the door, Ward stopped at a very ordinary-looking cupboard and pulled out a camera. Of course, the body wasn't actually *there*.

The police station was meant to serve every village in the valley, but it was such a ramshackle inadequate place. Equipped for dealing with little more than driving offences and the occasional drunken or drugged-up teenager, it was about as likely to house a mortuary as it was to contain enigmatic shining corridors. If Theresa – *Theresa's body* – had passed through, she would have been hastily whisked on.

But Richard's relief was short-lived. Although the camera's screen was small, by the time Ward took it back, Richard was scared he might drop it, he was trembling so badly.

And it wasn't just the shaking. His hands felt filthy as if the screen's gritty images were rubbing off, leaching through his palms. Then the dirt was moving up his arms, pushing its way under his skin until his whole body, looking at *her body*, felt invaded. Wave after wave of grime swelling up towards his gullet.

It was like the reverse of putting his clients into a trance state, of leading them, one deepening breath at a time, down that passageway. "With each step," he would tell them, "you'll feel easier and emptier. Let your body fill with light."

But as powerful as the sensation was, it did nothing to block out the camera's pictures. There was such a lot of blood.

In every shot, Theresa was shown sprawled on her back in her bungalow's narrow hallway. Richard knew her home well, but it was hopeless trying to focus on that; it wasn't just Theresa that had been transformed. The wallpaper's pattern of birds was spattered and streaked, the rug underneath her lolling legs looked dipped in thick red oil, and it took him a while to recognise the vintage kimono that she wore as a dressing gown. The fabric was ripped into tattered strips and soaked. The blood was everywhere.

Only Theresa's kneecaps and the soles of her bare feet seemed to have been spared. They glowed palely, caught in the camera's flash, and because the skin there was less marked, less changed, than the rest of her, Richard tried to concentrate on her knees, but it was impossible. There was no avoiding the mess that had been made of her torso and her poor ruined face...

Richard couldn't stop looking at her face.

As even now, while in another world his fingers went on trailing over his daughter's silky scalp, he couldn't turn away.

In life, Theresa's hair had been untameable. An auburn tangle forever shaking free of its clips and bands, it was as unruly as the laughter that would spill from her wide brightly lipsticked mouth, but on the camera screen, it had been remade. Darker than it should have been, it was matted into sickening clumps and her mouth – her full, lush, laughing lips – her mouth had been torn open.

There was something horribly roselike about it, her bottom lip a wet shredded petal merging with her opened jaw. Theresa's face seemed to have been destroyed so easily as if it had never been anything more than a flimsy mask. Her right cheek hung loose, the skin reduced to a flapping rag that revealed the meat inside and a glint, perhaps, of bone.

The knife, Ward told him, was serrated. They had found it at the scene. Despite the damage it had done, it was a plain and practical kitchen tool, which had quite possibly belonged to Theresa. And still staring at the screen, Richard could only nod, though it struck him that he knew that knife. He might have even held it.

While he had managed to shake Theresa free of most of her old defensive habits, she'd refused to give up the last of the knives. She kept them hidden around the bungalow "just in case", and there had been one tucked under the small heap of discarded shoes next to her front door. But with the camera trembling in his soiled hands, Richard couldn't explain, he could only look, and in the worst image, the close-up, Theresa was gazing back.

Somehow, her left eye remained untouched. It was still wide open, the mahogany-brown iris huge and shining. But the other eye, the other...

"Dad, what are you doing? Dad, *let go*."

Richard's hand, he realised, had tightened. He was clutching, tugging, a fistful of his daughter's hair and though he prised his fingers open, it took an enormous effort. As Caitlin turned to face him, it was hard not to think about the things that lay underneath, the blood pushing up behind her cheeks.

"*Dad*," she kept on, a new whine to her voice, and he could tell her mood had changed.

"Dad, what were you going to say?"

"Caitlin..." he started.

But now, as he took in her wide blue eyes and her young smooth skin, marked by nothing worse than tear tracks, his intentions crumpled. There was a different kind of ugliness shifting through him and as irrational as he knew it was, at least he recognised his anger.

Why should he have to deal with his daughter's hysteria, this *tantrum*? Her angel hair seemed suddenly mocking and her supposed distress as selfish as it was clueless. The girl knew nothing. *She hadn't had to see–*

"What were you going to tell me about Livy, Dad? Please, Dad... I just really need her back."

Livy, Richard thought, and though he had imagined he'd successfully slammed the door on his own fears surrounding the girl, his pre-prepared speech was collapsing along with everything else. How was he meant to explain the detective's suspicions about Theresa's daughter who Caitlin supposedly loved...

But Caitlin – so small and weak and self-absorbed – what could she possibly understand about real life and real pain? What did she honestly know about love?

Still, as she went on staring at him like a greedy child, it dawned on Richard that there might be more to her angst than he had thought. Considering how close Livy had kept her, was it possible that Caitlin might already harbour some suspicions of her own?

He stood so abruptly the room went wheeling and as he struggled to catch his balance among the swirl of posters and cosmetics and discarded clothes, his shin struck something hard poking out from under the bed. He glanced down and saw, between the flounces of an untucked sheet, the polished wooden board with its familiar carved numbers and letters, the ornate panel in one corner that read "*No*".

He bent and dragged the Ouija board out, his movements clumsy with disgust. She hadn't even bothered to hide it properly.

"Your mother told me about this," he said. But he barely

knew what he was saying anymore, where one outrage ended and the next began.

"How dare you take my things? You, of all people, should know better. I don't know what you're turning into, Caitlin. What were you thinking? Do you ever think at all?"

And with the board gripped like a shield to his chest, he strode away from her, heading for the door.

"Dad," she called. "Please, Dad, what–"

"Irresponsible," Richard barked, without looking back. "And *stupid*. You stupid, reckless little girls..."

He couldn't spend another minute in that room with her. He would talk to her later, or else Jill could–

Except, *God*, Jill... Right now, she was in the kitchen, sipping a too early glass of Chardonnay and waiting for him to reappear, expecting a full report. And behind him, Caitlin went on snivelling.

"Dad, please," she was still begging. "What about Livy? What did you want to say?"

It was all too much – *too fucking much* – he refused to turn; he wouldn't go back. The demands were relentless, hemming him in from every side. And of course, it wasn't only Caitlin and his wife, there was Ward as well, and even now, with his temper flaring, Richard was scared to shut his eyes, dreading the return of Theresa's face.

Chapter 6

Caitlin

23 December 2017

On the off-chance anyone's watching as I leave the house, I glance back over my shoulder. I don't want to look like I'm storming off. But the windows are blank, the curtains don't twitch, and I drop the hand that I had lifted, readying myself to wave. Obviously, nobody's about to call me back, to ask if I'm okay.

Nonetheless, I linger, turning to take in the pale imposing walls and the dull-gleaming roof, the awkward jutting tower room, which gives the row of chimneys a cockeyed look, protruding from one side. Despite the weird angles, or maybe because of them, the house remains impressive. The woods rise, soft, behind it. A blur of knitted grey.

Even when I lived here, there were moments when the building would catch me just like this. On twilit evenings coming back from school and especially during that last summer when I often sneaked in like a burglar in the pearly light of dawn.

With its age and eccentric grandeur, my parents' home sometimes felt like a dream house, but not in any estate agent's kind of way. Set apart from the rest of Underton where the road weaves through the woods, the dust-coloured stone might have emerged from the misty trees and hills, or else been dreamt up by the locals. After all, shouldn't every respectable village have a haunted house? And with its history, it was perfect.

The building stood empty for years before my parents bought it, but it had previously belonged to Evelyn Hansworth and the Hansworths were once a pretty big deal around here. Great-granddad Hansworth owned the Valley's mills and though his mills and most of his money were lost by Evelyn's time, her bloodline would have provided her with a certain mystique even if she hadn't turned out to be so satisfyingly bonkers.

Evelyn was a recluse, living out here alone for decades. Her only visitors were the delivery drivers who dropped off her groceries and it might have been months before anyone realised that Evelyn had disappeared.

But it didn't take long for the rumours to start. The mystery of the deserted house was irresistible and it soon became the place kids targeted every Halloween, toilet-papering the driveway and daring one another to creep up to the weathered front door, though they didn't start smashing the windows till later.

But the house wasn't a total spooky wreck when we moved in. At some point, a construction company took it over and the renovations were nearly complete when the firm went bust overnight. There was talk of illegal investments, but of course, the locals knew better, especially since Evelyn had finally shown up. When the builders began clearing the garden for the kitchen extension, they discovered her skeleton.

Naturally, Underton's gossips went into overdrive. The state of Evelyn's remains prevented any conclusive cause of death and they were convinced that the house was jinxed.

There was talk of witchcraft as well as murder. *They didn't just find her body*, Ali told me the week we arrived. *She was surrounded by babies' bones.*

But the stories didn't get to me. At twelve years old, I was already stubbornly sceptical and I was also incredibly pissed off about being dragged away from my London friends and so it's hard to recall my initial impressions – although surely I must have felt something? That stumpy turreted tower room still looks like it's out of *Scooby Doo.*

Dad, being Dad, was charmed by the house and even Mum was excited. The high corniced ceilings and original feature fireplaces provided an ideal showcase for the interior design business she was intending to launch back then. She would work from home alongside Dad, who was transitioning completely to private practise. In addition to bagsying the tower for his study, the second reception space would become a therapy room for his growing list of troubled businessmen and fawning elderly ladies. Dad had no problem convincing his richest neediest clients to travel out to the sticks; it would only enhance the therapeutic process.

Transform the pain of the past, his brochures had seriously read for a while. *Heal your history,* beside a sunlit photo of the house.

Of course, the whole haunted house thing tickled Dad for other reasons too. In contrast to his rational professional side, there was what he called self-mockingly his "esoteric interests". He was fascinated by the psychological aspects of spiritualism and more generally with superstition. Along with an extensive library, his collection included tribal masks and a spirit cabinet, as well as his treasured "ectoplasm", which was basically just an ancient cloth decaying in a jar.

Easily bored, Dad's obsessions were a way of channelling his restlessness. In the therapy world, he was renowned for pushing boundaries and his energy could be surprisingly physical. He completed much of the leftover work on the house, rehanging doors and sanding floors and beating back the ever-encroaching woods, and he built the treehouse for my thirteenth birthday. The best gift I've ever had...

But I never should have allowed myself to get sidetracked. I'm no longer admiring my old home; I feel stuck here now, with the house glowering over me, and I brace myself for the grief that can still come rushing in. An oddly warm and liquid thing followed inevitably by guilt.

Because it wasn't just Mum I neglected, staying away for all this time. After everything that happened with Livy, my relationship with Dad was temporarily derailed and at first, I wanted to keep him as distant as the rest of the village. And though we patched things up years before his fatal second stroke, I still felt selfishly relieved that I wouldn't have to return here for Dad's funeral, the family plot in Highgate letting me off the hook.

But I can't let the guilt take charge. It's as pointless as it's exhausting, and hasn't there already been more than enough? Not only last night but this morning, with Mum's carer, Bethany, joining in. The pair of them dismissing me as if I'm still a wayward child.

And the house is just as indifferent. It goes on gazing steadily past me, its thick walls unforgiving, the dark panes unimpressed. If the building understood my intentions – yes, I had in fact been storming off – it clearly doesn't care.

But isn't it better to feel ignored than watched? After yesterday's paranoia in the garden, and at the station–

Out of nowhere, Livy's giggles flutter through my head.

For fuck's sake, get over yourself, Cat, and get a move on. You're such a drama queen.

"So, you decided to come home then?" Bethany had said, rising from straightening Mum's bedding to spray an acrid haze of cheap "pine" air-freshener across the living room.

Blinking to clear my eyes, I struggled to reply. There was no sign of Mum, and this bustling blunt-faced woman had been the last thing I was expecting when, sleep-befuddled and clumsily dressed, I groped my way downstairs.

Just a couple of years younger than me, Bethany – "not Beth, *never* Beth," she insisted – couldn't have been further from the lazy teenager I'd imagined. While she talked, she smacked the cushions mercilessly and flung the windows wide. She only paused in her tidying once, interrupting our awkward introductions to scold my leftover biscuit crumbs: "What are you lot doing here?"

Despite the twice-daily visits, it was clear it was a lack of time rather than determination that kept the house from sparkling like it used to. But that didn't stop Bethany from trying, and it wasn't just the room she was taking to task. She gave me a couple of brief but intense once-overs before claiming to remember me.

"I'd know you anywhere," she announced, briskly lifting the seat of the chair I'd occupied for two hours yesterday without for a minute suspecting it was Mum's commode.

"Hmm," I replied, trying to focus on Bethany's stiff coiled brown hair and meaty forearms rather than the hidden bowl. But there was nothing about her I recognised.

"You and your mates always intrigued us," she ploughed on, "even before what happened."

And *fuck*, I thought, *already?* I blinked faster, my tongue drying in my mouth. *For fuck's sake, don't go back there yet.*

But Bethany was too practical to notice my discomfort.

After snapping on a pair of rubber gloves, she attacked the commode, everything about her ruthlessly efficient. Even with the gusto of her scrubbing, her wiry hair refused to move and the small sprig of heather pinned to her blouse barely quivered. But while I hovered at her side, not knowing what to do with my empty hands, I wondered if I might remember her after all. There was something about those disciplined curls and her clumped mascara. The judgement in her eyes.

She could have been one of the interchangeable village kids who'd heckle me on my way home from the station. Gathered in the bus shelters but going nowhere, "Snob," they'd yell or "Rich bitch", my plaid skirt and bottle-green blazer marking me out, like Sam and Ali, as one of the select teenagers who commuted to the city to attend the posh girls' private school.

But "You lot seemed so cool," Bethany said, surprising me. "Alternative types, always keeping to yourselves, so secretive, though you never tried to hide your smoking or drinking like the rest of us. You and your friends didn't have the same rules. You seemed braver or wilder. Sort of glamorous, I suppose."

She paused to laugh self-deprecatingly and when she spoke again, her tone remained deceptively light.

"We all thought you girls would have it made, especially you. Brains *and* looks. All that long, blonde hair... We thought you'd turn out famous or super rich or something. Some glittering, big city career that kept you away from here... Well, I suppose you can never tell."

The dig was so deliberate I felt pinched, and a petty urge ran through me to snap right back, some bitchy comment about village girls who'd never left, paid to clean up their neighbours' shit. But the thought was instantly shaming. Surely I hadn't ever really been the snob they had believed I was? And besides, it was my mother's shit.

Obviously, I should have risen above her snide opinions.

What did it matter what she thought? But though I knew better than to try to overplay my inconsequential jobs or the degree I'd given up, I found myself gabbling on about Scarlet, trying in some pathetic way to justify my life.

But I'd hardly begun to explain my daughter's acting talents or great grades and sense of humour when Bethany interrupted.

"You got married then, did you?"

I started to nod, but Bethany hadn't finished.

"To a man?" she asked.

Heat bloomed across my stupid face, anger and embarrassment muddled up with something else, but my reply was lily-livered.

"Yes, to a man," I murmured.

"But she's getting a divorce."

Suddenly Mum was there. Her walking frame filling the doorway, a dangerous gleam to her eyes.

"My poor granddaughter," she continued with a predictable sigh, and I could only watch as Bethany concurred, shaking her wire-wool head in sympathy. It was the type of hair, I mused, that would probably crackle if you pulled it.

"It's always the children who suffer," Bethany said, her gaze hardening as it flicked from Mum to me.

I didn't bother to hide my clenching fists. What the fuck was going on? Mum was one thing, but who did this Bethany think she was? Bustling past me, she unpeeled and pocketed her rubber gloves in a distinctly nurse-like manner and then she was reaching out with her practical hands, clasping hold of my mother's shoulders.

"Don't upset yourself, Jilly," she said, with a significant squeeze. And while she helped Mum re-angle the frame, easing her path into the room, I turned away, biting my lip, but still wanting to strike back.

Instead, I took in the bed's neat hospital corners, today's

newspaper folded on the table, and the thoroughly bleached commode. I couldn't fail to see how much Bethany had done, how much she *did*. Hopelessly, I pictured my own living room with its haphazard piles of books and yellowing plants, the dusty Christmas cards carelessly arranged across the mantelpiece–

"But where's Christmas?" I blurted, swinging back. "Your candles, Mum, and all your beautiful decorations. The glass angels and the ribbons and the star-shaped lights."

Mum and Bethany paused mid-shuffle. They wore the same wary expression, plainly both thinking I'd gone mad.

"It isn't right," I said. "You always made such an effort, Mum. The way the house would look..."

And though it was true that my mother would go to town each year, transforming our home into a giant, magical snow globe, I knew I was grasping at tinsel straws, but, "It's not good enough," I blundered on. It made no difference knowing how absurd my behaviour was; "I'm going out!" I shouted as I stalked past Bethany. "I'm going to get a fucking tree."

But the Gilmans' farm, with its annual Christmas Tree Sale, lies on the other side of Underton and I hadn't considered how it would feel to cut right through the heart of the village. As soon as I set foot on the high street, the past starts closing in.

Other than a queue of elderly women outside the butchers, everything's predictably ghost-town quiet. The Peking Palace has become Lucky Buddha Dining, but it's basically the same old shoddy takeaway and the dead rabbits outside The Hunters Arms are looking as gruesome as ever and the sign's still missing its apostrophe. Nothing's changed enough.

I'm briefly cheered up by the tie-dye and crystal dragons

filling the window of an unexpected New Age gift shop, but I don't feel the same relief when I pass the chintzy tearoom that's replaced the steam-ridden greasy spoon. Livy's mother, Theresa, sometimes worked there and I quicken my pace and cross the road, ignoring the rub of my impractical boots.

But on the other side, the council's Christmas lights are depressingly familiar – ropes of plain white bulbs, unlit at this hour – and while there aren't any kids about, the graffiti illuminating a bus shelter seems eerily unchanged.

I look up, staring determinedly past the shops and lights, but though the village shrinks around me, the sky's a vast grey pressing lid and it isn't only Underton that feels oppressive. I'm so tired of being me.

Stop it, Cat, I tell myself, *just keep going*, but when I glance back down, I stumble, realising where I am.

Having left the shops behind, I've reached the twitchel, which runs between the village hall and the cricket ground, providing a shortcut to the hidden council estate and as I hover there, gawping, the wind picks up. It ruffles my hair and crawls inside my coat collar, but for the moment, I can't go anywhere.

At the far end of the twitchel, beyond its mossy walls, there's a blur of orange brick and in a rush, Livy's bungalow comes back to me. I remember the front garden with its riotous plants and the poky brightly painted rooms inside. All those art nouveau posters and faux fur cushions, everything clashing but trying its best to match.

Theresa wanted to make her home as welcoming as she was, but she never truly fitted in. Like my parents, she arrived here as an outsider, without any tangible ties to Underton, but there was more to her neighbours' distrust than that. Obviously, there was Livy.

The villagers couldn't ever get their heads around Livy. That beautiful, moody, fatherless girl, who slunk through the woods like a fox at night. Theresa could be as hospitable as she liked, throwing open her doors for coffee mornings and barbecues and a short-lived book club, but her visitors mainly came for gossip's sake. Theresa's warmth, like her home, was always obscured by her daughter. Livy's shadow everywhere...

I wonder what's become of the bungalow, if the garden's been uprooted and paved over and the walls reduced to a bland magnolia, but then it strikes me that it's probably been torn down. After all, who would live there now? No matter how much concrete and paint you poured, you would never be able to conceal its past. That unforgettable night when my house's haunted reputation was so thoroughly eclipsed–

But there's no way I'm returning to that night. Gathering my strength, I start backing off, and then before I understand what I'm doing, I'm spinning away. I'm running. Trying to get as far away as fast as I can from Underton's infamous Murder House.

When I eventually make it to the Christmas Tree Sale, I wander through its fake forest in a kind of trance. Passing through the gates, I try to convince myself I am calm. I'd stopped running and mostly stopped panicking, but it's taken longer than it should have to realise how different the farm is from the place it used to be. Unlike the rest of the village, it's been radically transformed.

A sign reading "Belleview Bed and Breakfast" hangs over the barn's startlingly crimson doors, all the cows and sheep are gone, and I wonder what happened to the Gilmans. I suppose I ought to feel relieved that the fir trees are still here.

But I'm struggling to cling onto this stupid mission. While the new car park surrounding me is littered with trees, they're stunted, withered things, already shedding browning needles. It's another thing I've left too late, and I've no idea what I'm doing. *Why the fuck did I come back?*

Mum's hardly been tap-dancing with happiness to see me. Before I showed up, she had her routines and Bethany, and all I've done is upset her with my messy life and my messed-up head, and the last thing she probably wants is a Christmas tree. Especially one of these.

But I need some time before I can face the village again, and isn't it better to be doing something – anything – other than freaking myself out? And at least Belleview is deserted.

Apart from a row of fibre-optic dwarf snowmen, turning from acid-green to neon-yellow, there's no one about to witness my tired dragging feet, and as I shamble between the scraggy branches, it occurs to me that I could simply take my pick, such as it is, and walk off without paying.

"Go on," Livy would have said. "I dare you..."

And for fuck's sake, I need to stop thinking. *Just make a decision. Either choose a tree or go.*

But when I look up, I'm no longer alone. A woman has materialised outside the barn and having clocked me, she's already marching over.

Her arms are laden with a great shuddering heap of mistletoe so I can only make out her edges. Underneath her bunched sticks, a sturdy pair of mud-splashed thigh-high boots, and above them, the bobbing black fur of a Russian-style hat.

But then "Can I help you?" she calls, and I go rigid. I don't need to see her face.

I'd know that braying voice anywhere, and there's no hope of retreat. I scan the car park, but the trees and flaring snowmen seem to have formed a barricade, and when I look back, she's started jogging towards me, scattering leaves and berries in her wake.

"Fuck," I mumble, inching backwards.

But suddenly, she's right here, in front of me, and she's opening her arms, giving up on her mistletoe altogether.

And "Oh my God!" she exclaims. "*Caitlin Shaw*, I can't believe it's you!"

Chapter 7

Sam

11 August 2002

Sam groaned as she followed Ali's large swaying rump up the treehouse ladder. She was struggling to keep a firm grip on the ropes. Her hands were sweating, her arms protesting, and she felt generally off-kilter. Mrs Shaw's tin was wedged under one crooked elbow and the rucksack kept dragging at her shoulders. It thumped and clinked against her spine each time Ali made the ladder jolt.

There were only thirteen rungs in total and they must have made it to the ninth or tenth, but with the midday heat pressing in around them, it seemed to be taking forever. She'd hoped for some relief in the thickening canopy, but the sun cut easily through the deep green shade. Gleaming threads ran like solder between the branches, and Sam blinked, feeling dizzy, whenever she looked up.

"Ali!" she called. "Could you go any slower? My head's stuck halfway up your arse." And then, because she thought it might make her feel better, "Your *lard* arse," she added, but it didn't really help. It wasn't just the heat or her awkward posture; if Sam was being honest, she'd rather have been anywhere else.

The entire way up, she'd been thinking about her bedroom, or Ali's, somewhere cool and dim where you could draw the curtains tight. Even the Shaws' kitchen would have been preferable, as bright and tense as it had been.

While she waited for Ali's next painstaking manoeuvre, Sam leant back as far as she dared, trying to ignore the rucksack's tug. She craned her neck and twisted, but the house remained a pale shape through the weighted branches, even vaguer than the hazy lawn. There was no sign of the patio doors, or of Caitlin's mother flitting back and forth behind them. As soon as she'd shooed Sam and Ali into the garden, Mrs Shaw had started up again. A manic, cleaning shadow puppet, whipping through the kitchen's glare.

"Piss off, Sam," Ali said, her delayed reply as weird and detached as everything else. Between the liquid dashes of sunlight and the ropes' muffled creaking, Sam was beginning to feel unreal.

There had been occasions, climbing up here, when the wind had shaken the tree so violently it was like being surrounded by the ocean, waves thrashing through the boughs. Wild, witchy drinking evenings when Sam's dad thought she was safely tucked up at Ali's house. None of the parents had a clue about their treehouse nights.

About a year ago, they had been caught in a proper thunderstorm. As well as the booze, they'd been smoking Livy's weed, and Ali freaked out, but while she ended up huddled in the treehouse's sturdiest corner, Caitlin and Livy had given themselves up to the downpour. Rushing out onto the railed platform, they shrieked joyfully at every flash and rumble, cheering on the squall.

It had been a couple of months before Caitlin and Livy had given up pretending they weren't really doing what they were doing together, but though Sam was stuck inside with Ali, she had guessed that night.

At some point, Caitlin and Livy stopped squealing, and as Sam had sat there, listening to the rain and the thunder and Ali's whimpering, it was like they had disappeared. And when they eventually returned, soaked to the skin and giggling, she could feel the electricity between them, as if they'd brought the lightning in...

The rucksack clinked again, but the ladder's swaying was changing, and "About time," Sam muttered. Ali had reached the top and she seemed to have dredged up some last-minute energy. Sam watched her trainers kick as she squeezed through the splintery hatch and before she'd finished heaving herself onto the decking, she'd already started to yell.

"Caitlin, hey, Caitlin! It's us! Surprise!"

It took Sam longer to scramble up. She had to shove Mrs Shaw's tin ahead of her and by the time she made it through, the platform was empty. Ali must have joined Caitlin inside the treehouse. There was nowhere else to go.

Built around the oak's massive ancient trunk, the treehouse was undeniably impressive. Over the years the weathered boards had merged with the twisting branches, and it appeared both organic and magical, much more than a windowless box. Except Sam knew that was basically what it was, and on a sweltering day like this, it would have morphed into an oven.

Caitlin hadn't even knotted open the grey sacking that served as the treehouse's door – they usually did that; it was so dark inside – and shrugging off her rucksack, Sam deliberately turned away from its wilted folds, toeing the edges of the hatch.

But as badly as she wanted to, Sam couldn't slip back down the ladder. She'd promised Ali she would stay. Strolling through Underton that morning, Ali had talked and talked until Sam had given in. The day had already been too hot for an argument, and Ali was insistent. Whatever they were feeling, or fearing, it was Caitlin they should be thinking about. They couldn't let her down.

Although Sam and Ali had known each other forever, they'd been friends with Caitlin for most of high school. From the start, they'd liked how she'd taken the piss in Drama and History, and during their daily commute, they bonded over their boredom with village "life". Caitlin had been enlivening their train trips with games of Truth or Dare long before Livy came along.

And why did she have to come along? Why did we let her in?

It was hardly the first time Sam had wondered, but as she turned grudgingly back to face the treehouse, her sweat ran cold. Everything was too still and way too quiet. Without any breeze, the heavy leaves hung in pitiful clumps and the heat seemed to have knocked the birds out too. There weren't any of the usual territorial flaps or squawks, and that was creepy enough, but it was the treehouse's silence that was truly unnerving. Its greenish walls weren't that contained, and Ali could never shut up for long. But what if, when Ali had gone blundering in, she'd found more than just Caitlin? What if this was where Livy had been hiding?

Hiding, Sam thought, *and waiting for us. Like she might have waited for her mum.*

Half an hour and a wine bottle later, Sam knew she should have given up the idea, but it was driving her crazy. If Livy had been holed up in there, Ali would never have left her behind when she'd dragged Caitlin out onto the decking. But still Sam's gaze kept snagging on that doorway. She hadn't seen inside.

"It's roasting in there," Ali had declared when they emerged. "I thought I'd boil alive!"

But though Ali's ginger curls were lank with sweat, and her round, freckled face had indeed looked cooked – swollen and gammon-pink – she'd been grinning, the weary climb, along with so much else, apparently forgotten.

"I told her!" she had said. "She can't be alone, not today of all days." Then, swooping past Sam to grab the tin from the platform's edge, "Caitlin, look!" she yelped. "Your Mum made you a cake!"

Staring at the tin, Caitlin had turned as pale as Ali was pink, and for a second Sam was sure she was about to tell them to piss off, and honestly, that would have been fine with Sam. They could have been languishing on Ali's beanbags by now, laughing at the sex advice in her mum's old *Cosmos* while making their way through the wine at a happier, less desperate pace.

But it was the wine that had persuaded Caitlin to let them stay. Though her mother's cake had clearly appalled her – she'd refused to touch the tin, let alone open it – when Ali unloaded the rucksack, she suddenly perked up.

"Okay," she said, picking up the bottle. "But no birthday shit. I don't want any of that. Let's just have a fucking drink."

And in that moment, Caitlin had sounded so incredibly like her usual self, Sam almost dismissed the idea of Livy hovering close. She even wondered if ever-optimistic Ali had got it right for once. Maybe things would be okay.

But the whole time the three of them had been lolling on the platform, swinging their legs between the railing's posts and passing the bottle back and forth, Sam's thoughts had kept circling back. Ali's endless mindless chatter about clothes and bands and boys had seemed the safest way through at first, but after a while, it just made all the unsaid things feel more urgent, and the Merlot wasn't helping. Sam had drunk too much too fast. Her mouth felt full of glue.

She had nicked the wine from her dad's cellar, and it was

meant to be something fancy, but it was overly rich, as well as sticky, and whenever she glanced at Caitlin's red-stained lips, it was impossible not to think of blood.

Still, she'd gone on swigging, and while Ali babbled, Caitlin's quiet had intensified until Sam began to visualise it, and it was nearly as bad as her vampire mouth. An opaque thickening bubble, keeping her stubbornly apart.

But inside her bubble, Caitlin looked so fragile. Sam had always been thin, all stringy running muscles, but Caitlin was skinnier and she'd obviously lost more weight. Even the baggy cotton of her oversized vest dress couldn't disguise her ribcage when she reached for the bottle and now, as she tipped back her head to swallow, Sam had to turn away.

Caitlin's throat, with its delicate bones, reminded her of the gutted fish at her dad's restaurant. The chefs extracting each fine, feathery skeleton with a few expert flicks of their razor-sharp knives–

She hastily blurred the image. She didn't want to think about knives any more than blood, and the treehouse felt suddenly enormous, looming over them. She couldn't sit there any longer.

Crazy as it was, she needed to prove to herself that Livy wasn't lurking inside, biding her time, but when Sam struggled to her feet, the light swung with her, a queasy kaleidoscope of greens and golds and red, red, red, and turning towards the doorway, she stumbled. Behind her, Ali laughed.

But Ali didn't call her back, or even ask what she was up to, and feeling absurdly pressurised into it, Sam flung open the sacking and plunged inside, and the heat was just as bad as she'd imagined. The air felt solid. It reeked of dead leaves and baking wood, and Sam could already feel herself melting. Sweat crawled through her fringe into her lashes, but at the same time, her mouth was so dry, it was tricky to swallow. Her throat felt stuffed with scorched sawdust, and the shadows were cloying. They clung heavily to the corners and streaked the boards like grime, and before Sam could grasp what was happening, the sack-door flapped shut. The darkness came bowling over her in a suffocating wave.

And in her panic, battling to hook the sacking back, the shadows appeared to condense. There was a sense of a figure growing out of the dirt and dark, and horrified, Sam remembered the Ouija board and the thing that Ali had claimed she'd seen that night – the same night Theresa died–

The daylight flooded in. Sam had somehow found the nail and hung the sacking open, and there was nothing filling the treehouse but her dumb imagination and the massive branch, which formed the main roof-beam, hanging ominously black and low.

Obviously, the treehouse was empty. Livy wasn't here, and there were no such things as ghosts. Unlike the rest of Underton, Sam had never believed Caitlin's house was haunted, and she hadn't believed Ali's story either. Besides, just like blood and knives, she wasn't meant to be thinking about the Ouija board. In Caitlin's room that night, it had been insane, and Sam still wasn't quite certain what had happened afterwards, when Mrs Shaw had driven them home...

"Get your head straight," Sam murmured. "Get it straight right now."

But while she forced herself to circle the walls, trailing her fingertips across the smouldering planks, she went on talking to herself – "Forget it, Sam, forget it" – as if her words could create a barrier against all the spooky stuff. Except nothing could block out the stark reality of Theresa's death, and kicking through the mothy cushions Caitlin had heaped into the furthest corner, Sam stopped muttering, wishing she could overturn her thoughts.

But as the cushions tumbled apart, they revealed a pale wad of paper, and gazing down at the fluttering pages, Sam felt sick. But it was a sad kind of sick, rather than scared-sick; she knew what those papers were.

Both Sam and Ali had seen Livy's "art" before. They had, in fact, spent several sleepovers giggling about her pictures – "Life drawings, *yeah, right*" – but it was different seeing them here.

According to Mrs Shaw, Caitlin had stalked off to the treehouse early that morning and the idea of her curled up for hours, alone with those sketches, was utterly depressing. It was time for Sam to go.

As soon as she'd given herself permission, she hurried to the doorway, hoping she wouldn't look too freaked out. But when she stepped outside, her friends didn't even glance over.

"No," Ali was saying to Caitlin in a stage whisper. "He's down there by himself."

She was sprawled on her front, gazing towards the garden, with her hair dangling into the leaves past the decking's edge, and her arse – *her lard arse* – bobbing in the air. But though Sam was tempted to whack it, she didn't.

"What's going on?" she asked.

"Shh," Ali said. "It's Caitlin's dad. He's acting weird."

Sam leant on the rail. Her vision was blotchy after the treehouse's dim and it took a moment to see beyond Ali and the layered green branches. The lawn shimmered like a fairy-tale pool and Mr Shaw seemed to be rippling too, drifting in and out between the trees.

"He isn't doing anything," Sam said. "Just wandering around."

"Exactly!" Ali replied, and Sam couldn't disguise her groan.

She knew how Ali felt about Caitlin's dad. Whenever he spoke to her, her face turned pink with a different sort of heat and quite frankly, Sam thought the whole thing was disgusting.

Mr Shaw might have been fit when he was young or in a certain light, but he was over forty, properly old, and Sam wasn't about to encourage Ali's fantasies. But then Caitlin drew her in.

"The policeman was out there with him this morning," she said. "And he came over yesterday too."

On the other side of Ali, Caitlin wasn't looking out at the garden but into her lap, her dress tented between the poles of her crossed knees.

"Really?" Ali said, shuffling to sit up as Sam sat down. The decking whinged. "What was the policeman saying? Did he talk to you as well?"

Despite the heat, Sam felt a small shiver of shock. She couldn't believe that kind, diplomatic, chattering Ali had dared to ask. Sam was usually the brutally honest one.

Caitlin didn't answer. She reached for the wine – there was less than half a bottle left – and as Sam watched her take a long, slow slug, she imagined all the unsaid things between them widening into tunnels. Endless, bottomless black holes.

But Caitlin set the bottle aside, and after wiping her red mouth with her bony knuckles, the words came tumbling out.

"I spoke to him yesterday, but he's useless. It was just the same questions over and over. It didn't matter what I said. He hasn't got a clue about what happened to Theresa. And no fucking idea where Livy is."

"What questions?" Ali said, and Sam felt doubly impressed. She knew if she'd asked it would have sounded wrong, but Ali kept her voice gentle. She sounded surprisingly mature.

"Stupid things," Caitlin said. "*How often did she confide in you? How would you describe her relationship with her mother? Would you say she was aggressive? Have you ever felt threatened?* Honestly, he's such a wanker. I can't believe he genuinely thinks that Livy..."

"What?" Sam blurted. She couldn't help it. "Did he actually say that Theresa – that it was Livy who–"

Caitlin jumped to her feet, and Sam felt momentarily dazzled by the swinging arc of her hair – it was so, so blonde – but then Caitlin was pushing past Ali and crouching next to Sam, and before Sam could register what she was about to do, she had reached out and seized Sam's wrist.

Sam laughed instinctively, but there was nothing playful about Caitlin's tightening grip, and then she was hauling Sam towards her, and "Don't," she hissed, with their faces hovering inches apart. "Don't you ever say that. Don't you even fucking think it."

They were pressed so close Sam could see the new grubby pores scattering her friend's hollowed cheeks, and there was something metallic, maybe menstrual, cutting through the smell of her sweat. But Caitlin's eyes were the very worst thing. They were bigger than ever and very dark, the pupils eating up the blue.

Black holes, Sam thought again, gazing helplessly into them. *Black holes, black holes...* She couldn't break their stare, and after a moment, it wasn't Caitlin looking back at her; it was Livy. Sam yanked her arm away.

"Hey!" Ali said. "Hey, you two, *stop*."

She'd scrambled gracelessly to her feet, and as she nudged in, squatting between them, her trainers clanged dully against the cake tin and Sam thought briefly of the pink marzipan "18" inside and then of Caitlin's mother's face. She had never seen Mrs Shaw look that way before. Handing over the tin, she'd appeared both ancient and childlike, and precariously close to tears.

And it was *everybody*, Sam realised. Mrs Shaw wasn't Mrs Shaw anymore, and Caitlin wasn't Caitlin, and Sam herself – she couldn't deny it any longer – she'd never felt this scared.

Theresa's murder had been mind-blowing, and the investigation was far from over. Like everyone else, Sam needed Livy to be found.

But it wasn't Livy's safety that concerned her. It was Livy's mood swings and her temper. It was the same joyous glitter that danced in her eyes whether she was fighting or laughing, and it was what she'd once said about hearing her dead father's voice. Weaving, like smoke, inside her head.

"Don't worry, Caitlin," Ali was cooing now, looping an arm around Caitlin's shoulders. "No one believes that Livy had anything to do with it."

But though Caitlin already seemed calmer, Sam felt her own hot thoughts shift, her fears giving way to exasperation. She flashed Ali a warning glance, but Ali wasn't looking at Sam.

"That policeman," she was saying, nodding towards the garden, though Mr Shaw was still alone down there, still pacing his lawn in slow motion. "I heard he's been over to the traveller site, and he's probably questioning Livy's dad's side of the family. It can't be long till they find out…"

While Ali's soothing words spun on and on, Sam kept her face carefully averted. But as she watched Mr Shaw dump an armful of sticks onto the grass, her anger flared. She couldn't hold it down.

He was building a fire, she realised, as if the day wasn't blazing enough. Even Caitlin's psychiatrist dad appeared to have lost it, along with the rest of the world – but maybe that made sense. After all, wouldn't he know better than anyone how truly crazy Livy was?

"She's okay," Ali continued. "She's run off, that's all. She'll be lying low, in shock, somewhere. But they'll find her, I know they will. And when they find her, she'll be fine–"

"Will she?" Sam said, turning back.

Caitlin's face was striped with tears now, but though her

eyes were glistening blue once more, Sam was past the point of sympathy.

"That's not what people are saying or thinking," she snapped. "And that's not what we've been thinking either."

Ali released a high-pitched gasp, then gawped at Sam, but Sam no longer cared. She was tired of all the pretending and utterly sick of feeling scared. She watched as Caitlin scrubbed the tears from her face, and *yes,* Sam found herself thinking, *wake up, Caitlin. Wake up.*

"What she means," Ali began to explain. "Sam just means..."

But Caitlin was shrugging her arm away and Ali faltered going on.

"We... we were only talking about that night. You know, *that night,* when Theresa... But before we knew... Those freaky things the Ouija board told us–"

"Fuck that, Ali," Sam interrupted. "No one thinks that Theresa was stabbed by a fucking ghost."

There was a moment, a heavy, humid moment, before Caitlin spoke. But when she did, her tone was cool and measured and emotionless, slicing cleanly through the heat.

"So, Sam," she said, "tell me," and each word was a separate blade. "What exactly do you think?"

Chapter 8

Caitlin

23 December 2017

There was a time, I think, *when I hated you,* and I realise how intently I'm watching Sam as she pushes through the throng to order us more drinks.

The Hunters Arms is heaving, an obstacle course of ruddy faces and air-kisses, slapped backs and brimming glasses. It was always busiest around Christmas but never quite like this. The entire village might be here.

I shrink further into the shadows of our corner table, though I'm careful to keep Sam in sight. Even with the crush, it's not that tricky. Sam's a lot bigger than she used to be and there was never anything small about her voice. It rises above the carols crackling from the battered speakers and the general chatter, her laughter so much louder than the rest.

She seems to know everyone. "Merry Christmas!" she calls and "Darling! How are you?" and an affectionate "Screw you, Bill." But when she makes it to the bar, I wonder about her braying confidence. Propped up between the beer taps, she looks unexpectedly nervous, her fingers digging through her hair.

I take note of the new dulled streaks, the grey that's

spreading from her roots, and as she tugs and ruffles it, I'm sure she's conscious of my gaze.

I've hardly stopped gawking since she grabbed me among the Christmas trees, her dumped mistletoe whisking around our boots. I don't know what surprised me more, her appearance or the ease of her embrace. But despite how Sam's body has softened, her grip was firm, as if behind that extra padding, she was still her young, lean, muscled self, and when her arms eventually loosened, I found myself searching her features for similar clues, trying to see past the puffiness and laughter lines to her true face underneath.

Her grey eyes were just as I remembered, except they were sparkling, glossed with tears, and with a start, I realised I was blinking back my own. As we gazed at one another, the last thing I was thinking about was hatred. I was shocked by the rush of love.

The pathetic little tree Sam foisted on me is wedged behind my chair and I can't help smiling whenever its scraggy needles catch my hair. It's astonishing how happy I am, though a small superstitious part of me seems genuinely concerned that Sam might vanish if I look away from her for long.

It's a struggle believing in any of this. Everything's colliding. Although the pub's mood is totally different, there's so much that hasn't changed: the wallpaper's garish mauve flock and the ceiling beams, which might well be bound with the same old plastic holly and half-dead fairy lights. I definitely recognise the moth-eaten velveteen robins perched on every table, but more than any of that, it's the smells that take me back. A distinct brownish mixture of beer and cheap musky aftershave, and cigarettes, never mind that the smokers have been relegated to a huddled cloud beyond the door.

It appears that the bar staff don't turn a blind eye to underage drinking anymore either. The rowdy atmosphere has nothing to do with age; Sam's far less grey than most of the pub. She's hemmed in by weathered skin and tweed and tasteful chiffon scarves, and while I don't think I know these people, I don't let my gaze stray far. Sam's more than enough of a blast from the past and as if that wasn't already overwhelming, she's summoned Ali, jabbing out a text.

She was insistent it should be the three of us. "The whole gang," she said, and though I winced, I didn't bother to correct her. Sam, I've quickly gathered, is as clumsy as she used to be. And even more of a drinker, I suspect.

It isn't just the two Pinots we've downed since arriving between our nervy, splurging chatter. The second time she hugged me, it wasn't her extra flesh I noticed but the fumes on her breath, and now, as she comes weaving back through a noisy group of ageing lads, who clearly appreciate the bump of her broad hips, she's wielding a shining ice bucket.

"I thought we needed some bubbles," she says, "to celebrate your return!"

She dumps the bucket on the table and pulls the heavy bottle out. It isn't cava or Prosecco, but Moët and I remember how Sam's family liked to splash the cash. They were the richest in the village and probably the most hated. Around the time I left, they'd seemed determined to buy up and gentrify most of Underton, but judging from the high street, their plans didn't quite succeed. I'm about to ask Sam what she's doing selling Christmas trees when the champagne cork erupts.

"Whoops!" Sam says, licking her wet wrist and laughing. Then she's swinging the bottle recklessly over our glasses, filling them to the top, and before the foam has settled, I'm reaching out. But maybe this isn't the best idea?

I'm already light-headed. It's everything – Sam and the robins and the dense brown air – but it's also those Pinots. I don't drink much these days.

After Phil left, I knew I'd need my clearest head to do right by Scarlet, but it wasn't only that. I suspected that blurring the edges might prove too tempting. After all, I'm ironically aware of what I'm like with avoidance and wouldn't it be so easy to attempt to muffle the pain, to drift, and then keep drifting, till I practically disappeared.

"To you, Caitlin Shaw!" Sam declares, her round face tipping close, her glass singing against mine. "To coming home, and to coming together. The prodigal returns!"

And *fuck it*, I think, clinking back. I'm off duty. Scarlet's two thousand miles away while I'm stuck here, *so weirdly stuck*, and yes, everything feels easier as the champagne goes sparkling down.

After knocking back two fast mouthfuls, Sam grins. "Show me the girl!" she says.

For an instant, something clashes in my head, but it's followed rapidly by a tumbling relief. She means Scarlet, no one else.

I dig out my phone and while I scroll through the pictures, showing off my daughter – gap-toothed in an old school photo and dancing on stage, looking bashful astride a horse – I go on drinking steadily. *Fuck it, fuck it.* Scarlet's fine. Just look at her... And when Sam insists on exchanging numbers, I ignore my flash of fear. It's going to be okay.

When we first arrived at the Hunters and she started with her questions, I'd considered making up an imaginary version of my life, something smooth and happy and successful. I thought about at least inventing a better job or presenting my fantasies about returning to university as if they might actually come to pass. But this was Sam – *really and truly Sam, in front of me* – and I'd never lied to her. Not often, anyway.

And she was being so kind, so genuinely attentive, I ended up divulging the whole sorry tale of my divorce.

"*Men*," Sam said, nodding sagely, when my babbling had eventually dried up. "They're all the same. Every one of them a dickwad, the whole narcissistic lot."

And once more, I had found myself feeling for the true bones buried inside her when she'd reached out to squeeze my hand.

But though Sam seems just as loyal and feisty as she used to be, as she beams down at my daughter, I realise I've done most of the talking. I've learnt little about her life, all the things that must have happened over the past fifteen years while I was busy pretending that Underton didn't exist.

"Sam," I blurt. "Do you have kids? Did you marry? What about uni? Work? Did you ever leave?"

She doesn't look up, just shakes her head to each rattled-out question. She seems utterly absorbed in Scarlet, only meeting my gaze when she finally hands me back the phone.

"She's so like you," she says.

"No," I begin automatically, and Sam interrupts, laughing.

"But she really fucking is," she says. "Exactly like when I met you. Isn't she about the same age? She's not quite as blonde, but everything else. Those eyes and that funny little twisty smile... Do you remember when Ali and I first came knocking? Wanting to know all about the new girl who'd come to live in the haunted house..."

I fumble for my glass, concentrating on the champagne crackling on my tongue as I smile and nod. It's my turn for a vague response.

It's not that I've blocked out everything. Her words bring back an image of two girls jostling on our doorstep, chattering in high-pitched voices as their gazes skittered past me, straining to see inside the house.

There's nothing threatening about the recollection. For nearly three years, it was only Sam and Ali. Livy didn't arrive until I'd turned fifteen and surely the early memories should be safe. Except so many of the things I did with Sam and Ali – hanging out after school, and the giggling sleepovers, turning the treehouse into our HQ – seem, in retrospect, a kind of run-up. And if all paths lead to Livy, "Do you remember?" could prove a dangerous game. But Sam isn't about to be deterred.

"That day, we were both a bit in awe," she says. "Not that we'd have admitted it. But there you were, living in that freaky house, without freaking out, and your mum was so classy and your dad a fucking *psychiatrist–*"

"Psychotherapist," I correct Sam for possibly the thousandth time in my life, but she isn't listening. She's laughing again and then plunging on.

"And you were so pretty, all that amazing hair, and at first, you seemed so completely together, so *London*, I felt like a fucking bumpkin! Before you came along, I'd always been the coolest. The sassy, bolshie one–"

A voice interrupts, low but steady. "You're still a bolshie bitch."

I look up sharply, pine needles prodding the nape of my neck, to the woman hovering behind Sam's chair. A woman with gaunt freckled cheeks and a wild mass of vividly red hennaed hair. She's wearing a fringed suede jacket and a necklace strung with shells, and when she blinks, her eyelids flash a coppery green. Her lips are painted gold.

I stare and that gilded mouth twitches, then parts to reveal neat, white teeth, which curve into a smile.

"Long time, no see," she says.

I feel my eyes stretch wide. The shock shouldn't be as great as it was meeting Sam, but I'm turned inside out, completely unprepared.

"Ali?" My voice sounds distant. "Ali, is that really you?"

The woman giggles, and in that giggle, I briefly hear the big, warm girl I used to know. But Ali's even more camouflaged than Sam. She's so colourful and so ridiculously thin – and how did she get that thin? It's as if my old friends have swapped bodies. Ali's a ghost of her former self.

But then she's sweeping around the narrow table, trailing that fiery hair and an unmistakable waft of patchouli, and there's nothing spectral about her circling arms when I give in to her embrace.

My face flushes, hot and wet again, and I wipe my eyes as she disentangles. She tosses a huge, tasselled bag under the table before bobbing into the empty chair that Sam's miraculously produced.

"Ali," I'm saying. "Ali... and Sam... I thought I'd never–"

"Actually," Ali overrides me, "I'm using Alice now. I've left little – well, big, fat – Ali, far behind."

"Besides, it goes with the shop," Sam chips in. "She's called it Wonderland."

"Shop?" I ask.

Then Ali – Alice – is talking fast, gushing on like she always did. Unlike Sam, she's not shy about bringing me up to speed about her life, filling in the blanks. It turns out that she owns the village's new hippy gift shop, and as well as selling her trinkets, she invites in specialist guests. Readers of runes and palms and tarot cards and experts in candle healing.

"Whatever that is," Sam interrupts, splashing out more champagne.

But Ali only giggles again, and then goes on to explain how her interest in spirituality began when she was backpacking around the Far East, a supposed gap year that turned into four.

"The people I met," she says, "and the things that I heard and that I saw, and felt... Naturally, I gave up on the idea of uni. What was the point? I was getting a far more truthful education.

Not just learning about myself but about the life force, the *connections*. Everything that's hidden underneath."

And though when we were young, my dad didn't pay Sam and Ali much attention, I think how much he would have enjoyed this new transformed Ali. But Sam lets out a guffaw.

"All the drugs you took!" she says.

Ali doesn't appear to mind. She's smiling, and as she reaches out with her bony, heavily ringed fingers to squeeze Sam's chubby wrist, I wonder if there's something more than the old camaraderie between them. But regardless of their obvious affection – catching each other's grins, their general ease – I don't think it's that kind of intensity. Nothing like the heat I felt for Livy.

I'm quick to shut the rogue thought down, but still, I'm grateful when Ali starts asking about my grown-up life, and while Sam makes yet another trip to the bar, I go through it all a second time. The marriage, the divorce, and my daughter, even the pictures on my phone. But when Sam returns – "More bubbles!" – the whole thing about resemblances is rehashed again and I feel my nerves return.

I take a large swallow, then hastily put my glass down and pick up our table's robin. I squeeze so hard my thumb punches through the ancient velveteen to its polystyrene heart. But the bird's already missing its beak and everything else is still okay, the conversation safe.

The memories Ali chooses to unearth are mostly to do with school. She brings up Mr Haywood, who'd go purple, enraged at our gossiping in Maths, and the assembly when Sam walked out, and that time we got caught smoking on the hockey field. I begin to suspect Ali's being deliberately careful, and I'm more than grateful now. I'm overcome. *Their exact same kindness, despite my missing years...*

I sit back, releasing the robin, happy to watch Sam and Ali

reminisce, and as they discuss our failed attempts at home tattooing and the fire caused by Ali's hair straighteners, I feel an urge to stroke Sam's laughing cheeks and tousle Ali's crazy hair. These wonderful women – these incredible, irrepressible girls – what was I thinking, leaving them behind?

After I escaped Underton, or thought I had, they both tried to stay in touch, but when Mum mentioned she'd been throwing out their letters and cards, I didn't complain, and I repeatedly deleted their Facebook requests. But what selfish madness that seems now. What a total fucking waste.

Except maybe it's not too late? With the champagne fizzing through me, and Sam and Ali glittering brighter than the fairy lights, perhaps I can tell them I'm sorry. *My old friends, my realest dearest friends...*

But when I tune back in, Sam's moved on to our shoplifting missions and I can't interrupt any more than I can join in. It was Livy who dared us into stealing and though I harden myself against the memory, something flickers through the pub's warm glow. Her shadow is too close, and I jump to my feet – or try to.

As I stand, I flail, and it's only the wedged tree that stops my chair from toppling. I didn't intend the melodrama, but the ceiling's swaying towards me like the beams of a pitching ship and the robin's lying on its side, knocked off its plastic feet.

"I've drunk too much," I say. "Toilets..." And yes, I'm slurring.

Sam and Ali stare up at me with sympathy, but their shining eyes are too much now. I stumble past their chairs.

Somehow I make it through the pub, negotiating jostling elbows and slopping drinks and three giant bald men roaring "Silent Night" to crash through the door to the Ladies. But while I'm grateful that the toilets appear deserted, the checkerboard tiles keep slipping out of place and I think I might be sick.

I stagger to the sink and yank the taps on, then splash my cheeks, willing the nausea to pass. But when I straighten, I'm panting, and as my reflection smears the mirror, I'm struck again by the frantic thought – *what the fuck am I doing here?*

Too late, I realise my mistake. I try to keep focusing on my dripping chin and smudged mascara, but it isn't me, now, who's floating in the glass. It's the girl I used to be, and then it's not just me. Livy's here as well.

I'm seventeen years old, and she's bundling me through the door, leaving it swinging so that anyone in the bar might see, but we don't care. *I* don't care because Livy's all dark hair and dark eyes, and dark, dark, hungry mouth, and nothing else matters as she grabs me and pushes me up against the sinks. The enamel's cold against my back where my shirt's come untucked, but everything else is summer-hot. The air, our hair, my skin and hers, and, fuck, *oh, fuck,* her hands...

They're all over me, sliding from my face to my breasts and then down to my Levi's. She's tugging the buttons undone and her fingers are warm, so warm, as they slip inside, and her mouth is pressing mine. There's a taste like sherbet lemons from the alcopops and then the nudge of her tongue, and all the while, she's stroking me, pushing closer, pushing deeper.

And I'm laughing and gasping between our kisses, though the kissing hardly stops. There are noises coming from the stalls, a flush and then a rattling lock, but I still don't care. *I don't give a flying fuck.* Nobody's ever wanted me, loved me, not like this, and Livy's hands–

"Hey, duck, are you all right?"

And it's gone. She's gone. The memory is sinking as rapidly as it appeared and I'm gone too. I feel completely lost.

In the mirror, I'm far from seventeen and the woman behind me, with her brassy hair and novelty bauble earrings, couldn't be anything less like Livy.

"Duck?" the woman says again.

But while her expression appears friendly enough, there seems more to it than simple concern and there's something about her hesitant approach. She's almost circling me, the way you would a feral cat.

I realise I must be laughing. I can feel its helpless hysterical swell. But the woman's shaking her head, her baubles spinning, and then "Oh, love," she says. "What's happened? I could hear you crying from outside."

I'm going to leave. I'm going to fuck right off. I'm not even going to stop to say goodbye, and let's all just forget about the fucking Christmas tree.

But as I scurry out of the Ladies, swiping at my hair and face, Sam's there, blocking my path. She lurches towards me and before I've opened my mouth, "Oh no, you don't," she says. "You're not going anywhere, not yet."

Then she's thrusting her arm through mine, dragging me back through the raised drinks and the noise and past the huge, bald, singing men, and she's right, I'm going nowhere. Sam always had a powerful grip.

"I told you," she says to Ali when we reach our table. "She was just about to bail."

And Ali looks up at me with such pained regret, I immediately start to apologise. "I'm sorry," I splutter. "I'm sorry. It's the champagne. I'm not used to drinking like this. I can't. I don't–"

"*Sit down*," Ali says, and as her face contorts, I realise what she's feeling isn't disappointment. She's furious. But then she turns away, pouring me another impossible drink. I sink into my seat.

"One more for the road," Sam says. "Before you go running off again. You owe us that much, don't you think?"

The champagne tastes flat and sour now, but I take an obedient sip, trying to hide behind the glass. I can feel my tears threatening to return and when I set the drink down, I catch Sam and Ali exchanging glances.

So what? I think. *Who cares?* And while I know my reaction's a totally petulant teenage thing, for the moment, I go with it. *They always talked behind our backs...*

But Ali has her expression under control again. There's no sign of hurt or anger, and when she talks, she sounds composed. There's the air of a practised speech.

"We understand – well, we can guess – what's kept you away from here, and it's obvious there are things you'd rather we didn't mention. But, Caitlin, don't we know you? And how can we be back together, doing this, if we don't address–"

"The elephant in the room," Sam blurts. "The *Livy*-shaped elephant!"

I flinch, and so does Ali in a smaller way, but she quickly resumes her script.

"Most people fall in love with someone they shouldn't. It's not like we've never had our hearts broken. But staying away, letting one thing rule your life like that... We could have helped if you'd let us. We were going through our own shit, but we understood and you knew we cared. But you turned your back. You cut us off. And we didn't just lose her, Caitlin. It really hurt losing you too."

"I'm sorry," I start again–

"But this isn't only about you," Ali says, "or us. We all know what Livy did, and yes, it's still unthinkable. It was horrible. She was horribly sick, but it was such a long, long time ago, and you were the one who supposedly loved her... Did you ever think what it was like for her, locked away, alone, for all these years?

All the things she's had to struggle with... Can you imagine how she's felt?"

"What?" I ask, and my mouth's gone cold. I feel suddenly icily sober. "What are you saying? What do you know? Have you – are you in contact?"

Ali laughs, and there's nothing familiar about her laughter now. I stare hard at her burnished lips.

"You weren't the only one I wrote to," she says. "I've been in touch with Livy on and off for years, though I haven't heard anything since October. But what about you, Caitlin? Are you finally talking to her? Is that the real reason you've come back?"

"October?" I ask, though I've no idea what I'm saying, or thinking. My head's a rushing wind tunnel. "What happened in October? What's happening?"

But Ali doesn't answer straight away and as she pauses, biting her golden bottom lip, Sam leans forward, taking over.

"October," she says, and her grey eyes gleam. "October was when Livy was released."

Chapter 9

Karl

14 August 2002

When they told Karl they'd be keeping the girl following her arrest, he'd thought that they were joking. Not because he believed Olivia McKinnell was innocent, far from it, but because she so obviously belonged in the city. The Valley's main station was even more poorly equipped than he'd imagined nearly a whole bloody week ago, driving out here to the sticks.

God knew where they'd dump the girl tonight, but the basement cell they had provided for the interview was a perfect example. High-ceilinged but so narrow it could hardly accommodate the table where she was sitting, it looked like something out of a museum, the sort of Living History space where tourists came to experience "Gaols from the Past". As well as its ominous angles, the once white paintwork was peeling and blistered, and as soon as Karl unlatched the hatch in its battered steel door – a predictably Victorian-looking rusted hatch – he was hit by a cave-like waft of damp-riddled air. He rubbed a tired hand across his face.

The headache had descended the first day he arrived and though the pills he crunched mostly reduced its throb to a low-level thrum, he hadn't been able to shake free of it entirely.

Everything about this place made his skull close in, not just the old-fashioned station, or the tatty B&B they'd put him up in, but the entire sodding Valley. The "picturesque" rolling hills and protected forests had started to feel inescapable and even the sunshine was verging on oppressive.

But it was undoubtedly the case that had muddied his view of the place. Karl should have been delighted when the girl was picked up, but seeing her now, in that archaic cell, only added to his depression.

Not that Olivia McKinnell seemed bothered by her surroundings. She was sitting very upright, her hands clasped demurely on the tabletop. Her dyed black hair was scraped away from her face, tied up in a high bushy ponytail, and she had made some attempt to scrub her make-up off. But though her mouth was stripped bare, the bold lipstick gone, her eyes remained smudged and as Karl followed her blotchy gaze across the table to the pair of folding chairs propped against the wall, he felt the pressure in his head building. One of those chairs was meant for him.

Telling himself he was keen to get the interview over, Karl had come along early – a mistake, he realised now. This watching and waiting was only making things worse, and he couldn't enter the room alone. The girl had vehemently refused to see the duty solicitor, but Karl still had to wait for his new colleague, Alma, and *get a move on*, he found himself willing her. *Let's just get this done.*

But though Alma was the Valley's only female senior-ranking officer, Karl didn't share the general belief that the fact she owned a pair of sagging breasts would be enough to get the girl to open up. From everything he'd gathered, Alma wasn't exactly a gentle touch. Along with that sack-like figure, she had a harsh, lined face, a smoker's cough, and a matching hacking laugh. Still, *get your arse down here,* Karl kept thinking. He needed to go home.

He wasn't even supposed to be here. He'd been sent in place of Walker, his DCI, who was tied up with another gang-related city shooting, and since the McKinnell case had taken its latest turn, it was unlikely that Walker would show his face at all. It would be down to Karl to see it through to the end and there would be about as much satisfaction in that as there had been in every dismal development so far. Karl had felt like a bystander, useless, from the start.

By the time he arrived in Underton, Forensics were finished with the house and the search for the girl was already underway. Karl had been told he'd lead the press conference, but the locals had taken that over too. Coleman, the Valley's Commissioner, had squeezed into a dressy three-piece suit for the cameras, and positioned behind him, Karl had done his best not to grimace while the man talked too much and smiled too much, trying not to begrudge him his fifteen minutes. Except Karl had and still did. Yet another petty desperate moment to add to his growing list.

His headache was definitely expanding, its drone becoming darker and angrier, stirring like a nest of wasps. His fingers returned to his forehead, massaging the bridge of his nose, while beyond the hatch, the girl's face remained as stiff and still as the rest of her, her expression as creepily blank as a porcelain doll's.

Karl didn't think she was aware of his watching, but really, it was impossible to tell. Behind that seamless mask she might have been concentrating, trying to contain her own multitude of buzzing thoughts, or else her head could have emptied entirely. *Nothing left inside at all...*

He had seen that happen before. People, though usually victims, so sunk under an avalanche of shock they practically disappeared.

Frozen, Karl thought, but then as if she'd heard him, the girl moved, breaking the spell, and he started away from the hatch. As if he'd been the one submerged in some distant elsewhere place and Olivia McKinnell was in charge.

There had been a weird sense of that from the outset. While the girl was missing, he had done the rounds, interviewing the neighbours and Theresa's friends, and they'd all responded with a similar enthusiasm, not so much worried as excited. Each one of them, including those who had joined the search parties, had been convinced of Olivia's guilt and yet they appeared more awestruck than afraid.

Like the Commissioner, everyone seemed to relish their bit parts in the girl's grand drama. Mrs Abbot, who owned the café where Theresa had sometimes worked, topping up her benefits with a little extra cash in hand, launched into an extravagant monologue as though Olivia might have been hiding nearby, listening from the wings, just waiting for her cue.

Only at the traveller site had the reaction been more measured. For the first time, Karl had encountered genuine concern for Olivia's safety and an alternative explanation for Theresa's death. The travellers seemed to believe the killer was a local man, but they refused to offer a name or any specifics, and there was clearly no love lost between them and the villagers. They didn't think Underton had treated the McKinnells well, but again they'd been vague, and before Karl left, they began to defend Olivia like she was some sort of martyr. She'd attained mythical status even there.

Perhaps it wasn't surprising that long before Karl set eyes on her, the girl had left him rattled. But it wasn't like him to feel so invested or so unnerved. As ugly as her mother's murder was, he had dealt with worse. The machete gang victims, not just butchered but hung like meat, and the baby he found three days too late, still floating in the bath... And as screwed up as Olivia

McKinnell might be, she was basically a kid. There was no reason to feel this jumpy.

The girl hadn't even changed her position much. She hadn't turned to look at him, she had simply raised her hands, and when Karl peered back through the hatch, she was still holding them open in front of her face. She could have been studying the scratches on her palms, although unlike her fingerprints, those marks had nothing to do with the murder weapon. The cuts were consistent with her story about a broken glass and besides, she might have just been admiring her nails. She had painted them electric-blue.

And staring at those very teenage fingernails, the thought came whining through Karl's wasp-nest head: *what if she's innocent after all?*

It wasn't the first time the idea had struck him, but he was all too aware of how untrustworthy supposed "instincts" could be, and again, he regretted turning up early. Hadn't that decision been inspired by his gut? If – when – Alma found him here, she'd probably laugh her rasping laugh. *I didn't think you'd be so keen, Ward. I can't, for the life of me, figure out why...*

But while Karl could admit, to himself at least, that his curiosity wasn't entirely professional, he was sure it had nothing to do with the girl's appearance, as attractive as she was. Didn't he know, better than most, what some women were capable of, especially the lookers?

No. Both his fascination and his confusion came from somewhere else. He had thought some of the unease would lift once Olivia McKinnell showed up, but reviewing the CCTV footage from the petrol station shop, where the uniforms eventually found her, had only left him more disconcerted. Before her arrest, the girl had been sidling up and down the narrow aisles, and watching her nonchalantly pocketing a can of Diet Coke, Karl had been reminded of his daughter.

Since Elise had turned six, she'd developed a sneaky little magpie streak, collecting – well, stealing – pretty, glittery things. Just last month, when Karl had gone to fetch her for his weekend, he had caught her rifling through her mother's jewellery box, and though he made her return the rings and necklaces, he had felt more amused than angry. There had been such a comical intensity to her shining eyes and delving fingers, and something almost charming in her utter lack of shame.

For the first few minutes tracking Olivia McKinnell's brazen progress through the shop, Karl had found himself questioning everything. Never mind the girl's fingerprints, or the timeline, or how she'd fled the scene, as she stuffed a sandwich into her jacket, she had appeared as guilelessly naughty as his own disarming child.

But the petrol station footage was grainy. There had been a stutter to her movements and the subtleties of her features were obscured by her tangled hair and heavy make-up, the theatrical face paint adding to that sense of naivety. She looked like she was about to go trick or treating. It was only when she stopped and raised her head to the camera that Olivia McKinnell transformed.

Her cleavage came abruptly into focus, but that didn't shock Karl as much as her expression. After shaking her hair away from her face, her full dark lips curved into a smile, and it was such a confident, self-possessed smile. No child's grin could be that knowing.

Pausing the tape, it had dawned on Karl that the girl was fully aware of what she was doing. She wanted to get caught.

If it hadn't been for that unwavering gaze and adult smile, Karl might have assumed that Olivia's behaviour, offering herself up so blatantly, was driven by her conscience. It wouldn't be the first time an investigation had been solved by guilt. A few months ago, there had been the junkie who had called to confess to strangling his girlfriend, though he'd still half believed, or hoped, that it was another of his paranoid dreams, and more recently, the "Killer Crime Lord", as the tabloids crowned him, who had come shuffling into the station. In reality, just a frail and weepy old man, too tired, he explained, to go on...

But though Olivia had been on the run for days, sleeping rough in the woods, or so she claimed – those unchipped blue nails might tell a different story – the arresting officers had mentioned nothing about exhaustion, let alone remorse. While she had steadfastly refused to discuss her mother's murder, they said she'd seemed at ease in the back of the car. Even chatting about the bloody weather as she tore into her stolen sandwich, which no one had thought to take away.

Obviously her behaviour, both casual and audacious, was bound to be misleading. Karl had spent hours reading up on her, the GP and school records and the thin sheaf of notes that he'd finally pressurised from Shaw, and it was clear Olivia hadn't had it easy. She'd had to grow up tough.

Her father had been a total waste of space. He'd probably done her a favour by dying from a heart attack four years ago following some mindless nightclub brawl. Steve McKinnell wasn't exactly a family man; he had worked occasionally, picking up casual carpentry jobs, but spent most of his pathetic life inside. He'd been sentenced for both ABH and GBH and though there weren't any reports of domestic abuse, Theresa's medical history listed an excessive number of trips to A&E resulting from "accidents" at home.

Poor dead Theresa McKinnell. For a while, especially after moving to Underton, she might have imagined she'd escaped her violent past, but when Karl glanced over the photos added to her files, he had felt more wary than surprised. As vibrant and striking as Theresa had been, there was something about her face, so eager and open, so willing to please, that he'd come across before.

Despite their physical resemblance, she was an altogether different type of good-looking woman to her daughter. A misguided, unknowing type, her shine partially undermined by need. Again and again, Theresa's photographs revealed that sense of unguarded hope, and the FLOs could think whatever they liked, it had become increasingly evident to Karl that some women were magnets for tragedy.

In the interview room the girl was moving again. She had twisted her ponytail over one shoulder and still seemingly indifferent to Karl's presence, she was brushing its bushy tip across her mouth, and though her face contained nothing of Theresa's desperation, she was distinctly her mother's daughter. They shared those voluptuous Bardot lips, as well as the other more obvious curves. There didn't seem to be any trace of Steve McKinnell in Olivia at all.

But of course, abusers breed abuse, except that usually happened with the sons. The girls tended to end up a different way, the Theresa-way. Clearly not in Olivia's case.

She had been shunted from school to school, repeatedly suspended and then excluded, and by the time Theresa brought her to Underton, the girl had withdrawn entirely from formal education without completing a single GCSE. She was supposedly studying by correspondence but as far as Karl could tell, the only subject she was keeping up with was an overpriced and rather dubious-looking foundation course in Art.

At school, there had been regular truancy issues and a general resistance to authority, but it was the acts of aggression that interested Karl, the "lack of impulse control". Up until the final classroom incident, Olivia's physical fights appeared to have been exclusively with boys. Only the last most shocking assault involved another girl, apparently a previous best friend.

The attack had been premeditated – Olivia brought one of her dad's old chisels into school – and its viciousness was revealing. According to the report, even as her teachers tried to restrain her, Olivia kept going, slashing at the air.

But though there had been a hospital visit, stitches to the other girl's hands, her parents decided against pursuing an investigation and there was no indication, at least officially, of anything happening lately. Still, it was hard to forget that weapon and the fact that she wouldn't stop.

But as damning as Olivia's history was, it would never be allowed in court without more recent evidence. Olivia's prints on the knife had been enough to make the arrest but the CPS wanted more before Karl could charge her, especially since so much of the forensics was compromised when the local-yokel first responders went blundering into the bungalow.

Karl had hoped the girl's therapist would provide what he needed. Involving the man so early had felt like a shrewd decision, but perhaps it was just another useless gut instinct? It certainly didn't seem to be paying off. Shaw had been frustratingly ambiguous during their meetings, refusing to speculate about Olivia's current mindset and her possible extremes. He might have been equally protective of his other clients who, as far as Karl could tell, were mostly wealthy retired executives, but Olivia was clearly different. Shaw seemed to have taken her on as a charity case and perhaps his reticence had something to do with knowing the McKinnells personally. Maybe even therapists could suffer from survivor's guilt?

The girl was chewing on her ponytail now, sucking and nipping at the strands. The bites looked gentle, an absent gesture rather than an indication of nerves or impatience, and *why* Karl wondered as he watched her. Not why she might have so savagely attacked her mother, but why did she turn up at the garage shop, practically handing herself in.

What is it that you want?

Everybody wanted something, and in a rush that felt like inspiration, *bugger Alma,* Karl thought and reached for the door's heavy handles. The bolts released with a series of clanks – more Living History – but Karl ignored them, just as he dismissed the small blinking light of the ceiling camera, which was unlikely to be working anyway, to focus solely on the girl. This pretty, scrubbed-faced, dangerous girl, who was still sitting there passively as Karl barged in. She didn't even bother glancing up.

"Olivia," he said. "Olivia McKinnell."

And still she took her time, meticulously extracting the wet twist of hair from her mouth before meeting his gaze. But then she was staring at him as purposefully as she had confronted the CCTV camera, only she wasn't smiling now.

For a second, Karl imagined something passing between them, something dark and fast and fluttering, but that might have been down to his aching head. The pain was intensifying though the girl hadn't spoken and her stiff expression remained unchanged.

But this close, he could see that her face was far more than an empty mask. There was a strange concentration to the composed blankness of her features, and Karl didn't think that he was imagining the icy wave of her contempt.

"Olivia," he began again. "Olivia, what–"

She interrupted him. But though her voice seemed as firm and level as her gaze, her words didn't make any sense, and with the wasps in his head growing busier. "Hold on," he said. "Could you tell me that again?"

Olivia slowed down to repeat herself, laboriously enunciating every syllable as if Karl was hard of hearing, or just plain thick, and to his astonishment, he hadn't misheard her.

"I want to see my cat."

Chapter 10

Caitlin

24 December 2017

I wake up wincing. I didn't bother with the curtains last night and the morning's flooding in. After all the days of relentless grey, I ought to be grateful, but the sunshine does nothing to help my hangover, and worse than that, it feels like it's gloating, exposing every detail in the room.

I never wanted to be back in my old bedroom. I'd have preferred a guest room, or even Mum and Dad's abandoned suite, but like so much of the house, they've been locked up. I didn't have a choice.

Trying to make the best of things, I've used the room strictly for sleeping, escaping to the bathroom to put on my face and brush my hair and change, but leaping out of bed isn't an option right now. My head is pounding and when I try shutting my eyes again, the light easily penetrates my sticky lids and "Fuck," I mutter, remembering the cocktails. As if all that champagne wasn't bad enough.

For a moment, I see Sam with a tiny pink parasol propped behind one ear, and Ali pausing to lick her gilded lips, her tongue stained Curaçao-blue. But mostly, Ali's mouth keeps talking and talking, and the cocktails make more sense than the things that she's telling me. Livy has been released–

I sit up fast and the room swerves with me, and there's no comfort when it settles. Although Mum probably tore down my posters the second I left, the lilac walls have never been repainted, the old mirror goes on looming over the dressing table, and the shelves are still crammed with my books. I take in the top row – *Atkins' Diet Revolution* squeezed in between a revision guide to *Animal Farm* and an unread copy of *Atonement* – before my gaze drops to the floor, and now I'm fighting the urge to heave.

The floorboards are strewn with paper and "Fuck, fuck, fuck," I say between sour swallows as more of last night returns.

I remember the reckless longing that dogged me home. Staggering along the high street, I kept searching the dark beyond the blurry white trail of the council's Christmas lights, and in the woods, it was even worse. A kind of madness overtook me; I was almost praying I was being watched.

But the memories melt together, revolving, and abruptly I'm back in the Ladies, confronted by a worried stranger, and then I'm staring into Ali's knowing face as she reveals that she tracked Livy down several years ago, and *what?* I'm demanding and *why?* and *how?*

I couldn't get my head around any of it. Not the timeline, nor Ali's curiosity, and especially not the fact that they'd been keeping in touch via email – that didn't seem possible – and my confusion made Sam laugh.

"What did you imagine?" she asked. "Some Bedlam place, with the inmates rattling their chains or the bars of their cages and howling at the moon?"

And *yes*, I realised, recalling a series of nightmares I'd had where Livy was bound to a chair and screaming, that was exactly what I'd thought.

But the papers scattering my floorboards aren't email printouts, or letters, or anything like that, and as my gaze shifts to the narrow drawer underneath the wardrobe I've left gaping, my hands rise to touch my face as if it might still be slick with tears.

As soon as I got in last night, I started searching and it was as bad as in the pub toilets. I couldn't stop remembering and I couldn't stop crying. By the time I found what I was looking for, I could scarcely see–

Livy, literally laid out bare, before me.

In my last week living in Underton, I was ruthless, destroying most of her gifts, but I couldn't bring myself to rip up her life drawings. I thought hiding them in the dark would be enough, but for all these years they've been waiting and after the way I fell apart last night, I should finally get rid of them for good. Except I don't. I can't. I'm already reaching down and scooping up the two nearest sheets.

Like so much of Livy's art, they're self-portraits and though the first is sketched in faint grey pencil lines and the second's cruder and darker, its charcoal smudged, the resemblance in both is remarkable. The papers tremble in my hands.

In the pencilled one, Livy's drawn herself lying on her stomach wearing nothing but a grin and a pair of ankle socks. In the other, she's also naked, but her body's mostly obscured. She's curled in on herself, her arms roped around her bended knees, and only her face is clearly exposed. She's peering out at me.

Pushing aside my covers, I slump to the floor and give myself up to her entirely. There's no excuse – I'm not drunk now – but *just one more*, I keep telling myself as I sift through page after page of Livy's endless gaze and seductive curves until suddenly she disappears. But though I shake my aching head, I should have known. I was always going to find myself.

There's no mistaking my young features. My dopey eyes

and needy smile and that absurd amount of spilling hair. Livy always spent a long time recreating my hair and in this picture, it's a swirling waterfall. I raise my free hand self-consciously towards my head, but as I stare in wonder at my teenage body, my fingers change track. I trace a soft path from my throat to my cleavage.

It's like looking into some freaky time-warping funhouse mirror. *Here I am and here I was.* In the sketch, my breasts are small and high, my waist's so thin it looks like I've had a couple of ribs removed, and my wrists are tiny glassy things. Livy always loved my bones.

I didn't think I'd forgotten her talent, but with the evidence right here, it's startling – and heartbreaking. *Oh, Livy, what a waste.*

A genuine artist, she often captured something beyond the physical, but though in this particular sketch, my expression's bordering on angelic, my stripped body's far from ethereal. I'm crouched, doglike, on all fours.

But what comes back to me now isn't the crudity of those sessions but Livy's patience, the care she'd take arranging my limbs even when we had been drinking, or smoking, or popping pills. As she worked, she would grow cooler, increasingly distracted, till I'd inevitably take her distance as a challenge, and attempt some distraction techniques of my own...

But *no.*

No, no, no. I can't let the memories overwhelm me and while I go on scanning picture after picture, still unable to let them go, I try to focus on the more playful images where our nudity is contrasted with silly hats and joke-shop wigs.

I don't know how I could have forgotten that phase when Livy brought out her props. Along with the fancy-dress accessories, there's one where my body's puddled with what looks like milk, and in another, I'm wielding a rolling pin and straddling a mop like a witch's broom. But just as I feel my face twitching, wanting to smile, the next picture turns me cold.

There's a knife – a long, serrated kitchen knife – clenched between my gritted teeth.

With a gasp, I crumple the paper and then I'm scrabbling about, trying to gather up the rest of the drawings without looking at them. I don't want to see, or think, or feel anymore, but I'm being too rough – they're starting to tear – and because I'm dropping as many pictures as I'm clutching, I'm still helplessly surrounded.

And it isn't only the pictures or my oppressive bedroom: the ground floor is roaring up from underneath me, the whole house closing in.

But though I quickly realise it's just the Hoover, that Bethany must be back, that's all, I remember something else from last night. The other mess I left behind.

When I eventually make it downstairs, the house is quiet. Sunlight slants across the hallway and fills the blue glass bowl on the table with a perfect inky pool. The old landline used to sit next to it and I recall how, desperate for privacy, I'd carry out my conversations in code, watching myself whisper in the antique mirror. But the mirror, like the phone, is gone, and there's no faded patch to reveal its long-lost ghost. Everything looks ordered and settled and clean.

My coat isn't lying in a heap on the parquet where I tossed it. It's hanging primly from the rack, and my kicked off muddied boots have been partially concealed, shoved into the shadows underneath. More importantly, there isn't an incriminating trail of twigs or broken branches and the creamy walls aren't scuffed.

Any evidence of a drunken madwoman dragging a dead tree through here has been totally wiped out.

Still, I pause for a moment at the foot of the stairs. I thought I'd pulled myself together, but despite the toothpaste, my mouth tastes poisonous. I've spent the last ten minutes throwing up and I hold my body warily as I step into the hall.

Each door looks purposefully, pointedly shut and I ignore the living room in return, not ready to face Mum yet. But before I make it to the kitchen, thinking only of coffee and ibuprofen, I'm stopped in my tracks. There's something caught on the skirting board. A small tangle of soft black strands.

As I sink to a crouch, I'm shaking, though up close, the tangle is neither black nor soft, and I don't know what's the matter with me; I'm so fucked up. It's just a clump of pine needles that Bethany has missed. There's no reason to remain hunched here, trying and failing to battle another swell of tears. It's nothing at all like Livy's hair.

In the kitchen, the light is harsh. It hits me with the cold. The patio doors have been flung open and with the dazzle from the frosted garden, it takes a moment to understand that the bearlike shape hovering there is actually human, or almost. Bethany's silhouette is muddled by the glare.

But it takes her longer to notice me and when she does, she visibly jolts, throwing out one clumsy paw. As her cigarette whirls away, I feel a surge of petty victory – *Caught you! Ha, ha, ha!*

Although Mum might have changed in some ways, I sincerely doubt she's relaxed her smoking rules and the sight of Bethany trying to jam her incriminating Zippo into her pocket while fumbling to shut the doors is incredibly gratifying.

But when she turns to me, she's grinning and "Beautiful morning!" she announces, never mind that the air's abrasive. "You should've seen it earlier before the sun cut through. The mist was that thick, it was like a blanket. You'd never guess it now."

"Smoky, was it?" I ask.

But her smile refuses to falter and the flush of her cheeks might be down to rude health rather than embarrassment. Meanwhile, my hangover goes on rotting through me and I wonder if I stink.

"I don't suppose you were up that early," Bethany says. "Not after your adventures yesterday."

She cocks her head to the corner of the kitchen, and for several seconds we both contemplate my dumped Christmas tree. It looks even sadder than I remembered. All brown sagging fronds and balding sticks.

"There weren't many left," I mutter.

Bethany laughs. "No kidding! It took me ages to get those needles up."

As she sidles towards me, I glance from her ruddy face to the matching red of her festive jumper and I'm pleased to see how uncomfortable it looks. A sequinned snowman is painfully stretched across her breasts, his carrot-nose misshapen.

"I didn't mean to make such a mess," I start, but she's talking again.

"Like I haven't got enough to do."

She flutters one hand, magician-style, towards the table and as if it's really a trick, it's only now that I register the chopped herbs and a mixing bowl full of breadcrumbs, and a grubby spill of potatoes escaping from their bag. And at the centre of it all, in pride of place, an enormous uncooked turkey.

"Shit," I say, as I take in the bird's pallid pimpled flesh and it strikes me, like a cartoon dumbbell to my dumb head, that today is Christmas Eve.

"I'm getting the prep done now," Bethany explains. "That way Jilly can just bung everything in tomorrow."

"Right," I say, and from over her shoulder, there's a dainty skittering sound as another round of needles drop.

"I'm sure she'll be in better spirits by then," Bethany goes on, and for a bewildered second I think she's talking about the tree.

"What do you mean?" I say, then catching on, "Is something up with Mum?"

Bethany reels in her grin and solemnly shakes her head. "Just another of her bad nights. She was in a right state when I got here this morning. Poor thing, upset, and all alone…"

I drag a chair out from under the table and sink wearily into it. Refusing to rise to the bait of that "alone", "What happened in the night?" I ask.

"Well…" It's a weighted *well*, and with it, Bethany takes a heavy step closer. "I've only been here a couple of times to see it in person…"

She's lowered her tone to something hushed and conspiratorial. It's infuriating and I reach out for a potato, batting it back and forth across the tabletop while, spy-like, she goes on.

"But she's told me about the other times. It seems to come in phases, and it's been especially bad these last few months."

"What?" I ask. "What's been bad?" Round and round, the potato rolls.

"*Night terrors,*" Bethany stage-whispers. "You know, like little kids get. When they wake up screaming, and they don't understand who, or what, or where they are, only it's worse than that… Seeing a lady like your mother sobbing and pulling her hair. It's frightening. She's not herself at all."

"I don't understand. What's Mum got to be scared of? What's she dreaming? Does she tell you about her dreams?"

And as if I'm not feeling tense enough, Bethany looms right over me, reaching down like she's about to take my hand. But I'm loyal to my spud, I don't let go, and though her breath's puffing against the nape of my neck, I refuse to look at her directly.

"Can't you guess?" she murmurs. "All that stuff that happened, all those years ago. What your friend did and everything else. The papers, and your father helping to put that girl away... I know it was a terrible time for you, but you weren't the only one. And she couldn't go running off."

I don't say anything, but I squeeze the potato hard, flashing back to Ali's accusations in the Hunters.

"Jilly and Theresa were such good friends," Bethany says. "No wonder she's never got over it. Sometimes she calls out when the nightmares come – *Theresa, Theresa* – she'll say it again and again."

My knuckles turn white with clenching. I'm trying desperately to think. Were Mum and Theresa ever truly friends? I'm struggling to remember them together and the images I eventually recover – the pair of them chattering lightly on the doorstep and Mum frowning at some party, topping up Theresa's wine – don't exactly offer much insight. Maybe Bethany's making this entire thing up? She's so possessive over Mum.

"It's a worry," she says. "I worry that Jilly might hurt herself, what with her heart and all. I worry about her heart. Somebody has to, I suppose."

And though I'm tempted to throw the potato at her stupid yakking head, I let it roll away, but as I scrape my chair away from the table, Bethany's forced to step back. I jerk to my feet.

"But I'm here now," I say, "and so you don't need to worry."

I'm copying her tone deliberately, carefully ladling out each word. "You've already done too much."

"Oh no," she begins.

I cut her off. "All this," I say, and it's my turn to wave at the table. "It's really kind, Bethany, really considerate, and thank you so much for setting up, but I can get everything sorted now. You're not needed anymore."

"But..." She seems to be addressing the mixing bowl. "But... But... The stuffing's hardly started, and I was going to cream the parsnips. The tatties aren't even peeled–"

"I'm sure I'll manage."

I take my time considering her broad flushed features. The dirt-like specks of stray mascara and her wobbling jaw, the slight nicotine tinge to her teeth... And as I lean across to give her arm an oh-so casual squeeze, my hangover's finally abating.

"Honestly, Bethany, it's fine. You've done enough, and isn't Christmas all about family? I'm sure you've got your own lot waiting. You shouldn't be hanging about with strangers. You can get off now. You're free to go."

"But..."

"Really, Bethany, I insist."

"Well!" She's glaring at my hand on her sleeve. "If that's what you want. I'll just have a quick word with Jilly before... I'll just make sure..."

I shake my head. "That might not be the best idea. I'll be looking after Mum from now on, and we don't want to disturb her if she's resting. Not after the awful night you said she's had."

Lips tight, Bethany shrugs me off. There's a small powdery patch of potato dirt dusting her jumper where my fingers were and I don't bother to hide my smile.

"I was going to make pigs in blankets," she mutters. "And onion gravy..."

But I go to the kitchen doorway and gaze steadily into the

hall's serene gold light while she clatters about behind me. There's the bang of a cupboard door and when I glance back, she's gathered up her gloves and an enormous bag and she's huffing on her coat.

"I'll call Jilly later," she says. The heathery sprig she was wearing yesterday is pinned to her coat collar, but its petals are wilting and faded a dishrag-grey, and as she stabs her buttons into their buttonholes, it looks about to shake apart.

"Nice flower," I say.

She pushes past me. "Just make sure you tell Jilly," she growls. "Tell her I'll ring her. *I'll be in touch.*"

I watch her stomp away, ready to spring into action if she tries doubling back to Mum in the living room. But she makes it to the front door without misbehaving, and after she's opened it, "Bethany," I call out. "Merry Christmas! Happy Christmas to you and yours!"

There's a moment when she stiffens, but she doesn't turn around and as she slams the door shut behind her, I add a cheerful, "And fuck the lot of you."

It's like dusk in the living room. Mum's thick curtains are tightly drawn, keeping out the sunshine that's taken over the rest of the house. But though the shadows offer the respite I've been seeking all morning, I roll my eyes. Even the light defers to Mum.

But I need to get over this adolescent attitude. It might have proved useful while dealing with Bethany, but my mother's my mother, and she's old, I remind myself, and vulnerable. She looks so small tucked up in bed. She barely lumps the sheets.

"Hi, Mum," I murmur from the doorway. "It's me. It's Caitlin... Hey, Mum, are you awake?"

She clearly isn't. She's curled up, stilled, between the shadows, and I realise that I'm holding my breath and listening for hers.

"Mum?"

I ease my way past the chairs and the coffee table, but when I reach the bed, a memory floats up through the twilight. It isn't about Mum, though, or Livy. For once it has nothing to do with my teenage years. What comes to me, unbidden, is an image of my father before his funeral when he was waiting in his box.

He was wearing a neat, finely pin-striped grey suit and an elegant silver tie. He was always a stylish dresser and despite everything else I was feeling at the time, I wondered about his outfit, if he'd chosen it in advance.

But Dad wasn't meant to die. The first stroke had been minor and his recovery impressive, at least as far as I'd been told.

Mum had sounded reassuring when I called. "The doctors say he's doing wonderfully. There's no real loss to his mobility. The left side of his face is still a bit stuck but he's doing fine."

And when she passed the phone to Dad, he had seemed his usual good-humoured self. I'd imagined him smiling at a slight angle, but he didn't say anything to worry me or slur a single word.

But Dad could be an expert in concealment and there had been more than one occasion when he had seemed to know things he shouldn't.

"My esoteric talents," he used to joke whenever he sniffed out trouble among the neighbours or successfully predicted a friend's divorce, though his instincts undoubtably arose from his work. All that delving about in his clients' heads... But after Theresa's death, Dad stopped mentioning his hunches. I don't think he ever got over feeling so blindsided.

Still, Dad didn't look at all surprised laid out in his coffin. In fact, he looked shockingly healthy and as well as wondering about embalming techniques, I couldn't help remembering the handsome ageless vampires in the old horror movies he used to love. Leaning in to kiss his cool, dry cheek, I half expected him to break into a grin and wink. I'd badly longed for that.

"Mum, *wake up.*"

My own voice startles me, but it does the job. Her snowy hair shifts on the pillow. She frowns and when she opens her eyes, her gaze is both disapproving and confused.

"Kitty," she says. "What are you doing here?"

"Oh, Mum..." Preparing to explain, I sink to my knees and reach out to touch her bird-bone fingers. The way she's clutching the blanket's ribboned trim reminds me of Scarlet as a toddler.

"I'm staying for a bit," I tell her. "It's Christmas tomorrow and I've come to visit. You've not been well–"

"For Christ's sake," she rasps over me. "I know that. I'm not an imbecile."

Then she's sighing – of course she's sighing – and sitting up impatiently, shaking off my hand.

"What I meant is, why are you in here? I was sleeping. Has something happened? Where's Bethany?"

She cranes to look towards the doorway and I turn with her, almost expecting to see Bethany blocking the hallway's glow as if I'd never sent her packing.

"She's gone," I mumble. "She had to go. It's Christmas Eve. She had a lot of stuff to do..."

Mum's frown deepens. "Really? I had something for her, a little gift. Perhaps she's coming back?"

"Perhaps."

My hands are suddenly busy, pulling free a hospital corner, then trying uselessly to tuck it back. "She said you had a bad night and that you've been having nightmares... She told me they've been happening for a while."

Mum starts wheezing. She doesn't seem able to catch her breath, but when I look up from the untucked sheet, she's holding a hand girlishly across her mouth, and I realise that she's laughing.

"What?" I ask. "Was Bethany lying? I thought she might be making it up or exaggerating."

My mother shakes her head, but though she's bitten back the laughter, her eyes keep glittering, amused.

"Kitty," she says. "Nobody's making anything up. No one's telling lies."

"What is it then, Mum? What's so funny? I don't get it."

"It's just..." Her thin hands flap. "Look at you, my Kitty-Cat. You haven't changed a bit. Always worrying about all the wrong things and always so bloody melodramatic."

"But, Mum," I try to backpedal. "Bethany told me you've been dreaming about that time before I left. About Theresa, she said... And it's horrible, Mum. I understand, I really do. The nightmares haven't stopped for me either."

And as I go on babbling, the dream images flicker around me. There's Livy screaming and Livy bleeding. She's tied up in a cell and she's crawling towards me through the treehouse with her hands outstretched... But then the nightmares begin to merge with her sketches – that knife clenched between my teeth – and my voice, I realise, is rising. Everything's jarring in my head.

"Livy," I'm saying. "She's never left me alone. She keeps on coming back."

Mum's face has paled behind its creases and "Stop," she hisses. "Kitty, stop. For God's sake, what's wrong with you?"

"Mum," I say, and I want to cry, but there's something predatory about her glittering eyes now.

"Stop," she says again. "I won't hear that girl's name, not in my house. Not after what she did."

107

But I'm still not myself. "Did you know?" I'm practically yelling. "Did you know that Livy's out?"

I'm not sure what confirms it, the sideways flick of my mother's gaze or her lifted hands warding me off.

"Caitlin," she says. "*Just stop.*"

For a moment, there's nothing but the sound of our ragged breaths. I can't tell mine from hers, though when she continues, I hear her exhaustion, the effort that comes with every word.

"Didn't you hear what I said?" she asks. "We will not speak of her. Or think of her. After what she did to us all, that girl's dead to me. She's deader than the mother she killed... As far as I'm concerned, the McKinnells never existed."

With another thinner sigh, she closes her eyes, her wan face sinking back onto the pillow, and I feel like I'm sinking too.

What was I thinking? What was I saying? She looks so frail and empty, and I realise she's right; I've gone about everything wrong. She needs me and what have I been doing? Obsessing over Livy, as if she might reappear at any moment, never mind that Underton's got to be the last place on Earth she'd want to be, and that she's the very last thing I should be talking to Mum about. *For God's sake, what's wrong with me?*

"Mum," I whisper. "I'm sorry. It's all too much. I didn't mean to... I'm not here because of any of this. I came back for you."

"Hmm." She doesn't open her eyes.

"Please, Mum. I shouldn't have brought her up, and I won't again..."

I pause to rein myself in, then "Everything's going to be okay," I say more firmly. "We'll have a proper Christmas, you and me."

But though I haven't a clue why I'm still clinging onto the Christmas idea, Mum's eyes open. She almost smiles.

"Bethany told me you bought a tree," she says, and my relief is stunning.

"I did!" I say before hastening on. There's no way I'm about to describe it. "And there's tons of food. We'll have a feast. I'll finish getting it ready this afternoon. I need to mash the parsnips and make the gravy..."

I wonder if I've gone too far. Mum's frown has returned. But she's simply distracted.

"The angel, and the rest of the decorations, I remember boxing them up... I think they're in your father's study, somewhere among his junk. We'll need to find the key."

"Yes, the key," I echo, the words chiming out of me. It feels like she's offering me so much more than Christmas and when she allows me to clasp her little hand, the gratitude forms a warm lump in my throat. Perhaps, for once in my life, I'll be able to make my mother happy. All I have to do is stick to my promises and maybe they'll come true.

Chapter 11

Jill

15 August 2002

When Caitlin insisted on going in alone, neither one of them had put up much of a fight. After all the days the girl had spent moping, Jill didn't have the energy and Richard seemed to think the fact she'd accepted their lift to the school to collect her results was a major achievement in itself. From the moment that Caitlin climbed into the back of his Bentley, he'd been looking smug, and if Jill had asked him – which she'd certainly had no intention of doing – he would probably have given her one of his sage nods. "Baby steps," he might have said.

But though they were meant to be waiting patiently in the car park, Richard had lasted less than five minutes before erupting, and as he stalked off across the tarmac, Jill directed her glare at the sweat stains patterning his shirt and made no attempt to call him back.

Throughout his outburst and the banal speech that preceded it, she'd held herself perfectly straight and still, refusing to utter a single word. She wasn't surprised at his behaviour – he no longer had the power to surprise her – and quite frankly, it was a relief he'd gone. She might even have orchestrated it herself.

As soon as their daughter had slipped out of sight, sloping her way towards the main school building, Jill had snatched her hand from Richard's knee and turned away, the force of her sigh making her shudder. The effort of performing for Caitlin was exhausting, and too often, lately, a single glance at her husband's face could leave her feeling drained.

She couldn't bear his swollen eyes or his quivering mouth and how she kept having to remind him to shave. Was he deliberately trying to drive her mad?

"Please, Jill," he'd said after Caitlin left. "We've got to stand together, provide a united front. I've never needed you so much." And then, within seconds, he was slamming out of the car. It was almost laughable.

Well, good riddance. Perhaps now Jill was free of him she'd finally find some peace.

She kept praying for that, for a quiet half hour, or just ten minutes, when the tension would let up. She'd thought it might come following the news of Livy McKinnell's arrest, not from Caitlin of course – there would be no quick end to her theatrics – but Jill had hoped that Richard would regain some degree of composure, for appearances' sake if nothing else. He could at least pretend to be a man.

But Richard had cancelled his clients for the next three weeks, locking up his therapy room and retreating to his study. He claimed to be working on his book – the official teaching guide and not the other manuscript, obviously – but as far as Jill could tell, he was spending most of his time staring moodily into space or snivelling. Just two days ago, she'd caught him hunkered over his desk, all snot and tears, his shoulders racked. He was as bad as Caitlin, worse in fact. A red-faced spoilt child.

For Christ's sake, how could this have happened to them? What was still happening to him? After everything he had put her through, Richard's self-pity was outrageous and yet Jill had

111

been forced to pick up the slack as usual. Even during the darkest patches of their marriage, and there had been several, she didn't think she'd ever felt quite this thoroughly used, or so utterly alone.

In the rear-view mirror Jill saw how her face had tightened, her jaw clenched, her blue eyes narrowed, and her skin flushed an unbecoming pink. And though she was quick to rearrange her features, her colour refused to settle and that was also Richard's fault. His precious clapped-out Bentley was ridiculously hot.

On the passenger side, the window stuck so Jill leant across the cracked cream-coloured leather of the driver's seat, reaching for the door he'd slammed. But the moment she touched the handle, she pulled back, gasping. The world turned white with pain.

"Christ, Jilly," she muttered. "You silly girl." Foolishly, *so bloody thoughtlessly*, she had somehow forgotten the enormous blister deforming her right hand.

The pain was vicious, searing through her palm and wrist and flaring up her arm. For several stretching seconds, it was more consuming than her anger and accompanied by a quicksilver fear that flashed her straight back to the morning after Theresa's death. For a moment, she was back in the kitchen, clutching a knife, and even as the pain subsided, she thought of other sticky hands groping towards her. The air shimmering, transformed.

"Oh, Jill," she said shakily. "Poor silly Jilly." But as her vision cleared, she stared bravely at her thumb.

The blister was huge and alien-looking. A rubbery yellowish bubble, not at all like human flesh. Jill had burnt herself the previous evening dragging the lasagne from the oven – and what a waste of time that had been. The dish was supposedly a family favourite, but Richard and Caitlin had barely picked at it, literally adding insult to injury.

Jill hadn't eaten much either. Along with the blister's sting, the ingratitude had ruined her appetite and she'd also been frustrated with herself. She'd used a cloth rather than the gloves and it wasn't like her to make such sloppy basic mistakes. That was usually Richard's job.

But what came to Jill then was far from the worst of her husband's lapses. Although the pain of her burn was easing, she found herself thinking about Richard's bonfire, recalling the reckless way he had sloshed on petrol, his face lit up like a Halloween mask.

"Richard," she'd yelled, hurrying over. "Be careful! *Why can't you take care?*"

Except then she'd seen the papers stacked among the dead wood behind him still waiting to be burnt.

Pictures, she thought at first, her running slowing to a creep. But inching nearer, she couldn't see any images, only densely scribbled words. They were Richard's case notes and rather than yanking him away from the pyre, she snatched up her own handful. Together, they fed the blaze.

It had felt like entering some sort of trance state, standing beside him. The flames were bewitching. The lawn and trees rippled through the smoky haze, and floated over everything, the house appeared majestic. Jill's heart seemed to catch along with each thrown page.

Our home, she had thought, *this life we've built*. She would never let anyone take it away. It couldn't be destroyed.

And when she turned to Richard, he was smiling and though his smile was slightly manic, she imagined that he felt the same. Side by side they would raze a path back through the nightmares; they could still somehow be remade.

If only Jill had been able to hold on to that moment, not just the brief sense of solidarity but the idea of moving on, this whole summer reduced to ash. But within an hour of leaving the garden, Richard had returned to that shadow version of himself, keeping all of them trapped... The car's heat was becoming oppressive.

Jill leant back across the driver's seat, carefully using her left hand to crank Richard's window open while her right went on burning, cradled in her lap. She lifted her face to the gap and took a breath, but the breeze, such as it was, smelt of melting tar and baking metal. The car park was nearly full.

Squinting out, Jill saw several other vehicles with their windows or doors flung wide revealing restless silhouettes. But the thought that she and Richard weren't the only parents who'd been forced to wait outside didn't offer the reassurance it might have. As high as the stakes might feel for those other families, Caitlin's A-level results had come to mean so much more. Practically a matter of life or death.

At the start of sixth form, there had been such high hopes, even talk of Oxbridge, but that was when Jill and her family still existed in a bubble that resembled normality, an entirely different innocent place. As the months rolled on and Caitlin had gone spinning off, Jill was forced to rethink her ambitions and now, with everything that had happened, *and was still happening,* she no longer cared where Caitlin ended up. The lowliest ex-poly would do, so long as it was far from Underton.

And on this, Richard was in agreement for once. As much as he'd have liked to have believed he could solve Caitlin's problems, they both knew the best hope of getting their real daughter back came from letting her go. They had to get her out.

Jill spotted Richard then. He was extracting himself from a group of smokers huddled under a glossy awning outside the refurbished PE block. The smokers were exclusively male, Jill noticed, and as she imagined her husband cadging a cigarette from those ordinarily worried ordinary dads, she turned from the window in disgust.

Far more than Richard's smoking – of course she knew he'd taken it up again; she wasn't an idiot – what incensed Jill was how he'd have insinuated himself, exuding camaraderie. As if he wasn't the same Richard who had gone slamming off like a teenager, or the man-child she'd caught weeping in his shamefaced cowardly way.

Bastard, Jill thought. Why could he pretend for other people and not for her? He wore so many masks.

No one understood what Richard was truly like, the things he was capable of. How he could tear your world apart just as easily as he could turn on the charm–

"Want to change your luck?"

With a start, Jill swung back to the window. A grey-haired woman was stooped beside the car, peering nosily inside. Despite her age and the heat, she was heavily made-up, her cloudy eyes crudely outlined with kohl, her wrinkled cheeks spotted hectically with blusher.

"Pennies for luck," the woman said. "Lucky heather and roses for wishes."

Then without any warning, she was reaching through the window, shaking a bunch of flowers into Jill's face.

Their scent was pungent, but not remotely natural, as if they'd been sprayed with tacky perfume. An attempt perhaps to disguise how the straggling blooms – neither heather nor roses as far as Jill could tell – were so incredibly wilted they had probably started to rot.

And before Jill could shove them aside, she felt them brush her jaw. The woman had somehow managed to lean even further in and she'd used the flowers to touch Jill. To *stroke* her–

"Don't!" Jill cried, recoiling.

But though she shrank back as far as she could into the

passenger seat, the woman stayed where she was, her arm still outstretched, and her painted expression appeared to have frozen. Her mouth remained curled into something that wasn't quite a smile. Another discoloured wrinkle carved deep into her face.

"Luck," she crooned again, giving the flowers another quick shake. "You'll be needing luck today."

"Jesus Christ," Jill said. "You're the last thing that I need."

But it made no difference. As if she was pre-recorded, the woman kept doggedly on.

"A pound," she said. "One or two pounds, that's all. Don't you have a heart? It's not for me, it's for the children. Won't you spare a kind thought for the children?"

Of course, Jill had heard the rumours about the travellers. Her friend, Helena, had gone into extensive detail about their noise and rubbish and the way they were harassing the villagers, peddling from door to door. But Jill hadn't paid much attention. She knew how much Underton loved a scandal and even if she'd taken Helena's warnings seriously, she doubted if anything could have prepared her for this.

The woman's audacity was as outrageous as everything else about her. On top of the hammy performance and make-up, she was swathed in a flamboyant red dress. All she was missing was a pair of hoop earrings and perhaps a gold tooth, but other than that, she might have stepped straight out of one of the formulaic mysteries that Jill had loved as a child. Those crime capers where the Gypsies usually did it and always got their comeuppance.

Honestly, it was ludicrous, and on any another occasion Jill might have laughed, at least in the retelling. But it was too much today, *the final bloody straw*. Her head already felt invaded and the woman wasn't giving up. Waving her "flowers" about again.

"For Christ's sake," Jill snapped. "Didn't you hear me?

Won't you please just go? I don't want your bloody disgusting weeds. I'm not giving you a bloody penny."

But amazingly the woman still refused to budge and Jill found herself craning forward, enunciating into that clownish face – "*Get out.*" And before she realised what she was about to do, she had raised both hands. She pushed the woman's shoulders hard.

She was fleetingly aware of the dress's damp warmth and then the pain from her thumb exploded. But though it was worse now, igniting the whole of her, Jill didn't stop. She couldn't.

"Just fuck off!" she wailed and from somewhere behind the raw electricity searing through her, a slim observing part of her lifted a wry ghostly eyebrow. She sounded so much like her teenage daughter.

But Jill didn't care. The woman was out of the car at last and nothing else mattered, not the tears she could feel looming behind her face or her screeching nerve endings. Not even the sickening wetness coating her entire right hand where the blister had broken open.

"I see you," the old woman said. "You hopeless bitch."

And though she was picking up her red skirts and backing away, she went on talking, spitting out a final curse.

"You'll never get what you want. You're poison. But you'll get what you deserve."

Chapter 12

Caitlin

24 December 2017

What strikes me first is the dust; it's everywhere. It furs Dad's old scrolled desk and his cherished display cases, and turns the air to smoke where I've unsettled it. Here and there, the motes blink like embers, catching the last of the afternoon's light.

Although its circular walls are surrounded by sky, the tower room's always dimmer than you might expect. The windows are tall but narrow and every sill is heaped with books, an overspill from the crowded shelves. Trying not to sneeze, I squeeze between a wastepaper basket knitted with cobwebs and a battered leather trunk, and it's only as the door bumps closed behind me that I realise something's missing. But though I reconsider the mismatched furniture, I can't work out what's different, apart from the obvious. Of course, there's the gap Dad's left behind.

It had taken a stupid amount of courage just to come inside. Mum had given me such a heavy bunch of keys, I'd felt like Bluebeard's dumb curious wife or a nervous jailor. But the keys weren't the reason I felt so stuck. I knew which one would fit the lock. It was the door itself that stopped me.

I couldn't look at its oak panels or jutting lintel without

picturing Dad's stoop when he ducked inside and the way he would grin, inviting me in, as if he was the eager child.

The tower room was more than Dad's study. It was his sanctuary. While Mum rigorously remodelled the rest of the house, he insisted on holding on to its quirky angles and groaning floorboards, and for once my mother gave in. She was probably relieved Dad's stuff would be out of sight. It had been driving her nuts for years.

And though I'd worried that she might have had the room gutted after his death, I had also been anxious about confronting a shrine, but the dust's put paid to that. The musty library scent has deepened but there's not a whiff of my father's spicy aftershave or sneaky cigarettes, and I've never believed in ghosts no matter what his books and curiosities might promise.

Still, I can't shake off the sense that something's off. It might simply be that Dad's stuff has been rearranged, but with so much piled around me, it's hard to tell and my memory's hardly reliable. I've been away too long.

I pause in front of the main display case. Its glass doors are misted. I use my cuff to scrub away the smears and as soon as I peer inside, I feel the tension lift; my shoulders relax. I always loved my father's things.

Dad's hobby might have started as a scholarly pursuit, a fascination with the psychology behind beliefs in the paranormal, but at some point his interest loosened radically. He stopped acquiring books and artefacts purely for their academic worth. Claiming to be obsessed by superstition "in all its guises", his collection expanded to include a playful range of increasingly tacky props.

The case is home to several authentic antiques – a spiritualist trumpet and a scrying bowl and a Victorian conjuring mirror – but it also houses a plain brown brick supposedly recovered from Borley Rectory and a transistor radio, spewing wires, meant to capture spirit voices. There's a shrunken head, patently made of rubber, which particularly tickled Dad given his profession, and a moth-eaten rabbit's foot, and taking centre stage on the top shelf, the gift I gave him one Christmas when I was about eight or nine.

Knowing that Dad was on the hunt for just the right cursed doll, I transformed my favourite Barbie, hacking at her hair and dress, then melting her hands over the gas hob and colouring her eyes a garish red.

I had wanted her to be perfect and she was far from that, but when Dad tore off her wrapping, he'd laughed with delight.

"An excellent job!" he exclaimed. "Magnificent!" And when my mother sighed, "All she needs is a name," he said. "Perhaps I'll call her Jill."

I can't remember Mum's response, but I suspect she iced him out. My mother's disdain for his collection was probably why I got so involved. For several years, I acted as Dad's loyal apprentice, though he rarely wanted any practical help; my main role was to provide an appreciative audience. Every object arrived with a new supernatural story and on the whole, I gobbled up those tales. There was only one occasion when my excitement morphed into genuine fear.

I wasn't especially young by then. We had already moved to Underton and that particular story was inspired by the house rather than Dad's things. Like the rest of the village, he couldn't resist those bones.

Of course, I'd already heard the rumours and they didn't bother me, not even the ones about dead babies. After all, I'd been brought up to be made of sterner stuff, and up until Dad offered his own spin on the house, I had taken its creaks and shadows in my stride. I couldn't have imagined lying, sleepless, in my darkened room, sure that something was dragging itself through the hallway or slithering up the stairs...

I don't know what it was about that story. It wasn't original or especially horrible and I'd definitely heard worse. Dad simply told me that in the hurry to remove Evelyn Hansworth's remains from the property, a part of her got left behind. It wasn't anything major, just a single rib, or vertebrae, or knuckle, but it was enough to make her return, and keep returning, endlessly searching for what she'd lost.

Even now, although it's ridiculous, I shudder and I realise that the room's grown gloomier. While I've been daydreaming over my father's trinkets, the windows have filled with bruise-coloured clouds. It won't be long till dusk.

I ought to be getting on, trying to find Mum's Christmas decorations, not dwelling on the past. But picking my way back towards the light switch, I wonder if Dad missed me when I stopped joining him here and whether he blamed himself?

But it wasn't really his Evelyn story that made me pull away. I had a new life to deal with in Underton. A new school and new friends, not to mention a newly evolving body. A typical egotistical teenager, I was keen to replace childish hobbies with riskier excitements. I was more than ready when Livy came along.

When I flick the switch, nothing happens and while the dead bulb shouldn't surprise me, I try again and again, listening to the useless clicks and wishing I had more than the shadows to ground me. I shouldn't have let Livy in. The memories aren't ever done.

There was the afternoon when I sneaked her up here. It was early on in our friendship – we were still just friends – but even so I had wanted to impress her. And while I was no longer my father's willing sidekick, I imagined that Livy might appreciate some of his freakier artefacts.

During our village wanderings, she had startled me by avoiding ladders and three drains in a row and by cheering on black cats. But Livy's phases came and went, and I had clearly timed it wrong. She shrugged over Dad's collection, rifling disinterestedly through his precious books and charms, and as she pulled a face at the conjuring mirror she casually confessed that she'd seen it all before.

"I've already had the tour."

My father had apparently shown her around after they'd given up on a therapy session.

"I'm not always in the mood," she said. "But I reckon your dad was still doing his thing. He probably thought it would make me feel better if I knew what a weirdo he really is too."

And though Livy was calm, explaining, I couldn't get a grip on my emotions. As well as an unexpected urge to defend my father, I felt an ugly jabbing jealousy. I thought I was over being a daddy's girl but as it struck me how many hours they spent together, I felt usurped, and it wasn't just about him. I didn't want to share Livy either.

On a surface level, I was also disappointed. I had been looking forward to a giggling afternoon spent messing about with the crystal balls and creepy witch doctor masks, or playing with the spirit cabinet, bundling in, squashed close–

The cabinet, it suddenly hits me, *the cabinet's gone*. I scan the clutter again, but there's no way it could have got buried. Although it was narrow, it stood taller than the display cases and Dad used to keep it next to his desk as if for company. In its place, there's a stack of cardboard boxes and incensed, I stride towards them.

I can't believe Dad willingly gave his cabinet up. It was one of his proudest purchases, won at auction, a rare example of its kind. Spirit cabinets generally consisted of little more than fabric-covered frames or boxes, but this had been a proper piece of furniture custom made from wood. From the outside, it looked like a fancily carved wardrobe or cupboard. If you wanted to learn its secrets, you had to peer inside.

Behind the door, there was a ragged black curtain, and behind that, a stool where the medium, frequently a young woman, was meant to sit. Sometimes, to guard against accusations of fraud, the medium would also be roped and blindfolded. Channelling the dead was a serious business. There was a lot of money to be made.

And Dad's cabinet was so cunningly designed it could leave you stumped even after you climbed right in. It took patience, as well as a special knack, to find the hidden catch for the sliding panel that opened the escape hatch in its back.

I eye the boxes cautiously as if they might be a different sort of trick, but it's only their efficient brown ordinariness that makes them stand out in this room. Each box is neatly labelled and though my mother's stiff handwriting shouldn't come as a shock – after all, didn't she send me up here? – something slumps inside me and *Mum,* I wonder wearily, *what else of Dad have you replaced?*

But the labels are unapologetically pragmatic. "Spare China" and "Miscellaneous", and perched at the top of the pile, a box marked "Christmas". Mum's lettering looks smug.

With a sigh, which sounds unnervingly like one of hers, I grab hold of it. It releases a festive jangle as I tug it free, but it's heavier than I expected and I stagger, searching for a better grip. But it isn't the weight that makes me gasp; it's what I glimpse in the next box down, the one marked "Miscellaneous".

Instead of a lid, the box has been covered with a board. A board made of lacquered wood and engraved with numbers and an arcing alphabet, along with three separately etched words: "GOODBYE" and "YES" and "NO".

No, I want to agree, *no, no, no,* but I'm already dumping the

Christmas box on the floor at my feet and reaching out to seize the board.

As soon as I touch it, I long to drop it, but it's too late. It has cast its spell. I'm seventeen again and surrounded by candles, with Livy crouching at my side.

Enough, I think. *Let it go right now.*

But I can't. I can't move at all. Livy's hands are clamped over mine and though the glass we're using as a planchette is strangely cool, everything about her is warm. Not just her fingers but the press of her hip and thigh, and her breath on my neck. Her whispers in my ear...

Then the candlelight dips, the shadows unfurl like black roses, and the glass is sliding away from us–

"Enough!" I shout and I hurl the board aside, but for a moment, I'm still trapped. Still glimpsing Sam and Ali's screaming mouths – and then my mother's face comes flaring through the darkness. An angry bright white flame.

I shake my head until the images vanish but what I really need is to get out of here, *just fucking go*, but when I turn, about to snatch up the Christmas things, the "Miscellaneous" box draws me in once more. Without the board, there's a clear view of the stuff that was hidden underneath. There's an oriental vase wrapped in a gauzy cloth and a battered bronze dish, but what grabs my attention is much more personal, *far too fucking personal*. A colourful scattering of photographs.

As I stare, my thoughts return to Dad's beloved cabinet. How behind its door, there was a curtain, and behind the curtain, a stool, and beyond the stool, a secret panel... And while I know I should look away – what I've already seen is bad enough – I gather up the pictures and shuffle through them like they're one of Dad's tarot decks. Only instead of revealing any sort of future, they're unravelling the past.

They're Polaroids, faded by time, but not nearly as faded as

I'd have liked. Between their smudges and bleached patches, my mind starts to empty. It's the shock, after all these years, of seeing Theresa again. And not just Theresa's face.

And as I go on flicking through the images, I feel hypnotised; I don't know why I can't stop. From my first glimpse, it was obvious what they are. There's so much spilling flesh.

Again and again, there's the loll of Theresa's weighty breasts and gently bulging stomach and her dusky parted thighs. She's posed in a variety of positions, sprawled on her back and on her front and bent right over. In one shot, she's using both hands to hold up her heavy hair and laughing like a glamour model. But I can't concentrate on her lipsticked mouth or gleaming eyes, not beside all that shameless skin, and "What the fuck," I mumble as if I don't understand, though I'm trying not to think about the drawings strewn across my bedroom floor. About Livy equally exposed.

But Livy won't leave me alone. Between my panicked thoughts, I catch her husky voice.

Come on, Cat, I know you get it. Why do you always have to play so dumb?

But I'm still willing my head to make a different kind of sense. There must be some rational explanation for these photos turning up among my father's things. Maybe he found them after Theresa's death and hid them to protect her? And even if she gave them to him, that didn't necessarily mean that he wanted them. Weren't there other occasions when women had tried to blur the boundaries? Sometimes his clients got confused...

And while I keep staring – I seem to be stuck on a photo of Theresa sucking her thumb – I see past it to the time when a skinny red-haired woman turned up at our London house. Wild-eyed and ranting, she had banged on the windows when we refused to open the door, only slinking off when Mum threatened to call the police—

As I turn to the last picture, I freeze. I'm literally frozen. Goosebumps stipple my arms.

There's no lipstick smile here, no voluptuous curves, no sign whatsoever of Theresa. The picture shows a man in bed and though a sheet's covering most of his body and part of his face, I can't kid myself any longer. He's so obviously my dad.

All too quickly, I begin to thaw, but there's nothing good about the heat taking over. As my gaze moves from the faint fuzz of chest hair, where the sheet has slipped, to my father's familiar jawline, hot waves rise greasily through me, thickening my throat, and I'm sure I'm about to throw up again.

But there's so little left inside me, I can only dry heave and when I shut my eyes, I'm bombarded by another memory. Except this one has nothing to do with my dad or Theresa. What returns is the pale glowing square of Phil's laptop screen. There weren't any pictures attached to the email my husband had been composing to his latest pretty intern, but there hadn't needed to be. His message was loud and clear.

No need to stress, I'll be there tonight, and wear the black ones. Can't wait to strip them off...

In another world, I'm moving on autopilot. I place the photos on top of the Christmas box and then gather everything up, hardly feeling the box's weight as I sleepwalk through the dust and shadows towards the door.

On the threshold, I briefly hear my thoughts. *Dad, oh, Dad, how could you...?* But the question is faint, the muffled cry of a distant child, and it's only once I'm out of the tower room that I'm forced back to myself. The air reels with the sound rushing up from downstairs, the house quaking with my mother's screams.

Chapter 13

Richard

15 August 2002

It was time to face the music. Caitlin would be out with her results at any minute, and whatever happened, Richard told himself, they would make sure that she escaped. At the end of the day there was always Clearing.

The cigarette had helped to calm his nerves, though not as much as the cocktail of anxiety suppressants he had taken with his breakfast, which were finally kicking in. Feeling pleasantly distanced, Richard could return to Jill; he could ignore her rage. Perhaps he should have spiked her coffee too?

But he might have overdone it. When the hot morning's hazy clouds parted and the sun bounced across the car park, it didn't just gild the bonnets and windscreens; the whole universe ignited. A couple of rows of cars ahead, Jill vanished as the Bentley's windows blazed, and the old woman who had been tottering towards him looked like a martyr in a medieval painting, her red dress pluming flames.

Transfixed, Richard waited for the world to settle, but even with the light softening, Jill remained obscured. The car was full of shadows, and though the old woman was no longer burning, she went on throwing off a rosy aura. Richard rubbed his eyes.

He knew his self-medicating was verging on reckless, but these odd, disconcerting moments were vastly outweighed by the benefits. While the pills couldn't completely cushion him from the worst of his grief – it hit him now and then in unpredictable disorientating waves – much of the guilt had lifted and more importantly, his body was his own again. That terrible spreading pressure had been exorcised and only in his dreams was Richard still trapped at the police station. Still haunted by Theresa's ruined face.

But he had heard little from Ward since Livy's arrest and even his darkest nightmares could be contained to a degree. They were generally forgotten within an hour of tranquillising and he could manage the side effects – well, mostly. Richard was sure he would soon find the courage to return to his therapy room and in the meantime, he was keeping it locked.

"Something for your troubles?"

The old woman had come to a stop in front of him. "Lucky heather," she offered. "Just two pounds a bunch."

Richard blinked, but he wasn't hallucinating. The woman's aura had faded but nonetheless she looked surreal. The flowers she was clutching appeared to be dead or dying and in addition to her clumsy make-up, her red dress was remarkable, sagging to the ground in florid tiers.

Smiling, the woman lifted her flowers towards him and though her smile looked somewhat practised, Richard grinned back. It was another of the pills' advantages; they helped him to remember his usual warm, curious self. The man he was meant to be.

"Lucky posies, eh?" he said. "Did you bless them?" He was already searching his pockets for coins. "Does the blessing go both ways?"

"Two pounds," the woman repeated. "Two pounds a bunch. Won't you spare it for the children? You'll have good luck for days… For days…"

As her spiel faltered, Richard cocked his head, studying her more closely. He was trying to get a better look not just at the flowers but at her jewellery. She wore a pale-stoned ring on her left thumb – possibly an opal? – and while she was speaking, a pendant had shaken free of her ruffled collar. It appeared to be engraved, but he couldn't quite make out its markings.

"Go on," he prompted, nodding and grinning more broadly, but the old woman's smile had vanished. Despite the determined beeline she'd made across the car park, she suddenly looked bewildered as if she had no idea how she'd ended up here. Her gaze flitted away from him, her eyes shining against their sooty rings of kohl, and when she took an uncertain step backwards, Richard wondered if she was readying herself to run.

"Really," he pressed on. "I'm interested."

But as her gaze darted back to his, the day flared again, the air a scalding tide, and in its wake, Richard's grin grew heavy, an unexpected burden on his face.

"Mary?" he said, squinting, half blinded. "Mary, is that really you?"

For a moment, he felt as disturbed as he had been in the therapy room staring at the door's carved panels and imagining those sounds. There was no way the noises could have been real – they were such an obvious manifestation of everything he was trying to repress – and yet he had been unable to shake off the sense that something essential, but invisible, had shifted. Like a first-year psychology student, he'd kept thinking about Jung's exploding bookcase, and there was also that chapter from one of his pulpiest books about cracks in the universe…

But as peculiar as this woman looked, she didn't belong to

some separate dimension – unless that was how you viewed the past. The last time Richard had seen her, she'd been sitting at Theresa's kitchen table sharing a pot of tea.

"I..." she said.

But then she was turning away and before Richard could think it through, he had reached out to seize her shoulders. He couldn't let her go.

"Mary," he murmured, more blindsided, he realised, than blinded. "We've met. Don't you remember? I met you at Theresa's..."

The woman shook her head and a petal or leaf or something escaped her thick grey hair, spinning off like a dazzled moth. But ignoring both the head-shaking and the tension in her shoulders, Richard tightened his grip, resisting her attempts to shrug him off.

"I know you know me," he told her. "You were there at the bungalow."

It felt suddenly vital she acknowledged their meeting; the memory was so clear. A spring evening just a few short months ago, when Richard had been thrown by the sound of voices after letting himself in. He had thought it would be safe to use his key. Livy was out with Caitlin and Theresa was supposed to be alone.

But coming into the kitchen, he'd found a strange woman – *this truly strange old woman* – piling sugar into one of Theresa's chipped mugs and chatting merrily away, blatantly feeling quite at home.

And though Richard was standing in the school car park, sweating through the cotton of his shirt, neither the heat nor the pills could prevent him from returning to that scene; it remained so vivid. The women with their steaming drinks and the room hunched intimately around them, the particular quality of the light...

It had rained earlier, Richard remembered, and there was a kind of hopeful last gasp to the setting sun. The window had deepened to amber and a tangerine glow lapped across the sink and cluttered countertops. The light added an extra layer of glitter to the Klimt poster and when Theresa and the woman looked up at him, they were shining too. But their auras had been precarious that evening, hardly there before they were gone.

Richard didn't think Mary had been wearing any make-up, or at least nothing so extreme, and without it, she'd looked younger and her clothes – a baggy sweatshirt and a long denim skirt or jeans – had been boringly ordinary. At the time, it had taken him a moment to connect her with the new rebellious friend Theresa had mentioned. A female farmer living on the outskirts of Underton, who had recently caused a storm of controversy by welcoming the travellers onto her land.

"She's so funny," Theresa had said, "and fascinating. The stories she's told me! But there's also a kindness about her and a weird sort of knowledge. When we talk, I don't need to explain things. She's not like anyone else around here. She somehow understands..."

Apparently Mary had always had a witchy reputation in the village. An older woman daring to survive alone, she'd been a natural target for gossip long before she had invited the travellers in. There were stories about what she might be growing out there and about what she was feeding – as well as hordes of feral cats, there were rumours of foxes – and on any other occasion Richard might have felt intrigued.

But seeing her then, at Theresa's table, he was gripped by a petty pang of envy or something akin to it and he found himself glancing away as he approached them, turning to study the poster as if he'd never noticed it before.

An opulent merging of scales and skin and vine-like coiling

hair, the picture was one of Klimt's "Water Serpents", a slightly less predictable choice than his "Kiss", although that one hung predictably enough above Theresa's bed. But thinking about Theresa's bed, its rumpled sheets abandoned to the dusk, only made Richard's irritation worse.

Still, he'd been nothing but a gentleman as he clutched and then kissed the intruder's hand. "Mary, is it?" he said. "I've heard good things. It's great to finally meet you."

He didn't stoop to Theresa in turn. Lately, their smallest public interactions had started to feel dangerous. Even a simple air-kiss or casual hug could be enough to betray them and yet there was also something delicious about that sense of risk. Instead of touching Theresa, Richard leant across the table and grabbed her mug, and the air between them rippled just as he had hoped it would.

"What have you girls been up to?" he asked. "Sharing gossip? Telling fortunes?" He paused to take a generous slurp of Theresa's tea, aware of her gaze on his mouth, and then winked at Mary. "Perhaps you'd like to read my leaves?"

"Richard!" Theresa squealed.

Pleased, he watched her leap up to retrieve the mug, her magnificent breasts swaying in her T-shirt. She was pulling a face and rolling her wide brown eyes and though Jill also liked to roll her eyes, the gesture from Theresa was so different, so utterly playful, Richard's annoyance loosened and as soon as she began to laugh, it completely fell away.

The kitchen was instantly suffused with warmth. With her head flung back and her dark eyes flashing, Theresa easily outshone Klimt's glitter. Whenever she laughed, she made the cliché true, becoming the brightest thing in any room.

"The three of us sat down together," Richard was saying now. "We were drinking tea and laughing..."

And though he was returning to the present, to the parked

cars and his sweat-soaked shirt, it was the first time since the police station that he'd been able to recall Theresa's face as it was meant to look and he needed Mary to engage in the memory, to agree about Theresa's radiance. *She wasn't just some fantasy.*

"You and me," he went on, "and Theresa... Theresa talked and talked."

But Mary had managed to wriggle her shoulders free and her expression was no longer confused. As she stared – no, *glared* – at Richard, her face was stiff with hate.

"Get your hands off me," she said.

But he wasn't touching her anymore. Both his hands, in fact, had lifted, palms open as if surrendering, and "I'm sorry," he said. "I only wanted to... Theresa, that evening... I just wanted to talk about her. You knew her..."

As Mary drew herself up to her full height, still falling several inches short of his chin, Richard heard her strange dress rustle – and why was she wearing that dress? Was it meant as a joke on the conservative villagers or was it some kind of eccentric reaction to Theresa's death? She looked like an indignant crow ruffling her crimson feathers.

"I don't want to talk to you," she said. "Or listen to you. I don't want to hear you speak her name."

"Please, Mary–"

"Or mine," she interrupted.

But though Richard no longer knew what he was hoping to achieve – Mary was clearly disturbed – he couldn't stop babbling.

"At least let me buy some heather – or I could just make a donation? Something for the children? Is it for the children staying at your farm?"

This was obviously the wrong tactic. Mary's eyes had

turned to flint and "No," she snapped. "I don't want anything from you. Haven't you done enough? You—"

But her words were lost to a sudden outpouring of sound, the air electrified with high-pitched yelps and shrieks. The school had flung open its doors, unleashing the girls, but Richard didn't turn towards the building. His hands were reaching out again, but this time Mary had no problem evading his grasp and then her voice returned, cutting darkly through the noise.

"You're to blame," she said as she twisted away. "The mess you made, ignoring the boundaries and letting everything in. It all comes back to you."

Dazed, Richard watched her scuttle off between the cars, heading directly into the tumbling rush of girls. She didn't look back, and nor did she pause for the excited stream of teenage bodies. As they surged around her, a small, odd noise escaped Richard's throat, a hollow straining chuckle.

But this was also lost to another round of shouts and screams, and Richard stood inside the sound as if suspended, as trapped in the car park as he'd been in his therapy room, staring at the door while the scraping noises grew louder—

"Fuck that shit!" a girl screeched past him. "We're getting out of here. Three As! Let's get fucking wrecked!"

Shaking and slick with sweat, Richard watched the girl fly away, a whirl of hair and long, loose tanned limbs, but before her squealing friends could catch her up, he forced his heavy feet to move. Pushing his way through the heat towards the car, he dodged a hugging knot of quieter weeping girls. But though the Bentley's door was swinging open, there wasn't any sign of Caitlin and Jill looked uncharacteristically awkward climbing out. She was cradling her right arm and despite regaining her composure when she straightened, she seemed almost as out of place as Mary.

While the rest of the car park went on shrilling with young riotous life, Jill stood poised and pale and thin in the sunlight – and wasn't there something vulnerable in her stillness? Perhaps she felt as trapped as him?

But he couldn't afford to keep returning to the rabbit hole of his therapy room. At some point, he suspected, there would be no way out, and anyway, there was no sense of camaraderie in the idea of Jill feeling hunted too.

Instead, as Richard gazed at the perfect blank of his wife's perfectly made-up face, her ice-queen features such a contrast to Theresa's easy warmth, the thought scraped through him – *Why did I have to lose her? Why couldn't it have been you?*

Chapter 14

Caitlin

24 December 2017

"Mum, don't cry. Please don't cry. It's going to be okay."

But there's no holding back the tears. The words too clearly echo the things I said to my own mother less than an hour ago trying to convince her she was safe.

"You're breaking up a bit," Scarlet continues. "Can you hear me, Mum?"

The line's crackle briefly overtakes her voice. An eager buzzing that makes me think of mosquitoes and though it's night, I picture my daughter sitting beside a sunlit pool, her hair and shoulders sequinned with water, her skin baked a honeyed brown. But I don't imagine her smiling. She sounds unnervingly grown up.

I suppress a groan. What am I doing? As desperate as I was to hear Scarlet's voice, I never intended to offload like this. I thought calling her would help me regain some perspective, but instead I've been blubbing on about Underton. *It's so lonely here...*

Obviously I haven't mentioned any of my terrible discoveries. Scarlet has no idea about my history and there's no way that's about to change, and yet I've done an appalling job at concealing my emotions. I'm blatantly falling apart.

You're her mum, I tell myself, wrestling another holly-patterned napkin from the packet on the kitchen counter. *Be her mum...* The tissue shreds as I tug it free.

"Mum?" Scarlet says and the crackle's fading, but she still sounds small and muffled. So very far away.

"Scarlet, love," I say. "I'm sorry. I don't know what's got into me. I'm okay, honestly..."

But my head's still brimming with images, though I'm no longer picturing sunlit pools. I can't block out those repellent fleshy Polaroids and there's the strange stuck vision of my mother too. I keep seeing her shaking and crying in the living room's shadows, looking so breakable and lost.

"Take no notice, love," I insist, doing my best to quash the quaver in my voice along with Mum's terrified face. "I'm fine, really. Don't worry. I'm having a moment, that's all. It's just hearing you and missing you, and Christmas... I must be getting sentimental in my old age."

"You're not *old*, Mum," Scarlet replies and her ordinary exasperation provides a brief reprieve, but as she goes on, my tears return. It's her kindness; how did my little girl grow up to be so kind? Something in my chest has come undone.

"You're always too hard on yourself, Mum. It's silly. You're only human. You're allowed to get upset."

But *no more*, I think, resisting the full extent of the flood. Our roles are already reversed enough. She's only thirteen – *my little girl* – and for fuck's sake, it's Christmas Eve.

"I'm sorry," I repeat and I'm finally sounding firmer. "I should let you go. And I'm feeling loads better now so you're not allowed to stress. You have a great evening and get a good night's sleep. I'll talk to you tomorrow."

"Okay," she says, "if you're sure. Are you sure? Dad's giving me a funny look... Say hello to Grandma for me... And you know I love you, don't you, Mum? And I miss you too. It won't be long until we're home."

"I love you, Scarlet. I love you so, so much."

But the phone's dulled in my ear, my daughter's gone and that's surely for the best. Through my useless tears the kitchen is shining like it used to and *home*, I think in Scarlet's voice. But when I try to visualise our house – the home we've shared for years, which I'll fight Phil to hold onto – it feels like one of my vaguer dreams. Our warm messy rooms collapse beside my mother's glistening tiles and the black glare of the patio doors–

Enough, *absolutely enough.*

I set down the phone I'm still clutching pathetically and turn to brave the table. It's still heaped with Bethany's preparations for our festive feast, and what possessed me, I wonder, to chuck her out before she'd finished.

Trying not to sigh – *I'm not my mother* – I scan the herbs and breadcrumbs, unsure where and how to begin. Certainly not with the turkey, though its pink is starting to grey. I reach for the spuds, but the bag is heavy and I fight off a wave of exhaustion just juggling it over to the sink. When I release them, the potatoes drum against the metal – there are so many to peel – and it's only as I'm blasting them with water that I realise how much noise I'm making.

"Shit," I mumble. "Sorry, Mum. I'm sorry..."

I twist the taps to off and glance at the door I left ajar, but the hallway's quiet seems impenetrable. It's already forgotten my mother's screams.

Nonetheless, I listen harder, aware of the kitchen waiting too. While the potatoes bob in the sink, the fridge emits a low hum and my sad little Christmas tree goes on cowering in its corner, still endlessly dying and still hopelessly unadorned.

In my rush to reach Mum in the living room, I dumped the box of decorations at the foot of the stairs and as the Polaroids on top flew everywhere, I found myself scrabbling about once again, trying to gather up image after damning image. But the photos were far worse than Livy's sketches and I wasn't thinking straight. I should have gone straight to Mum. There was no let up to her screams.

Instead, I looked about wildly, searching for somewhere to hide the pictures. The door to Dad's old therapy room was locked, the blue glass bowl on the table too obvious, and I ended up stuffing the Polaroids into my empty boots, not knowing what else to do.

By the time I burst in on Mum, I was panting and horribly conscious of my hands. I felt sure she'd be able to tell with a single glance what they had been up to – but she wasn't looking at me. She was huddled on the floor next to her bed and even after I hurried over, I don't think she saw me there at all.

She was still shrieking and sobbing, but when I grabbed her bony shoulders – *so roughly, too roughly, I'm so sorry, Mum* – I understood her cries were more than senseless noise.

If Bethany hadn't told me otherwise, I might have thought she was screaming "trees". She screamed it over and over – *trees, trees, trees* – and for a second, I was struck by an incongruously summery scent. Only it wasn't sap, or leaves, or sun-warmed bark, but the richer sweeter tang of roses.

Within seconds, the smell was gone. The room held nothing but shadows and the usual wafts of disinfectant and stale pot-pourri, but as I followed my mother's horrified gaze to the empty space at the foot of her bed, I was pretty certain that, for her, Theresa was still there.

"Mum, it's okay." I wrapped her in my arms. "I'm here. It's just us here. There's nobody else, I promise."

But several long minutes rolled by before she grew quiet

and shivering against me, she felt so fragile. A woman made of glass.

"She came back," Mum told me later, when I tucked her into bed. The screaming had left rough cracks in her voice, but as she spoke, she lifted her fingers and trailed them gently across my cheeks.

"I felt her hands," she said, "and her touch wasn't cold. It was warm and real... I was scared she'd never let me go."

And why didn't I believe Bethany about the night terrors? She was right, they were horrifying, and perhaps she's been right about everything. After all this time, my mother's still haunted. It's never been just me.

But no more nightmares, not tonight at least. At Mum's request, I fetched her medication from the bathroom cabinet and after she had taken a couple of *Diaze*-somethings, she closed her eyes and her breathing eased. Like a child, she sank away.

I'm tempted to sneak a few pills myself. Although I'm so tired my bones feel weary, I'm not sure how well I'll sleep. But when I lug the turkey to the fridge, planning on simply stashing it out of sight, I spot a bottle of Sauvignon crammed in between the jam and milk, and *that will do*, I think. I don't bother with a glass.

Gulping down one cold mouthful after another, I wander over to the patio doors, thinking of Bethany with her cigarette and though I haven't smoked for fifteen years, I remember the craving.

In another version of my life, I'd have been so much kinder to Bethany. I would have listened to her properly from the start and, who knows, we might've ended up sharing a smoke, united in our worry. If only I'd acted my age instead of behaving like the self-pitying teenager I used to be, I could have let her love my mother too.

It's all Underton's fault, I decide, drinking and staring blindly into the night. Everything that's happened since my return – Sam and Ali and their Livy revelations, and unearthing the Polaroids – feels out of my control and weirdly fated. Like I'm part of some sinister plan.

Of course, the idea's totally far-fetched and I'm quick to dismiss it. But no matter how much I swig and swallow, I can't drown out those photographs.

What were you thinking, Dad? How dare you have done this to us – to Mum? Poor haunted Mum–

Then my mother's careful handwriting comes back to me. It wasn't Dad who labelled those boxes, but Mum would hardly have packed the Polaroids up for safekeeping. *No fucking way.* It makes no sense. And if she'd had the slightest suspicion they were in there, she would never have sent me up to the tower room – not unless she had wanted me to find them–

A sound intercepts my thoughts, a soft skittering like fingers tapping deftly on the patio doors' chilled glass and the darkness outside seems to flicker. The bottle knocks against my teeth.

But in the next instant, my brain engages and I release a barking laugh like one of Bethany's. There's nobody out there. There's nothing but the wintry night and I've got to stop jumping at shadows. I shouldn't have to keep reminding myself that Livy isn't about to reappear – that she's about as likely to come back here as Theresa – and besides any of that, the night shouldn't have surprised me. After all, it's Christmas Eve at my mother's house where Christmas was always so seamlessly choreographed. Obviously it was bound to snow.

The flurries are beautiful. As the flakes whirl, coming thicker and faster, it's hard to tell if they're falling or rising. But as much as I'd like to lose myself in their magical light, my head keeps spinning back to the Polaroids, and Mum, and inevitably to Livy.

And despite my resolve, I'm searching the windows' dizzying patterns for a face beyond my own. But of course, the night doesn't have any answers. As pretty as the snow might be, it's just another distraction. More confusion in the dark.

Chapter 15

Karl

17 August 2002

Ever since he had arrived, Karl had been trying not to watch the Shaws. Telling himself it was pointless, they didn't matter now, and staring over anyway.

He had a clear view from his barstool; the pub was far from bustling. Apart from Karl and the Shaws, the only patrons consisted of three obligatory elderly men nursing their pints at separate tables and a grim-looking ginger lad feeding coins into a machine. But though Karl hadn't exactly been discreet – walking straight past the Shaws on his way in and then doing little to hide his glances – they appeared utterly unaware of him. Both Richard and the girl were hunched over their drinks while the stiff-necked pearled and coiffed mother kept turning her perfectly made-up face to the bay window. She looked about as at home in The Hunters Arms as a peacock in a pigeon coop.

Still, if you didn't know any better – if you hadn't been watching the Shaws like Karl had – you might have imagined them content. Such an attractive, if self-contained, family, sharing a civilised early evening drink at the best table in the pub.

Not that The Hunters' best counted for much. The

beermats would still be sticky and their leather booth was scuffed, though not as openly scarred as the others. But the setting sun streaming through the bevelled glass provided the family with an extra rosy glow and the wine bottle blushed pink when Richard lifted it, chivalrously topping up his companions' glasses before seeing to his own.

Reaching for their drinks, the mother and daughter looked startlingly alike. They had the same blue doll-like eyes and neat matching figures with narrow waists and small high breasts. They were both immaculately blonde, though the mother must have had some professional help and the girl's hair was longer and several shades lighter, moonlit rather than gold.

In fact, as the minutes had passed, the girl had seemed to grow generally paler. There was a kind of haziness to her edges and her expression as if she was somehow less substantial than her parents, and when they clinked glasses, she didn't join them. She barely glanced up let alone spoke.

But from the outset, Caitlin Shaw hadn't been what Karl had expected. While she was undeniably pretty, it was a washed-out, wispy type of prettiness. Despite their similar features, she didn't seem to have inherited an ounce of her mother's oomph.

It wasn't just age or confidence. On each occasion Karl had met Mrs Shaw, he had sensed a steeliness about her, an underlying strength. She undoubtedly had a temper, but he couldn't imagine her ranting and raving; she probably seethed in private, keeping the worst of her rage in check. Mrs Shaw's emotions would be as controlled as everything else about her. Her sleek hair and expensive tailored clothes, her grand, classy, soulless house.

The woman's self-possession was impressive and she was obviously used to taking charge. When Karl had questioned her daughter, she had been polite – icily polite – but insistent, refusing to leave them alone and then cutting off the interview altogether the second she decided the girl had taken enough. And so few women stood up to Karl, he'd found himself contemplating what Mrs Shaw might be like in bed with all that glamorous armour stripped away.

Caitlin, in contrast, appeared to have no defences whatsoever. In the unhelpful minutes before their "talk" was curtailed, she had fallen apart. A fragile, weepy, needy thing, she was nothing like the girl who Karl had pictured when Olivia McKinnell had talked about her "Cat".

But as Richard Shaw had eventually made plain in his latest surprisingly forthright statement, Olivia's version of reality could hardly be trusted and after her last interview, Karl had to agree, though he'd initially been suspicious.

Like his wife, Richard hadn't wanted Karl anywhere near his daughter and while Karl could empathise – he would have been just as defensive of his Elise – something seemed off about the therapist's blustering. As useful to the investigation as it was, the sudden talk about Olivia's possible "Identity Disorder" made Karl wonder. There had been nothing like that in Richard's notes and was he trying to provide a distraction? What if, in some way, Caitlin held the key?

But that was when Olivia had still been stubbornly resistant and the fact that Karl had homed in on vague little Caitlin Shaw only showed the extent of his desperation. Now that he had witnessed Olivia's extremes for himself, he wouldn't have been surprised if the girls' relationship, at least as Olivia described it, had been warped by her fantasies, if not totally made up.

But all this musing was as pointless as Karl's watching. He didn't know why he felt compelled to go on studying the Shaws. *They don't matter anymore.*

With what he hoped was a solid sense of resolution, he turned back to the bar and his whisky – the single thing that came close to levelling out the pain in his head – only to find his glass empty. He had somehow managed to down two doubles in twenty minutes, but the barmaid, Maggie, was hovering nearby, already on the case.

"Same again?" she asked, leaning between the beer taps and showing off a creased expanse of sunbed-orange cleavage.

Karl hadn't met the barmaid before today. She wasn't part of the interviews, but he knew she was called Maggie because she had told him twice, giggling and gushing over his orders. In her own way, she had probably been eyeing Karl as intently as he'd been observing the Shaws. Her flirting was off the scale.

"Go on, treat yourself," she prompted now, raising one plucked eyebrow. Karl half expected her to wink.

Nonetheless, he returned Maggie's grin. Her performance might have been as clichéd as her looks – the low-cut top and the thick slick of lip gloss, all that brassy feathered hair – but she wasn't entirely without her charms and besides, he was meant to be celebrating. Although Olivia's eventual fate remained unclear, now that she'd been transferred to the secure hospital where she so clearly belonged, Karl's role in the investigation had shifted significantly. Apart from the relentless paperwork for the hearing, he could basically move on.

"Okay, Maggie," he said, his smile widening. "Treat me, if you like."

But as soon as the barmaid turned to the shelves of bottles, Karl's mood deflated. There was something undeniably tragic in the calculated sway of the woman's substantial hips and *poor sad cow*, he found himself thinking. *Small towns, small needs, small minds...* He felt his headache stir.

Nothing ever changed out in these villages. Everyone on the lookout for cheap thrills, however temporary or misguided. There had been drugs in the Valley for decades and while the wife-swapping rumours might have been replaced with dogging stories, it all boiled down to the exact same thing – these people were bored out of their skulls. It didn't matter how scenic the hills might be, they were always closing in.

That desperation, which Karl had felt from the beginning, had only grown more depressing as the investigation wore on. It was there again and again in the eager faces of the countless locals who approached him offering "advice", their faux concern barely concealing the bloodlust underneath. Before Theresa McKinnell's murder, Underton's outrage had been centred on the travellers and the old woman who had offered them her land, but such a savage killing, literally on their doorstep, was patently more exciting, a true highlight in their groundhog lives. Several of the villagers had even taken to wearing the old woman's posies – "for protection," they told Karl – and the superstition drove him nearly as crazy as the hypocrisy. No wonder his head refused to stop aching. He had definitely been here for too long.

But tomorrow he would be back in the city. He'd be able to celebrate properly with his usual team and next weekend he would have Elise, his real life starting up again. Quite frankly he hadn't any idea what he had hoped to achieve with this final tour of Underton. Richard Shaw and his ilk could waffle on as much as they liked, Karl would never believe in "closure" and being in the pub was nearly as draining as revisiting the bungalow. Even without the Shaws lurking in their corner, The Hunters was such a miserable dead-end place. Maggie could keep her crinkled cleavage to herself.

Still, he wasn't completely heartless. When she set down his whisky, he tucked a tenner into her lingering hand and "Have one on me," he said before downing the drink in one and turning from the bar.

"See you soon!" she called out after him.

He didn't reply and though he could feel her gaze plucking

at his shoulders, he didn't glance back. Maggie was as tiresomely transparent as everything else round here. Even the case had proved pathetically simple and Karl meant to walk straight out, away from it all. *Goodbye, screwed-up Underton–*

"Detective?"

It was Mrs Shaw who addressed him. Leaning out of her booth, she blocked his path, wine glass held aloft in one manicured hand. The glass was empty and for a second, Karl thought she was expecting him to take it from her like a waiter, and he almost did. But then she was balancing it precariously on the booth's worn arm and "Detective," she said again more loudly. "I thought it was you. How are you? How's everything progressing? Do you think you're getting close?"

"Mrs Shaw," Karl acknowledged, but he glanced past her to Richard who was hastily rearranging his features into a smooth bland smile. Just an ordinary dad out for an ordinary family drink, he acknowledged Karl with a nod and that was all, as if he hadn't been sitting right there, next to Karl, when Olivia had suddenly broken open, giving Karl what he'd needed.

Despite Richard's latest statement, Karl wasn't entirely sure what had made him call the therapist in, except that Alma was useless and Pathology were messing up. When Karl first called them, they had mentioned finding semen on Theresa's body and he had wasted a whole day trying to track down the man she might have been sleeping with. But even Underton's nosiest gossips appeared to be stumped and after Pathology made their official report, it no longer seemed an issue. The initial findings must have been contaminated or misread and anyway, Karl was convinced he'd made the right arrest. He had known it was only a matter of time until Olivia confessed.

But the extra time the CPS had granted him with the girl was rapidly running out and feeling the pressure, he had gone in hard, though he never expected the breakthrough to happen so fast and certainly not in the way it had. But then who could have imagined that?

Richard had looked as shocked as Karl had felt and yet he patently hadn't told his wife a thing about it. Still, *not my business*, Karl reminded himself. *Not anymore...* But though he didn't owe the therapist much – the small help Richard provided had almost come too late – Mrs Shaw was looking at him with such haughty detachment he decided to give the man a break.

"Going as well as can be expected," he said.

Richard's private motivations were his own after all, and shouldn't Karl have had his fill of dysfunctional families by now?

"Well, Mrs Shaw," he said. "I hope you're enjoying your evening. I didn't mean to interrupt. I really should be heading off."

"No rest for the wicked," the woman agreed, but then, slightly slurring, she gabbled on. "We're celebrating! It's so good to have something to celebrate. We're incredibly proud. In all honesty, it feels like a miracle... Thank Christ..." As she spoke, Mrs Shaw upended the last of the bottle into her teetering glass. "To my Kitty-Cat's A-levels! Three solid Cs!"

Karl watched her knocking back the wine, surprised by the slurring and guzzling. Was her previously seamless façade beginning to crumble? Regardless of his resolve, he was curious – unless it was just easier to think about the Shaws than about Olivia? Those things she had said. That thing she had done...

Karl rubbed his temples, trying to clear his throbbing head, but when he turned from Mrs Shaw to her daughter, Caitlin's glare threw him totally off-guard. This wasn't the girl he had met before, or the girl who he'd just been watching. The intensity of her stare brought everything about her into focus – her sharp chin and cheekbones and her gleaming hair – and

Karl felt exactly as he had looking into Olivia's eyes. To his shame, he glanced away.

The table in front of Caitlin was littered with beermat scraps. Having already destroyed two, she was picking at a third and her hands weren't anything like her mother's. They were paler and bonier, the nails bitten to the quick, and watching her restless tearing, Karl felt an unexpected pang for his Elise, for the soft sticky clutch of her fingers and her overall lack of self-consciousness, her untamed energy. He would never allow her to grow up into a girl like this. *So young and yet already so screwed up...*

As Caitlin fidgeted, Karl knew she hadn't once broken that stare; he could feel it crawling over him. *And what was it about their eyes?*

"Please," the mother was saying. "Won't you join us for a very quick toast? It's actually a double celebration. Not just the exam results but a birthday too. Our baby's recently turned eighteen!"

"Oh, I couldn't," Karl said. "I really do have to get on, but, Caitlin..."

The girl was still looking, still staring straight into him, and "Happy Birthday," he mumbled, thinking *not a girl then, but a woman*, and the idea of that just made everything worse. He had to get away.

But as he turned from the booth, the barmaid's gaze passed over him and though it was a world away from Olivia or Caitlin's, for a moment, her scrutiny felt as relentless, and *sick women*, the thought accosted Karl. *Sick women everywhere...*

"Goodbye," he managed to splutter at the Shaws. "Take care." Then in three long strides, he was pushing out of the pub, finally making his escape.

But what was the matter with him? *With everyone?* Drawing in a deep deliberate breath, he looked wearily up and down the high street, but there was nobody about, *thank God*, and in the last of the long day's light, Underton was looking its quaintest, the old stone buildings drenched a reddish pink, the shop windows winking softly. But though the postcard prettiness should have mocked Karl's fears, his head was pounding. He couldn't unknow the truth about this place. Couldn't unsee the things he'd seen.

And as soon as he'd allowed that thought, he realised his mistake. The dying light rippled and the smell of the sun-baked stone intensified, hurtling him back to that cave of a cell and yesterday's revelations.

At the start of the interview, when Karl first introduced the crime-scene photos, Olivia had stood her ground. "It wasn't me," she kept saying. "It wasn't me." The same broken record she'd been playing since her arrest, and Richard, sitting between them, hadn't added anything of use. He had argued about the pictures beforehand, questioning Karl's "methodology", but once they entered the cell, he appeared to forget his ethical concerns. He cleared and rubbed at his throat, but barely said a word, and Karl had persevered.

Results, he told himself, just as he'd told the therapist, and after he slowed right down, lingering on image after bloody image, Olivia's muttering grew muddled. "It wasn't me" became "It was him", and Karl pushed the camera screen closer.

"It was him," she repeated. "His shadows. *They did this.*" She leant across the table, practically spitting. "I've got to get them out."

And when she snatched up Karl's pen, a part of him seemed to know what she was about to do, but there wasn't time to grab it back or hold her down. She wasn't cuffed, *and why hadn't they cuffed her?* But perhaps it wouldn't have made any difference. She had been so driven, jabbing the pen, like a blade, into her face–

"Wait! Please wait!"

The voice, high and warbling, hit Karl from behind, shoving him back to the village's warm stone walls and the lapping light. Then a small strong hand grabbed hold of his shirttails and he thought of Elise again.

But the girl hanging onto him wasn't anything like his daughter, *not in any way at all.* As Karl rounded on Caitlin, wrenching free of her grasp, she was panting, her pale skin shining unhealthily, her mouth a trembling hole.

But at least her gaze was her own now, her eyes stretched wide and very blue. There was no sign whatsoever of Olivia – and yet Olivia refused to let Karl go.

He could still see her with that pen in her fist, not just piercing her skin but slashing and sawing. The slick flap of her cheek–

"I'm sorry," Caitlin was saying, half gasping. "Detective, I'm sorry. I know I shouldn't..."

But her speech was drowned out by Olivia's huskier rasp. It ran through Karl's head in a strange dark loop. *Get them out of me, get rid of them. Get them out, get them out...* And crowding behind those words were the others that came later when her voice had been muffled by the bandages and sedatives. Those things she had told him about her dead father inside her and the satisfaction of the knife–

With an effort, Karl wrenched himself back to Caitlin.

"What have you done with her?" she said. "Please tell me. *Please.* She's a victim in this too. It isn't fair. You've got to let her go."

As she spoke, Karl's headache seemed to radiate a rancid heat and then his shoulders and chest were also burning, his muscles tightening. There was an urge to seize hold of this glassy-eyed girl, to shake her like the clueless doll she was. He spoke in hissing bursts.

"Do you really have no idea?"

"What?" Caitlin began. "What do you mean?"

But he couldn't take her any longer, not her blue, blue eyes or her oblivious face, her cracked and artless voice.

"Your friend isn't going anywhere," he interrupted, "not for a very long time. She might be sick, but she's no more a victim than you are – though I'm sure that none of this is news to you."

Karl had been speaking without thinking, but as the girl flinched away, he knew he'd struck a chord and he stepped quickly after her, towering over her. Maybe Olivia hadn't been exaggerating their relationship? And what else could Caitlin be hiding? The feverish desire to take hold of her was only growing stronger.

"Olivia told us everything," he said, "and not just about why she did what she did to her mother. We know about all her other sick secrets. We know about you and the things you did together. Your supposed 'love'."

He was standing so close he could smell her bright young sweat, but though his mouth was twisting with disgust, Karl wasn't done.

"Caitlin," he said. "We know about the sickness in you too."

Chapter 16

Caitlin

25 December 2017

It's still night when I stir and I'm not quite ready to wake. I'm in some fuzzy half-dreaming place, recalling a time – well, so many times – when Livy shared this bed. Always the big spoon, she would tuck me against her, keeping me safe, as we drifted off to sleep.

The memory's seductive and for a while I give myself up to it, feeling the snug fit of her arms and her breath on my neck. Imagining the shivery warmth of one last lazy kiss... But when I roll over, there's only the fusty tangle of my bedclothes. Of course I'm still alone.

Resisting the wash of self-pity, I open my eyes, but the room's disorientating; the darkness isn't right. The windowpanes are black between the curtains, but there's a hazy glow un-knitting the edges of things. I glimpse the pale hem of a dress trying to escape the wardrobe's doors and an empty wine bottle abandoned on the bookshelf. The blushers and bangles on my dressing table come and go in waves, and I can't work out where the glow is coming from. Its thin quiver reminds me of tiny puttering flames, but Mum hasn't allowed candles upstairs in years. I squint towards the shelf again, confused by the bottle's glint.

But the light isn't growing any brighter and *forget it*, I tell myself, sinking back onto the pillows and pulling the covers over my chin. Then the floorboards creak.

I peer through my lashes, but the shadows appear to have settled, just as the house is simply settling; there's no need to worry–

The floorboards creak again.

This time, the noise is clearer. It's coming from near the door and when it's followed by a more definite thud that could be a clumsy step, *Mum?* I wonder, but I don't lift my head to see.

I can't imagine Mum making it all the way up here and besides, she's so thin these days and the noise is weighted. The next steps – if that's what they are – are louder but less distinct. They shuffle, slumping together, and my stomach cramps queasily. I feel woozy with recognition.

The sounds belong to my childhood nightmares, those dreams I had of Evelyn Hansworth creeping through the house, returning for her bones. Except I don't remember her ever shambling this close and though I know I mustn't look – *don't fucking look* – I sit up and stare into the shadows.

The figure is down on its hands and knees. It's dragging itself towards the bed, coming closer, inch by sickening inch.

But this isn't the Evelyn from my old bad dreams. Its body's a dark, dense, swollen thing, and as it keeps on crawling towards me, I can't tell if it's entirely human. There's something reptilian about the sway of its head. I feel sniffed out as much as seen.

And I can't move, not even – *please* – to shut my eyes. I can only watch while it lifts its long blurred hands and as it reaches out to me, I'm hit by the spoilt-sweet scent of rotting flowers and the house's cold–

And what if I'm awake?

I flinch back, baulking and blinking. The foul icy air briefly fills my mouth, but then as quickly, the dead taste is gone and when I shove aside the pillow that I must have pulled over my face, the room is as black and empty as it's meant to be. There's no weird glow and no one else here. Despite my sweating palms and racing pulse, I'm no more haunted than I usually am. It's just me alone with my nightmares again. So fucking alone.

At some point, somehow, I slept again – a solid dreamless sleep – but still, the minute I wake up properly, I double-check the room. The wardrobe is neatly closed, there's no bottle on the bookshelf and the only thing shining on the dressing table is Mum's jailor's bunch of keys. Everything is starkly illuminated in the morning light and there's nothing ambiguous about my hangover either.

While I don't feel as toxic as yesterday, it's an effort to sit up, but gazing across the sunny floorboards, I feel instantly lighter. It isn't just the nightmare that's gone.

Fuelled with wine, I cleared away Livy's drawings late last night. I imagined building a pyre in the garden and burning her sketches along with those Polaroids. I thought it would be therapeutic, like one of Dad's rituals, watching all our secrets go up in flames, but in the end I couldn't do it. It took most of my strength and the last of the wine just to finish gathering up the drawings and instead of performing some cathartic ceremony, I stuffed them back into the wardrobe drawer and then didn't have the energy to face the Polaroids. I'll have to dig them out of my boots later out of sight of Mum.

Unless that isn't necessary? I'm still wondering what Mum might know and what she might be playing at. Was I meant to uncover the photos so she could finally talk about Dad's affair? It hardly seems likely. She's always taken great pride in her privacy, no matter what the cost.

If she wanted me to find them, and that's still an enormous "if", she must have had other reasons and besides, aren't there more urgent concerns – like who else might have known about Dad and Theresa? Could Livy have known? And was that what sent her spiralling–

But, *no,* I'm not doing this. I can't, not if I want to stay even vaguely sane. I hurl off my covers, but the room's an icebox and I wrap myself in a blanket before climbing out of bed, the window drawing me over. The day is glaring through the curtains and when I open them, I raise a hand briefly to my eyes. Underton's transformed.

The woods aren't dark anymore. Every tree is glittering, and the hills and fields are swathed in white velvet. The Valley has become an enchanted place overnight, entirely remade with snow.

The view is so gorgeous it empties me and I draw in a long appreciative breath, gazing out, not back. The past needs to stay just as blanked out and buried, and whatever Mum is up to, she isn't well. She needs looking after, that's all, and she's probably awake and waiting for me right now. Her only daughter finally returned for Christmas.

But before I turn from the window to think about the dress I packed and the gifts I bought, I touch my forehead to the icy glass and "Please," I whisper to the new, clean, flawless world. "Please make it a happy fucking Christmas Day."

We're going to begin with a proper festive breakfast. I didn't pay much attention to the fridge's crowded shelves last night, but this morning I've discovered smoked salmon, which we'll be having with toast, and a whole magnum of champagne. There are also tons of satsumas so it seems impolite not to make Buck's Fizz and after we've honoured the day with a suitable start, I'll attempt to tackle lunch. Maybe I'll even string some tinsel around my tragic little tree.

Or maybe not. It's looking sadder and balder than ever, and "Sorry, Tree," I murmur, but really I'm happy to ignore it. I'm too busy bustling about the kitchen, squeezing juice and cracking ice cubes and wiping up the toaster's crumbs. The air is invigorating rather than bone-numbing like it was when I came in.

I must have left the patio doors ajar after peering out at the flurries last night and cursing myself, I slammed them closed and turned the key, determined to keep shutting out my worries as well. No more Polaroids, or nightmares, or Livy – and the light already seems friendlier. The cut-glass jug scatters diamonds when I slosh in the champagne and as I carry our breakfast tray into the hallway, I catch myself humming a carol. Perhaps I'm more like Mum than I'd care to admit? I feel unapologetically domestic. She's going to be so proud.

But it's still quiet outside the living room and pausing at the door, I wonder if it would be better to let Mum rest. When I came downstairs, there weren't any signs of life, but I was quite content sneaking past then, already formulating our breakfast plans.

But the toast is hot, the butter at a perfect golden melting point, and I'm able to turn the handle with one elbow without upsetting the Buck's Fizz. Nudging my way in, I call out in my cheeriest voice, "Merry Christmas, Mum!"

There's no reply. The room is muffled, the thick curtains making the shadows so dense that even the hallway's dazzle can't offer much respite.

"Mum? Are you awake? I've made us breakfast."

It takes a moment to locate the edges of the coffee table, but once I've set down the tray, I try again. I badly want to get this right.

"Hi, Mum! It's time to wake up." I manoeuvre past her vacant chair. "It's Christmas morning!"

But when I approach the bed, there's just more silence and stubborn darkness, and as I reach out to the black bundled covers, I'm only vaguely aware of my muttering. "Everything's okay, Mum..."

All at once, the shadows crash in around me. Before I've grasped the fact I've tripped, I'm falling. Tumbling head-first onto Mum–

Except she isn't there.

For a few dumb seconds, I scrabble about among her covers. A pillow whirls off into the dark. The eiderdown slithers to the floor.

Struggling upright, I blunder over to the window and yank the curtains apart and as the light pours in, I don't let go of the heavy fabric. I need something to hang on to while I scan the room. Mum isn't crouched in a corner with her night terrors. She isn't anywhere.

My gaze darts from the bed to the walking frame. It's lying on its side beside it, chrome legs spiking the air. It must have been what tripped me up, and "Mum?" I squeak. The frame looks as wrong as the empty messed-up sheets and after forcing my fingers to release the curtain, I'm tearing back across the room.

But in the hall, I come to a stop, my hands in my hair. I need to get my head together.

Calm down, I tell myself, *be logical*. There's no need for all this panic. Mum can't have gone far without her frame.

But though she'd never have managed the steps, I find

myself at the foot of the staircase, shouting up – "*Mum*, where are you? I'm coming!" – like some kid playing Hide and Seek.

So stupid. I back away. But then, just as senselessly, I'm turning and jiggling the handle of the door to Dad's old therapy room and of course, the door is locked. The key will be with the others Mum gave me yesterday, and then it hits me, thinking of keys – and of the kitchen and the garden's cold – *have I locked my mother out?*

I swing around, whipping into the coatrack and though I don't bother with a jacket, I grab my boots. I quickly give up on the zips, leaving them half undone as I race to the kitchen. But with the leather flapping around my ankles, I realise they were empty when I pulled them on. Like my mother, the Polaroids have disappeared.

"Fuck," I snap. "Fuck, Mum."

But it isn't her I'm cursing as I press up against the freezing patio doors and grapple with the key, straining to see through the glaring glass. How could I have been such an idiot, leaving the photos right there, outside my mother's room? I'm suddenly convinced that she knew nothing whatsoever about them before, but she's found them now–

For fuck's sake what have I done?

To my relief, the bolt releases with a simple click, but the doors resist me, pushing against a small avalanche piled up outside and "Mum," I cry. "I'm sorry."

Then, in a flailing rush, I'm through.

The lawn is stupidly stunningly beautiful. A deep, furred, sparkling expanse, it's so white it seems to surge with secret colour, and the monochrome trees are nearly as exquisite. Their branches are all black lace and icy feathers, and beyond them, the sky is a misted blue, the sun a ghostly eye. The air's so pure, it tastes like metal in my mouth and everything is unbearably still – but what the fuck was I expecting?

Mum planted like a snowman in the centre of the garden? Or maybe a trail of photos that would lead me to her like the pebbles and crumbs in a children's story? Instead, there's nothing – so much astonishing white nothing – and when I call out again, the cold swallows most of my voice. The tears on my cheeks are already crystallising and I can hardly feel my hands at all.

But swallowing hard, I stagger out in my foolish gauzy dress and flapping boots. Mum can't have vanished into space.

Within a few paces, I'm sinking. The buried patio must have given way to the hidden grass. There's snow collapsing in around my calves, my feet are soaked, and the hem of my dress is drenched and dragging behind me. But though I force myself on, there keeps on being nothing except my too loud hitching breaths and the cold that's seeping inside me. *Hopeless*, it trickles through my thoughts. *This is hopeless, you're hopeless, everything's lost* – and then something hooks my gaze.

Further out, across the lawn, the whiteness isn't as complete as it first seemed. There are small dull patches creeping out across the snow, uneven indentations where the glittering crust has been broken and only shallowly refilled.

"Mum?"

I hardly dare to hope, but as I stumble on, the marks grow clearer – definitely footprints – and "Mum!" I yell, trying to run. "Mum! Mum! *Mum...*"

There is something muddying the silvery light between the nearest trees that border the lawn, something other than the hooded mounds of bracken. A dark shape lying in the snow.

For a warped moment, my nightmare returns – that hideous, searching, crawling thing – but I shake it off. Mum looks so small and crumpled, and "Don't worry!" I shout, trying to wade over as fast as I can. "I'm here now, Mum! You're safe."

And *safe*, my heart beats, as I struggle towards her. *Safe, safe,*

safe, as I drop to my knees in the cold at her side. *You're safe. You have to be safe...*

I roll her stiff shoulders towards me. Her head lolls in my lap, but though her eyes are closed and her lids, like her lips, are a strange mauve blue, "I've got you, Mum," I tell her. "We're going to be okay..."

But my voice comes echoing back at me as if from far away and at the same time as I'm bending over my mother, trying to drag her to her feet, I'm floating somewhere high above the snow-covered canopy.

And while I can't hear Mum's breathing yet, or feel her warmth, I can see the waiting house and the frozen woods and white garden surrounding us, and just before I'm plunged back towards our bodies and whatever might be coming next, I glimpse our criss-crossed tracks.

But there aren't just the trails that Mum and I have left behind. There are more marks weaving past us into the shadows of the trees. A third set of footprints in the snow.

Chapter 17

Sam

21 August 2002

Lovely day for a funeral...

Sam had been thinking the same phrase more or less – *lovely day, lovely day for it* – since first thing that morning when she'd cracked and broken into the weed that Livy had tossed into her lap three weeks ago. *Forever ago.* How was it possible that so little time had passed?

There wasn't much left in the pouch, just a few crumbs and a tangled nub, but still Sam had been suspicious, wondering what Livy might be expecting in return. But at some point while she was crossing the hazy fields or drifting along the high street, she had come to see it differently. Maybe it was Livy's farewell gift.

But that was exactly the kind of thought Sam had been hoping to avoid as she sent smoke rings sailing across her sunlit bedroom. From the moment she woke, she had badly needed to loosen her head. Today was the day – *the lovely day* – that Theresa McKinnell would be burnt.

Approaching the church, Sam's footsteps slowed. Beyond the gates, the graveyard was rippling in the same way that the roads smeared into rivers when Sam's dad drove them from the airport to their holiday home in Greece. The yellowed grass and the tombstones kept melting and the clusters of black-clad figures were like the flies that stuck to their windscreen, distracting from the view.

"Shit," Sam muttered, coming to a stop. She had thought the effects of that clumsily rolled joint would have worn off by now, but the weed was far stronger than she remembered and the temperature wasn't helping; *it was such a lovely day*. Her scalp felt spongey, her hair was sticking to it like a swimming cap, and was that sour whiff coming from her armpits? Perhaps it wasn't too late to run.

But her polished school shoes only scuffed at the gravel in a heavy hoof-like way. Like Sam's ill-fitting dress, they weren't remotely appropriate for either the weather or a funeral. The dress wasn't even black but navy.

Sam had borrowed it from her mum who would no longer be attending the service, the heat having brought on one of her heads. When Sam had eventually ventured downstairs, yawning extravagantly in an attempt to disguise how high she was, her mother was already stretched out on the sofa in her underwear, staring blankly at the TV.

The sound was muted and it had taken a moment to recognise the Valley. Shot from above, Underton was all lush woods and rolling hills, the high street a pale grey snake winding between them. But then the image was replaced with orange brick and gaudy police tape. Theresa's bungalow.

A uniformed officer stood in the garden beyond the tape. His only role, it seemed, was to linger among Theresa's crazy flowers, trying too hard to ignore the cameras. Behind him, the bungalow's front door was covered up with an intriguing rubbery sheet. Sam had crept closer to the screen.

But then the cameras panned out and the other houses in the cul-de-sac looked dusty and exhausted. Every net curtain was sagging, and was it the heat or the presence of the film crew that made them hang so still? Those curtains usually twitched at the slightest excuse. Each time Sam had visited, she'd been aware of the peeking and prying, the vigilance always intensifying whenever Livy came out onto the street.

Perhaps, like Sam, those neighbours were glued to their televisions. There was something compelling about seeing the village exposed in this way, laid bare for public consumption, and before her mother switched off, Sam felt herself giving into it. *That's us*, she had thought, *we're famous!*

But that feeling was exactly why she had been avoiding the news. It was as shallow and shameful as it was irresistible, and weren't things confusing enough?

Sam squinted at the flies lurking outside the church's arched oak doors. Maybe some of them were reporters? And then she was wondering about pallbearers, but she couldn't imagine some grand procession. The coffin was probably waiting inside.

Up until the murder, Sam's favourite TV show was *CSI*. She had been fascinated by the way a dead person could be opened like a book and read for clues. But now she wished she'd never watched it. Before the funeral was announced, Underton's gossips had gone into overdrive, speculating about when Theresa's body would be "released". They might as well have taken bets at The Hunters and privately, Sam was just as obsessed. She kept picturing tubes and drains and rubber gloves. Scalpels flashing eagerly like a second knife attack...

She really hoped that the doctors had been respectful, stitching Theresa carefully back up after taking her so thoroughly apart, but as Sam's gaze shifted to the stained-glass windows, taking in their bloodlike glow, she knew there would be no way of telling. Inside the church and later, at the crematorium, of course, the casket would be sealed.

Her fingers rose to cover her hot face, but the day – *the*

lovely day – pushed through in harsh white slits and she still couldn't force her hooves to move. Why the fuck had she smoked that spliff?

"Sam! Hey, Sam!"

The white light pulsed. Her hands leapt from her face.

"Hey, Sam, *over here.*"

One of the flies had peeled free to wave at Sam and "Shit," she murmured as its orange hair blazed. "Okay, Ali, okay."

Now that she'd been spotted, there was no hope of escape. But resigned, Sam could finally push her school shoes onwards and as she weaved between the tombstones, her awkward steps sped up. As well as Theresa's body, she was trying not to think about all the others buried in the earth directly underneath her. *CSI* had been bad enough; she didn't want to start thinking about zombies. George A Romero totally freaked her out and when a gaggle of old ladies blocked her path, she kept her gaze fixed firmly ahead, doing her best to ignore their muffled moans and sobs and damp trailing strings of tissues.

But as Sam slipped past them, "It'll be much cooler inside," one of them rasped and she stiffened, anticipating the reply. *Well, at least it's a lovely day...*

"Sam! Oh, Sam!"

Ali bowled towards her, her ginger curls bouncing, but her big, freckled face didn't make Sam feel any better. It was splotched pink and wobbling and worse than that, Ali wasn't alone. Caitlin hovered behind her, staring down at the corpse-filled ground.

Like Sam, Caitlin was one of the few people in the churchyard who wasn't wearing black and the fit of her dress was also wrong. It swamped her bones, a washed-out grey sack that matched her greyish features. Even her hair had lost its shine.

Since that last disastrous visit to the treehouse, Caitlin had stopped speaking to Sam, refusing to return a single call, and if it wasn't for Ali, Sam would have given up by now. But Ali remained insistent – "She must be feeling so alone" – and because Ali was usually infuriatingly right, Sam tried to smile, though something inside her rebelled and she almost said it – *What a lovely day for a funeral!*

But Ali was all over her, squeezing her in a wrestler's embrace, while Caitlin just went on standing there looking faded, and "Is Livy here?" Sam heard herself blurt instead. "Did they let her come?"

Ali didn't reply except to rub her blotched face snottily against Sam's shoulder, but Sam's stoned brain was clicking into place. She probably shouldn't have been surprised.

Ali's silence confirmed what most of Underton had suspected from the outset. When Livy reappeared, the police had issued a statement explaining that she'd been found unharmed, but that was all, and their reticence was telling. It was clearly only a matter of time before Livy's guilt was made official.

With the thought, the graveyard's buzzing revved up, and Sam gasped as Ali released her. But nobody had been reading her mind. The church doors had simply swung open. The people in black were swarming in, and as Ali and Caitlin fell into line, Sam followed in a daze.

But though she shuffled inside obediently, once the three of them were installed in the last empty pew at the back, Sam kept looking over her shoulder at the light swimming between the gaping doors. Despite everything, a part of her still expected Livy to come bursting in. She could picture it so easily – Livy's confident stride and her wild black hair and big black eyes – it would be such a typically Livy-ish manoeuvre. But then the sunshine narrowed as the heavy doors were pushed closed, and Ali pressed a pamphlet into

Sam's clammy hands, forcing her to turn around and face the funeral.

And Sam had been right; the coffin had been waiting here all along. Beyond the rows of bobbing whispering heads, it shone through the stony dim, clouded white with flowers.

There were lilies and baby's breath and a huge heap of roses that might have been plucked from Theresa's garden. But while the floral display was undeniably impressive, Sam didn't like the way it was shimmering in the candlelight. The candles reminded her of Caitlin's flickering bedroom and the Ouija board. She shrank against the pew.

But Ali hauled her to her feet and with most of Underton rising and rustling around her, Sam fumbled to straighten the pamphlet that she'd somehow crumpled into a ball.

The "Programme of Service" was roughly stapled and badly photocopied, Theresa's pretty face reduced to grubby smudges. It hardly seemed respectful, but then the funeral had been arranged much sooner than most people had wagered. Lately, everything kept moving in uneven jolts. The organ was already wheezing and "Abide with Me" Sam read belatedly as the congregation broke into warbling song.

Apart from Mad Mary, hunched in the pew in front of them with her head in her hands, these people who Sam had known for most of her life – old Mrs Fielding and Mr Jackson who owned the fish shop, and Maggie from the pub – were wearing the same expression. With their mouths stretched wide and their gazes flitting to the vaulted ceiling, they were all pretending that they knew the words. Pretending that they cared.

Meanwhile, the roses on the coffin went on glowing, the shadows kept fluttering, and Ali started to sing. But her faltering voice didn't quite sound like the others.

"The d-d-darkness deepens…"

Sam didn't dare to join in. It was the candles – *the fucking candles* – returning her to Caitlin's room again, and maybe it was because she'd been so high that evening too? All four of them stoned and laughing when they first leant over the board, bound up in one another. Sam could still feel Livy's warmth, somehow separate from the rest, and then she was remembering the heat that seemed to rise from the glass as it moved. The blood surging through their fingertips.

"Earth's joys... grow... dim..."

Ali's singing mouth was a long dark gap, the words dripping out of it in oily clots, and Sam didn't need to glance past Ali to Caitlin, who was standing next to the aisle, to picture her face. She would look terrified and ghostlike in the candlelight, and with a start, Sam realised why she couldn't open her own clenched lips. If she did, she might start screaming, just like she had that night.

"Change and d-decay," Ali was singing now. "In all around I see..."

But there was no way Sam was going to think about the Ouija board's message, or the thing that Ali had sworn she'd seen, or the dread she had felt when Mrs Shaw had driven them home. She wanted all of it gone.

But then the doors groaned open behind her, the church was flooded with harsh yellow light, and she swung around thinking *Livy*–

But the figure suspended against the sunshine was small and thin and grey, and Ali had stopped singing to stare at the empty space on the pew beside her.

"Fucking hell," she said, snatching hold of Sam's arm. Then she was yanking Sam towards the aisle and as they took off running after Caitlin, the hymn, which had briefly paused, resumed – "Thou who changest not, abide with me" – and Sam refused to look back. Leaving the congregation and the coffin behind her, she practically leapt into the light.

Despite the heat and the headstones, the relief was overwhelming, but Ali was crushing Sam's fingers and "Over there," she yelped.

Caitlin was huddled in a narrow slice of shade next to one of the churchyard's oldest chest tombs. Her head was bowed to her bended knees, her gauzy hair falling in a curtain like some freaky corpse-bride veil.

Ali yanked Sam on, giving her no choice, and with their feet crunching through the bleached grass, Sam became aware of the stillness around them. But when she looked up, she saw they weren't the only people out there.

A small group was gathered just beyond the gates. Most of them were women, women of Sam's mum's age, of Theresa's age, who seemed to be talking quietly, but there was also a younger lad and a wiry-haired little girl, and they had both turned around to stare. Sam glanced away and then quickly back, registering the boy's lanky gait and distinctive features, a raspberry birthmark on his neck. She couldn't remember his name – perhaps she had never known it – but she recognised him from the traveller site. He was the boy who sold Livy her weed.

Your fault, Sam thought irrationally, though it occurred to her that she wasn't really stoned anymore. With the lad and the little girl watching her, she felt horribly hollowly sober, and Ali, she realised, had let go of her hand. She'd slipped ahead to crouch at Caitlin's side and Sam hurried to join them.

"Hey, there," Ali was cooing, sweeping Caitlin's hair aside. "Hey, there, now..." Caitlin's face was soaked with tears.

And while Sam had no idea if Caitlin wanted her there, she felt compelled to drop to her knees and reach out too, and Caitlin grabbed her arm.

Sam thought briefly of the treehouse, of Caitlin's digging fingernails and her burning gaze, but her clutch was very different now and "I'm so sorry," she was saying, "about everything. How could I have got it all so wrong?"

Then she slumped forwards, crumpling against Sam, her tears seeping through Sam's mum's dress.

"I should have known," Caitlin said and her "known" came out a moan. "What was it about her? I thought she was the best thing that had ever happened to me. Why couldn't I see who she really was?"

"It's okay," Sam said, though it blatantly wasn't. "She had us all fooled." Another outright lie, but thankfully Ali took over.

"It wasn't your fault," she murmured, rubbing Caitlin's shoulders. "How could you have guessed? You were in love–"

"*Girls,*" said a thin, sharp voice, "that's quite enough. We don't need your drama, not today."

And – *lovely day for it* – Sam's mantra returned, though she'd thought her mind had cleared, and she needed it clearer than ever with Caitlin's mother looming over them and Caitlin's dad sidling up behind her. *What now?* Sam thought. *What's next?*

She hadn't spotted the Shaws in the church, but they must have been there. They were dressed impeccably for a funeral, Mrs Shaw sporting a black silk blouse and Mr Shaw in a solemn suit, his silver tie neatly knotted. But when he raised his hands to wipe the sweat from his brow, Mr Shaw's face undermined his outfit. As old as he was, he never usually appeared this craggy, and he looked almost as broken as his daughter.

"Kitty," Mrs Shaw said. "Get up out of the dirt."

To Sam's surprise, Caitlin obeyed immediately, but there was something odd about her movements, a kind of collapsing in reverse, and it wasn't Mrs Shaw she turned to but her father. As Sam watched him enfold her in his suited arms, she felt a strange pang, an acute sense of the space where Caitlin had been pressed against her, and *black holes*, she remembered from the treehouse. *Black holes, black holes...* It was as inescapable as her stupid "lovely day". There was so much trapped inside her head.

Abruptly, Sam realised that Caitlin was leaving, and as Mr Shaw guided her off towards the gates, she didn't look back once, but her mother lingered.

"*Girls*," Mrs Shaw repeated. She took a prim step closer, becoming a shadow, silhouetted against the sun, and now Sam was thinking about the Ouija board night again. The angry drive back to Ali's house.

"We've all had enough," Mrs Shaw said, the words slithering from her blanked-out face. "In case you hadn't noticed, a woman – a mother – is being laid to rest today, and you might think you're helping Caitlin but you're not. You girls, with your histrionics and your supposed *closeness*... It isn't helpful and it isn't natural. It would be best if you kept away."

She paused, stepping back into the light and patting her perfectly pinned hair. "I hope I've made myself clear?"

Hunched next to Sam, Ali was nodding and nodding like a dashboard dog, the movement so distracting it took Sam a moment to realise how frantically she was nodding too, and even after Mrs Shaw had turned and started to walk serenely off between the gravestones, they didn't speak. They could only watch as Mrs Shaw caught up with her family and as she swept them through the gates, the people clustered there mostly backed away.

Only the little girl and the Dealer Boy stood their ground. The boy remained statue-still until after they'd passed and then he cocked his head. He spat.

Although the lob flew too high and wide to hit the Shaws, it was shocking. Ali gasped. But as Sam blinked after its impressive glittering arc, her voice returned in an unexpected burst of laughter.

"What?" Ali said. "What is it, Sam?"

Ali's confusion just made the laughter worse. For a few more seconds, Sam struggled to speak, but then "Caitlin's mum," she spluttered. "I didn't think she could get any scarier. What a totally fucked-up bitch."

Chapter 18

Caitlin

25 December 2017

I sit with my chair wedged right up next to the bed, holding my mother's hand. I clasp it loosely as if the slightest pressure might hurt her. An absurd idea after everything that she's been through, but I can't shake free of the need to be careful. I want to do right by her, as belated as that is.

I've fetched her thickest, softest blankets and turned the lamps down low. They glow a gentle amber, but her hand remains cool and grey in mine and it's so light it might be hollow. A papier-mâché glove.

As small and vulnerable as she's seemed over the last few days, she has never looked this emptied whereas I'm too full. Weighed down with guilt and longing and still so many tears.

But haven't I cried enough? I'm exhausted and the room curled duskily around us is making me drift. If I half close my swollen eyes, I could be back in Scarlet's old nursery. During those first stunned weeks following her birth, I spent each night crouched beside her crib, just watching while she slept.

Phil thought I was waiting for her to wake up needing my milk or my warmth, but that wasn't the reason I was there. In part, I was simply spellbound, bewitched by the silk of her lashes on her curving cheeks and by her tiny starfish hands. But really my vigilance was driven by something more basic. As if my gaze was willing her on, keeping her safe, I had to watch her breathe.

In the hushed dim, with Mum, there's a similar quiet awe. A sense of the edges of things unravelling and the connections underneath. But this evening, the magic feels sad and precarious. There's so little to our love and our bodies and our boundaries. The veils are very thin.

I release Mum's hand, but only to lean closer. I brush my thumb from her fragile jaw towards the corner of her mouth. Her lips and eyelids are a deeper mauve shade now as if they've been painted or powdered.

Except Mum would never have gone for that colour. When I was little, I was fascinated by her make-up, all those sleek pots and palettes with their glamorous names: "Mediterranean Dreams" and "Sunset Gold" and "A Night Out on the Town". I especially coveted the doll-sized brushes, though I was rarely allowed to touch them. Mum's dressing table was immaculately organised, a kind of altar, and I understood what a privilege it was to share her stool and mirrors. Nobody else's mother was as beautiful. Even Theresa couldn't compare.

My hand moves up to stroke her forehead and there's something about the fine feathers at her hairline that brings Scarlet back again, and at the same time, my own childhood goes on unfolding. Mum was so proud of my hair.

She could always make it do things that I couldn't, twisting it into Heidi plaits, or a single fishtail braid, or a grown-up lady's bun. She would comb and comb until my scalp crackled, my hair fizzing from roots to tips.

"Oh, Mum," I say. "The time you spent…"

I raise my hand from her head to mine, conscious of my

practical cropped layers, and "I'll grow it out," I promise. "I'll wear it long again. I'll do it just for you."

And though my mother doesn't smile or open her eyes, she goes on doing what I'm sitting here watching for. She keeps breathing in and out.

"You're incredibly lucky," the bearded paramedic had said and his clean-shaven younger colleague nodded, but I was too shaky to respond.

The long fraught wait for the ambulance had left me frazzled and Mum seemed nonplussed. Her cocoon of blankets kept shifting with her sighs.

Her survival was probably down to sheer bloody-mindedness. While I was dragging her back to the house, her feet had started shuffling next to mine, raking new furrows through the snow. Unlike me, she'd been dressed for the weather. She was wearing sensible wellies and Dad's old camel-hair coat.

Still, the paramedics were right; we were lucky. Despite Mum's clothes, she had been soaked through, but there weren't any signs of permanent damage. There was none of the dreadful discolouration that would have meant frostbite and her heart, which I'd been so worried about, was already resuming its normal rhythm. Somehow – no one knew quite how, though it was possibly to do with the particular way her body had shut down – Mum was going to be okay.

"And you've no idea how long she was out there for?"

It was the same issue the 999 woman had fixated on and I was forced to admit all over again that I couldn't even guess and my mother wasn't telling. By the time the paramedics showed up, she was able to talk, but her replies had been minimal, selective perhaps, and when it came to that specific question, she looked straight through them.

"What were you doing, Mrs Shaw?" the younger one tried later. "What made you go outside?"

He asked it casually while rolling flat his blood-pressure cuff and ziplocking shut a yellow bag marked "Sharps". They had given Mum some sort of injection, though they assured me that it was just a precautionary thing.

I had meticulously followed the 999 woman's hypothermia advice and everything I'd done before they arrived – the undressing and the blankets and the constant flow of steaming drinks – seemed to have left the paramedics with little to do. Maybe that was why they were so hung up about Mum's wandering?

"Why did you go outside, Mrs Shaw?" the young man asked again.

Mum peered out from her swaddled blankets. Her hands kept escaping to drift up to the knitted cap I'd clamped over her head. I knew she didn't like it, she was frowning, and I assumed she wouldn't reply.

But then "She came back again," Mum muttered. Her eyes were so pale they had nearly lost their blue and she licked her chapped lips before continuing. "She keeps coming back... Only this time, *I* followed *her*. I wasn't going to let her get away."

"Who?" the man asked. "Your daughter?"

I stared down helplessly at my feet, still numb inside their thick, clean socks. Although the paramedics hadn't quite got it right, they understood who was to blame, and I couldn't argue. After all, I had turned the key. I had locked Mum out...

But when I glanced up, Mum was shaking her head, properly annoyed, and "No," she snapped, pulling off the cap. "Not her," she said. "Not Kitty. It was trees. It's always bloody trees."

The men briefly exchanged wry smiles. They had told me to expect a certain level of confusion and then appeared thrown, almost disappointed, when Mum was able to tell them not just her name and the current prime minister's but the chancellor's too, and when they'd asked the date, she had rolled her eyes. "For Christ's sake, it's Christmas Day."

"Trees, eh?" the bearded man said. "Well, no more trees, Mrs Shaw. You need to leave them out there where they're happy. You stay tucked up in the warm." And he led his partner into the hall before turning back to me. "Better let her get some rest."

Just like that, they were leaving. I had wanted – expected – them to take Mum off to hospital for scanning, or monitoring, or something. But when I scurried after them, they mumbled excuses about a major traffic accident and a worrying lack of staff. Their radios started spitting static before they reached the front door, and outside, the snow was falling again. So much endless snow.

But I couldn't let go of the idea of a clean bright ward. "Please," I begged. "I'm not a nurse."

They smiled again – those condescending smiles – and "You're better than that," the bearded man said. "You're her daughter and for now she's better off safe at home."

***

Fucking safe, I think now. *As if this house is safe.* Those paramedics didn't have a clue. They were gone before I could tell them that the "trees" that led my mother outside might be something other than a symptom of her confusion or about the extra footprints that I saw for myself. Still, I ought to take their advice and finally leave Mum to rest because as much as I'd like to stay right here counting her breaths, aren't there better ways to protect her?

Once I've tiptoed away, I head upstairs and go from room to room switching on lights and checking that every window is closed. Where the doors are locked, I rattle their handles to test them, but at the end of my rounds, I'm stopped once more in the kitchen. It isn't easy to see the garden through the mirroring panes of the patio doors, but I think that the blizzard has subsided. The night seems stilled and that stillness might be reassuring if it didn't feel so much like waiting.

Trees, I think, *Theresa...* But nothing makes sense. Barricading the house won't stop a ghost getting in, and I'm already uncertain about those tracks in the snow. With the way I seemed to float out of myself, what's to say I didn't imagine them?

Dissociation, Dad would have pronounced, a not uncommon reaction to shock and trauma, and maybe Mum and I have both gone mad? In the window, my reflection shrugs, but as I step back, it's like she's whispering. *There's only one way to know for sure.*

Before I can talk myself out of it, I hurry into the hall and wrestle on my coat and sodden boots, but I'm still thinking about Dad and his diagnoses, and when I return to the kitchen, my reflection looks hazy.

For a second, I think I can see straight through my doubled self to the counters and cabinets – and what kind of psychological symptom is that? But both sets of our hands appear solid enough grabbing the key and then the click of the latch brings us together. Together, we drift out.

It's well after dusk, but the garden is glowing, the night half made of light. The lawn's a shimmering rink and as I glide across it, I wonder where I really am. If I rubbed my eyes, would I startle awake at the kitchen table? Or maybe I never left

Mum's room? I'm asleep at her side, not dissociating but dreaming...

And though I'm not really skating but stumbling onwards, the idea feels right. Despite the cold – the air so sharp it should bring you to your senses – the world's flowing around me like a dream. A monochrome dream, with the ground so bright and the sky so black. Up ahead, beyond the radiant lawn, the trees form a wide dark wall.

It's the place where the night seems most concentrated, but as I sweep closer, it ripples and parts and I'm underneath the boughs before I know it. The carpet of snow looks moth-eaten here. The dirt pushing through is merging with the shadows, but though the shadows keep deepening, I keep going.

I easily dodge the hidden roots and slipperiest patches of ice, and I must be dreaming because I'm sure I'm on the right path. When the ancient oak appears, nudging clear of the other trees, I'm not in the least surprised. It's exactly where it's meant to be, and the ladder – a pale scar knitted against the frosted bark – is waiting for me too.

I give the ropes a quick hard tug. They're stiff and thistled with ice, but when I start to climb, the rungs hold firm. The ladder barely sways, and in this dream, the climbing feels effortless. My movements are fluid, my body young again, and as the darker block of the platform emerges from the canopy, I climb faster, the night sounds urging me on.

Besides my thin breaths, there's the creak of ropes and wood, and every now and again the slither of dislodged snow as a soft cloud powders down around me. The frozen rungs crackle and I'm momentarily distracted thinking of the static from the paramedics' radios and of my mother combing my hair...

Then the base of the platform brushes the top of my head and I'm pushing smoothly through the hatch and pulling myself upright on the decking. But though the planks feel sturdy underneath my boots, they're sheened with ice and I'm suddenly nervous. The rail is sagging and when I glance over, there's only darkness precariously veined with snow. The ground has disappeared.

And if I fell or the platform collapsed, who would call the ambulance for me? Days, perhaps weeks, could pass before anyone came out looking. But as I inch along, I lean against the treehouse's walls and they're just as robust as I remember. And anyway, haven't I been here in my sleep a hundred times or more, and dreams can't really hurt you however lucid they might seem.

As I move towards the doorway, there's the familiar sense of invisible cords tugging me impatiently on and I reach out for the sacking. But my fingers clutch at air.

Where the sack-door should be, there's a yawning hole, a well of oily black. Naturally, the sacking would have been the first thing to rot, but the thought is troubling and when I look back out at the darkly glittering canopy, a tiny feather tumbles by. It's quickly followed by another and then another, and while this new snow doesn't worry me – the flakes are fine and far apart, they might not last – as I watch them twirl, I wonder. Has it ever snowed in my dreams before?

But the invisible cords are back. They pull me on and as I slip through the doorway, the shadows surging around me are tinged with a summery scent. Roses stirring through the night.

But with my next step, the sweet tang turns foul. My mouth fills with the taste of decay and as the darkness ahead of me shifts, gathering into an impossible inevitable shape, I hear my mother's voice again, her insistent "Trees", and *no*, I want to shout – *I've never believed in ghosts* – but my throat is clogged and I'm crying.

Crying and dropping to my knees. I can't look up. I don't

want to see what's left of her. I don't want to feel her ruined hands.

But her touch on my head is like a blessing. Her fingers stroke my hair before sliding softly, so softly, down my cheeks and as they gently lift my jaw, the dead smell fades and the shadows thin. I see her face–

And how could I have got everything so wrong? Of course Theresa isn't here; there are no ghosts here. The only resemblance comes from the way that the years have changed her, but she's still as beautiful as ever and when she leans down to kiss me, there's no mistaking her warmth or her playful voice.

"Hey, Cat," she says. "Wake up."

Chapter 19

Livy

Look at me. Don't pull away, Cat. I understand it's a shock, but there's no reason to be frightened. Perhaps another kiss would help...

There. Doesn't that make things better? And you've done so well, following me like I've been following you.

I know that you've felt me watching. At the train station and outside The Hunters and right here, in the garden. I thought you might find me the night you came home, but you weren't ready, running back to your mother as soon as she called. How patient I've had to be.

But so much of my life has been about marking time, about holding on. You've no idea how hard I had to fight to hold on to you when they wanted to take everything. Stripping me open layer by layer–

It's okay, Cat. You don't need to look so sad, or scared, or guilty.

Do you feel guilty, Cat?

Are you honestly still afraid?

Don't worry, I'm not expecting any answers – not yet – and besides, I coped. I found ways to get through and it wasn't so bad once I stopped watching the clocks, once I stopped counting. There was nothing in those places worth counting anyway, not the meals with their plastic forks or the never-ending group sessions and definitely not the visiting hours when nobody ever came.

But I'll let you explain yourself later, Cat. I'm sure that you've been lonely too... And what I'm trying to say is that I'm still me despite the things they did to me. The drugs and restraints and all the rest. Hemming me in with the most haunted women, though handling the women could have been worse–

Cat, honestly! There's no need to pull that face. Don't tell me that you're jealous!

Of course it was always you and only you. You were more than a hope, you were – you are – my faith. And just look how good I got at waiting. They taught me that if nothing else.

But it's funny how coming back to Underton threw my rhythm off. Maybe it was because I could feel how close we were. Before you joined me here, I struggled with the old restlessness and I might have got reckless, I was remembering so much. There was your house and your mother to deal with. Your mother waiting for you too...

In a strange way, we've kept each other company and there were moments when I almost felt sorry for her. There was no denying how she's aged and greyed, and how alone she seemed with her nightmares. Watching her sleep, I would feel an urge to reach out and touch her. I might have told her – like I'm telling you – I'm here. I'm really here. I'm not another dream.

But look at you, Cat, you're shaking. Let me take your hands. I'll keep you warm. The years have been so cold without you. So many locked doors and lonely rooms and corridors. Every day like déjà vu.

I've sometimes wondered what your dad would have made of it all. Your dad, with his visualisations... Maybe from that very first session, when he opened the door, he was planning to shut me in.

But who knows what our fathers really thought about anything? It's pointless trying to figure out what went on in their dark little minds. The freaky rooms inside their heads–

Cat, don't cry. I understand. Thinking about our fucked-up daddies is painful, isn't it? And is that because you'll never get over what they did to me – or are those tears because you lost yours too? Cat, look at me. Keep looking.

Yes, I know your father died.

Ha! Don't pretend to be so shocked. Didn't I tell you I've been watching, and not everything is like the dreams we've shared. It's not all telepathy or magic. In the last place they put me, they gave us internet "privileges" and you made it so easy with your social media. Once I started watching, of course I couldn't stop.

I watched you smiling and eating and dancing. Growing older but even prettier. And, yes I scrolled back and saw your wedding, Cat. That glossy video.

There you were, right there, on the screen in front of me, wearing that lily of a dress and looking so lovely. Too fucking lovely, with that man at your side. That bland-faced fucking man.

But let's not talk about your marriage and what that did to me. Just as we won't discuss the child. That girl you paraded over and over, who dares to look like you–

Please, Cat. Don't cover your face. I understand how alone you have been. We've both done things we're not proud of, just trying to survive, and at some point, I'll forgive you. Maybe I need kissing better too...

There, you see, we're okay. More than okay. Can't you feel the way my heart is beating? Exactly like the first time you grabbed me, and I know you haven't forgotten that. The leaves *in your hair, and your eyes, Cat – your eyes had never been so blue.*

Not that anyone would believe it was you who started it, not even Sam and Ali – and Cat, oh, Cat, what did you think, meeting up with them again after all these years, and isn't it funny what the years have done to them? Ali dressed in those bright hippy colours but meaning business, while Sam – whatever happened to our spiky Sam? *She looks so different now. Not just fat, but lost.*

I can't tell you how hard it was seeing the three of you together at The Hunters. How badly I wanted to join you, but I'm so glad I resisted. Tempting as it was, it had to be just you and me. This time round, I wanted to do things right.

For a short while after they released me, I had to keep playing their games, but it could have been worse. When they turned me out, they gave me my medication and some measly cash and an overworked caseworker called Julie. There was a bed in a hostel, though the hostel wasn't that different from those other places. There were still too many rules and too many lonely rooms, but I didn't have to go on marking time for long. After three weeks, I ran.

I took the money and some clothes and left the rest behind. Goodbye, pills and rules and goodbye, Julie! At the first river I came to, I threw the mobile phone she'd lent me out into the dark.

And how glorious it felt, being up on that bridge, with the darkness rushing all around me. The night tasted of rain and petrol and autumn leaves, and I knew how close we were. I could smell you in those leaves, and I bet you could feel me too.

That feeling only grew stronger as I kept moving. You were there in the cars when I hitched and in the sheds and alleyways where I rested, though I never slept for long. I was so scared they would track me down before I found you. I should have remembered how easy it is to run away, to seem to disappear.

It came back to me when I reached the Valley. In the woods, I might have been nineteen again. Flitting between the trees, my heart felt fit to burst – but this time, my head felt clean. There's no one scraping away at my thoughts anymore, or crawling through my dreams. Well, nobody but you.

Back then, my mind had been so crowded and between your dad and mine, I was terrified you might get hurt. It seemed safer to stay away and I knew that Mary would take me in–

What, Cat? What is it? I expected Underton to fall for that story, but surely you never believed I spent my "missing" days holed up in the woods with the foxes–

Ha, Cat! Really? Maybe you're not so clever after all... Oh, Cat, I'm joking. Just joking! It only goes to show how messed up you were. Obviously Mary let me hide out on her farm. She'd always liked her waifs and strays and Theresa had meant such a lot to her. Her love was almost as fierce as mine.

And wasn't that one of the very worst things that Underton and the rest of the world chose not to see? How much I loved Theresa, everything I'd lost... But I never imagined losing you and that's what kept me going. I came back just for you.

Except, Cat, this morning... What happened with your mother wasn't part of any plan. No matter what she is and what she's done, that wasn't right.

I only went into the house to fetch those fucking photographs. I had seen what finding them had done to you – yes, yes, I was watching then too – and I didn't want you hurting like I'd been hurt. But I never expected your mother to come after me. She had always been so weak before. So frightened...

Anyway, it was unfortunate and I'm sorry. But perhaps it's for the best. No one can get inside our heads anymore, not our mothers, nor our fucking dead fathers. It's just you and me now, free at last.

And do you finally feel free, Cat?

Can you let the others go?

I know there's still a lot to talk about. All the years we've missed and the choices you've made, but I've promised I'll listen to your excuses–

Okay, okay, Cat! Just one more kiss...

But really, you need to stop crying. There have been enough tears, and haven't I told you I'll forgive you? And surely my kisses should have done the trick by now. Isn't it time that you woke up?

Part Two

Chapter 20

Theresa

6 August 2002, 7.03am

The garden never liked to be contained and it looked much larger than it was, stretching luxuriously in the sunshine. The foxgloves bobbed high above the stubby fence and the hydrangeas sprawled across the path. The rose bushes dipped with the weight of their blooms and Theresa loved her roses most of all.

They ranged in colour from ivory, through cream and deepening shades of pink, to a theatrical dark red. Theresa was clueless when it came to their specific varieties, but she didn't need to know their names to appreciate their fat silky faces and blowsy scents. Their perfume always made her feel so alive.

Alive, and incredibly grateful. The garden, the first she had ever owned, was endlessly rewarding, especially on a day like this. Gazing up at the wide clean sky, Theresa stretched along with her flowers, enjoying the warmth on her arms and her arching back, her head still soft with dreams.

Theresa's dreams had been kind to her lately. The usual maze-like nightmare passageways had given way to vaguer gentler rooms and the people had changed, becoming benevolent figures with soothing hands. Her body would often tingle awake as if stroked into consciousness – but then hadn't she spent much of the summer tingling, constantly ready to be touched?

Theresa smiled, lazily unravelling while the garden stirred into life around her. Several small brown birds rippled past low and fast, and then next door's holly tree erupted with chirrups and the bees seemed impatient too. They zigzagged thirstily from flower to flower and while the rest of the cul-de-sac wasn't exactly buzzing, there were some signs of human life.

A distant plane chalked through the blue, a car rumbled on a street nearby, and when the window in the bungalow opposite swung open, Theresa's smile widened at the short plump figure solidifying behind the nets. Of course, Mrs Fielding was awake.

Like Theresa, she was an early riser, though she wouldn't emerge with her scrappy terrier, Hitch, till quarter to eight. It was the same routine every morning, but as Theresa imagined them fussing about in their kitchen – Mrs Fielding clattering her crockery, Hitch whining at her heels – she wanted to shout across, *What are you waiting for? Come outside and play!*

Instead, she raised a hand to wave, but as soon as she did, the window slammed shut so decisively she almost heard the net curtains gasp.

"Okay," Theresa muttered, "be like that," and turning back to her garden, she refused to give up her grin. There was some deadheading to do and she really ought to clear the path – she'd spotted strands of bindweed sneaking out from under the hydrangeas – but bending to pick up the secateurs, her body went on distracting her.

She wasn't wearing much, just jean shorts and an old bikini top, and her cleavage and thighs were baked a satisfying brown. But maybe all that tanned skin was Mrs Fielding's problem? She probably thought that Theresa had come out in her underwear.

But despite its age, the top's orange stripes hadn't faded and it was still strung here and there with sequins. Surely, it couldn't be mistaken for a bra, unless that was exactly the type of brash beacon-like thing Mrs Fielding expected of her. Theresa wasn't stupid; she knew how people thought around here. She had grown up in a place like this.

Although the geography of the small town where she'd been raised by her grandparents was very different – its winding streets cleaving to the wind-battered coast – it had been as narrow-minded as Underton, with possibly an even narrower, meaner heart. Officially designated as "Deprived", the canning factories had shut down years before Theresa's birth and while the few remaining fishermen looked like a gang of Father Christmases from a distance, there was no denying the snarls cutting through their cotton-wool beards if you dared to get too close.

In a way, the sour energy of the place kept everything grinding depressingly on, but by the time Theresa hit puberty, the petty grievances seemed more than an outlet for the town's general resentment. The constant bickering about unruly neighbours and unpaid debts provided a distraction, a means of covering up far deeper wrongs. After her nana died and things grew unbearable with her grandfather, Theresa packed up and left, becoming yet another of the region's pitiful statistics – a teenage runaway – but at least she had made it out.

For a moment, Theresa stared blankly at the secateurs before remembering the bindweed. Dropping to a crouch on the path, she parted the hydrangea's froth, then reached underneath to tug free the nearest strands. They felt sticky, disturbingly fleshy, but ignoring her small shudder of revulsion, she pulled them taut and started clipping. Until Steve came along and changed everything, Theresa had been an expert at moving on.

She had skipped from place to place for years, loving the

largest cities best where it seemed so easy to vanish. After fleeing her hometown with her first boyfriend, Mark – who at thirty-four was scarcely a boy; he had a car and a job in sales and most importantly, a flat in Manchester – she quickly learnt to survive on her own. Within six months, Mark was over, but there were other flats to share and a series of temporary jobs, filing and cleaning and pulling countless pints, which just about kept her ticking along. And aside from the practicalities, there was always something new and different around the next corner. Mainly new and different men.

Before Steve, Theresa had seen herself as a free spirit and it was only after Liv was born that she'd started wondering about her restlessness. Perhaps all along, she had been secretly searching for a home.

Shuffling on her knees towards the next hydrangea, Theresa drew in a deep deliberate breath, sucking down the heady scent of her reddest roses. She'd never have guessed that she might find a sanctuary here, but maybe in a funny backwards way, it had something to do with coming full circle?

While Underton was about as far from the coast as it was possible to be, there were certain things that took her back. Things other than the gossip and the screaming gulls that descended on the fields at harvest time.

The huge unpredictable sky sometimes made Theresa feel like a child again, gazing out at the roiling sea. The sea was the only thing from her past that she missed and she felt a similar nostalgia exploring the hills. She liked the way the rocks broke through the rich dark earth like bones, but nothing could compare with the dappled magic of the woods.

There were moments, wandering among the trees, when a kind of shivering promise seemed to dance through the slanting light and if Theresa was lucky, she would feel it glimmering inside her too. It had something to do with casting off those nomadic years, along with all the pain and loss that followed, but it also went beyond that. As if she was part of some invisible mystical pattern or on the brink of some great revelation–

Or maybe she was just in love again.

As the thought flashed through her, Theresa became abruptly aware of the morning's deepening heat and the mess she'd made. But though her lap and the path were littered with haphazardly chopped-up weeds, the secateurs hung limply from her hand and she glanced around self-consciously. She had no idea how long she had been daydreaming.

But Mrs Fielding's nets remained disapprovingly closed and there was no one else around to witness her embarrassingly girlish blush other than the bees and the little black cat who was picking his dainty way between the roses and ferns, pretending to ignore her.

"Hi, Puss," Theresa called, but her voice sounded morning-rusty and she tried again. "Hey, Puss, you're late today."

The cat usually appeared while she was watering. He would dash under the bushes as if fleeing the spray, only to dart back seconds later to glisten among the dripping leaves. He was clearly someone's pet – well fed, with bright gold eyes and that lacquered coat – but Theresa didn't know which of her neighbours he belonged to, and she hadn't asked. She liked to pretend that the cat was secretly hers, as well as the keeper of her secrets.

"Puss," she called. "Get over here!"

But he rustled among the bushes, refusing to come any closer, and Theresa should have known better; that the cat never responded directly was part of his charm. They had their rules and games, and she considered refilling the watering can. She could give him what he wanted and there wasn't any harm in offering her garden a bonus drink. Like the bees, the plants were always thirsty, and Theresa understood that too. Often, when she thought of Rich, the saliva thickened in her mouth, and even now, when she thought she had finally admitted how wrong it all was, she felt compelled to lick her lips.

When it came to Rich, Theresa's body frequently took control, and rather than heading off to fetch the can, she found herself stroking the cool side of the secateurs across her soft brown belly, then tracing the blades lightly over her ribs. Rich also liked his rules and games. Her breath quickened at the thought.

It was easy to imagine lying back on the path and snipping free her bikini top. Hidden by the hydrangeas, she would be able to feel the sun on her breasts while picturing Rich... But before she went any further, she made herself stop – because everything had to stop. The affair couldn't last much longer.

But that wasn't down to Rich's bedroom experiments. He understood her limits and he was playful, nothing like Steve. But though Rich was a world away from anything in Theresa's marriage, he had started taking chances and she couldn't allow herself to keep being swept along.

At the beginning, they'd been cautious, mindful of the village with its many eyes and spies, but as the summer progressed, their meetings had grown riskier. Rich was staying out longer and later, and there had been the evening when they ended up down by the river where anyone might have seen.

The prospect of discovery was unbearable. Whenever Theresa came close to thinking about it, her mind shut down. She couldn't justify her behaviour to herself, let alone imagine explaining it to poor Jill, or Caitlin, or her very own Liv who had already been through so much. But so far, none of that had stopped her, and how could that be? How could she keep gambling with her daughter's feelings when Liv was her universe?

Rich had talked about compartmentalising to Theresa once.

He had been leaning over her, absently licking the hollow of her throat. "People divide," he mumbled as his mouth came away. "They divide in an attempt to conquer. Rather than facing your responsibilities, you've been building up barriers, separating into different selves."

And what about you? Theresa had thought, surprising herself with her sudden outrage. How dare she act like another innocent victim of their relationship, just as betrayed as everyone else?

If the affair came out, Liv would probably hate Rich as much as she'd despise her own selfish, immature mother. After all the hours he had spent listening to Liv, "establishing a bond of trust", she would be destroyed. But wasn't it Rich's kindness that had drawn Theresa to him in the first place? He had seemed so capable and generous, offering her hope when she'd been on the brink of giving up.

Still, Theresa didn't like to think it was Rich and not Underton that had changed things for her. That theory gave him too much power and he already had quite enough. But when she arrived at the village – the result of an impulsive council house exchange – she'd been haggard with exhaustion. For the first time in her life, her survival instincts were wearing thin and Livy clearly needed help. Steve's death had sent them reeling.

Despite their separation, Theresa had never felt free of Steve – he'd left her with more than physical scars – but his death hadn't offered the liberation that it might have. Instead, her habits of self-preservation began to verge on compulsive – even now, she kept various weapons hidden around the bungalow – and worse than that, she'd started seeing Steve, and not just in her nightmares.

"An interesting phenomenon," Rich had said. "Grief can

often seem to take on a physical shape. Unresolved anger can do the same."

But Theresa could only nod in response. There weren't the words to describe the shock that seized her every time she glimpsed a certain walk or the particular shape and tilt of a turning head. The stranger who might emerge from a crowd wearing Steve's features like a mask.

But lately, Theresa had been "seeing" Steve less and less, and she had even started to remember moments from her marriage that weren't anything to do with his rage or her bruises. Times when things had been good.

In their early days, after Steve had moved her from the North to the Midlands, they rented a surprisingly sunny flat above a tattoo parlour where they had been so recklessly in love that even her unplanned pregnancy couldn't derail them.

In Theresa's blissed-out state, the idea of a child seemed to make sense, only adding to her happiness. She would spend entire afternoons spreadeagled naked on the carpet, half dozing and half listening to the needles buzzing from the shop below, her body thrumming too.

With the baby turning inside her and the light unfolding across her skin, she'd wait for Steve to return from some carpentry job, eagerly anticipating his grin and the smell of his sweat, the sawdust powdering his hands. At the beginning, she adored his hands, and maybe that was when she first started thinking about the meaning of home. For a while, he had loved her back.

"The best of all girls," he called her, and later, including Liv, "My very best girls in all the world," and throughout everything, did he ever stop loving their daughter?

His drunken anger was never consciously directed at Liv and though the last year of Theresa's marriage remained obscured by a haze of hurt, she could clearly recall him teaching Liv how to draw. With his big body curved over hers, he would offer advice and encouragement before rewarding her with one of his little wooden animals. Because he stayed up late carving all those bears and cats and crocodiles, Theresa often fell asleep to the sound of his chisel. A rhythmic scraping as patient as breathing, rasping softly through the dark.

And though reclaiming these memories might have been another effect of Underton's strange powers, Rich had actively helped to exorcise her ghosts and for that, Theresa would be eternally grateful. Despite the terrible risks their relationship ran, a small part of her had never felt so safe, and yet–

Theresa flinched.

Somehow, as she'd been hovering uselessly beside the hydrangeas, she had cut herself. She must have been pressing the secateurs to her skin again; there was a thin line of blood above her belly button. But hastily rubbing at the tiny gathering beads, she felt more shame than pain, and when she glanced up, flustered, the cat was standing right in front of her, staring, while absently clawing at the bindweed scraps.

"I know, Puss," she said. "It's all crazy. I'm crazy. A total mess."

But the cat's sceptical gold gaze made her laugh. *Yes*, he seemed to agree, *you're quite insane*, and then Theresa wasn't just laughing at the cat but at everything. Her roses shimmered with her shaking head as if they were giggling too, and *projection*, she found herself thinking in Rich's irresistible voice – except from now on, she was determined to resist him.

She couldn't let herself be swayed, no matter how badly she was tempted, and whatever happened afterwards, she would be okay. Didn't she already have everything she needed? And looking over at her small bright bungalow where her daughter was sleeping, she was hit by the same dazzling sense she felt in the woods, as if she was a tiny shining piece of some greater puzzle, and "Home," she whispered. "Home at last."

She turned her wet gaze back to the cat, but he had slunk forwards to sniff her blood-smeared skin and though he kept nuzzling closer, she didn't push him away. The tentative flicks of his tongue made her shiver, reminding her, like the roses, of just how good it felt to be alive.

Chapter 21

Caitlin

26 December 2017

I eventually persuaded her to come inside. There was no way I was leaving her out there alone and I thought that seeing her back in the house might finally make her real. But stumbling through the patio doors, it seemed just as likely that she'd disappear, melting faster than the snow clinging to my boots.

As she followed me across the kitchen, I still couldn't fully believe in her, not even when she took my hand. Neither her touch nor the house could ground me and I felt more seventeen than thirty-two, creeping out into the hall.

Although we tiptoed past the living room, I wasn't really afraid of disturbing Mum. I had the feeling that if I opened the door and peered inside, there would be no sign of her bed or commode or walking frame. The furniture would be elegant and neatly arranged, everything restored to how it used to be.

Maybe I was feverish? Hallucinating? My teeth were chattering and I kept shuddering, but between each shiver I flushed with heat and it might have explained the spell that went on deepening as she took the lead, guiding me up the stairs and along the landing.

In my bedroom, she let go of my hand to undress and while

I fumbled with my buttons and zips, I stared dumbly at her clothes piling up on the floorboards. Her jeans joined her jacket with a dull damp thwack, but when a tattered bra landed on top of them, I turned away. I couldn't look at that bra, let alone at her. Like I didn't dare to speak.

Since entering the house, we hadn't exchanged a single word and that was so different from the way we used to giggle, racing up the stairs; by the time we reached my room, we'd be helpless. Spluttering as we peeled off our clothes, or more often each other's, before collapsing onto my narrow childhood bed–

But there she was again, slipping underneath my covers.

Pulling off my sodden socks, I could feel her gaze – she had never liked to wait – but though I climbed in obediently beside her, I still couldn't look at her. I rolled over to face the wall – and that was when everything changed. She reached out and pulled me close.

Her thigh, covering mine, felt natural and I didn't shy away from her breath on my neck or the press of her breasts. The bed remained too narrow, but somehow we still fitted. I was her little spoon once more.

But as she cradled me tighter, a stubborn part of me kept wondering when this dream would end and like a child, I pinched myself. But she went on surrounding me, keeping me safe, and it wasn't long until I closed my eyes, giving in completely to her warmth.

But perhaps the pinching worked? When I wake up, I'm cold and alone in my single bed. I peer out at the clothes strewn across the floor, but I can't see anything that belongs to her and the images washing through me feel dreamlike. A soft-focused fantasy.

I picture her lying underneath me in the shadows. I'm propped up on one elbow and she's sliding her hands across her breasts, her fingers moving in slow circles. She's watching me watch her and *Come here,* she says, or maybe just mouths, and as she pulls me down, I'm purring like the cat I used to be. So eager to lap her up...

Swallowing self-consciously, I smooth my palms across the mattress, but where the sheets are untouched by my body, they're so chilled they're clammy and I'm afraid that I'm only imagining her dusky scent. Resisting the urge to bury my face in the pillows, I sit up, shivering, and wonder if the pipes have frozen. Then I'm shaking my head; am I going crazy? Crazier? The heating's hardly my main concern.

I glance at the door, which is standing ajar, but I can't see much of the landing other than a strip of faded rose-patterned wallpaper and I can't hear anything aside from the house's ordinary creaks and groans. I clear my throat, preparing to destroy the peace.

"Livy?" I call.

But my voice is barely louder than the floorboards' muttering and I realise it's the first time since she came back – or since I dreamt her back – that I've said her name aloud.

"*Livy?*" I try again. "Livy..."

There's no reply, but after a few seconds, there's a rattle from downstairs. It's followed by the whine of an opening door – and *Mum,* I think. Then I'm scrambling out of bed and shouting now. "Wait, Mum! Stay there! I'm coming!"

There's no time to properly dress, but I snatch up my dumped coat and try to pull it on as I career along the landing. But I'm still wrangling with its damp sleeves when I hit the stairs and at first, I can't register what I'm seeing in the hall.

Not Mum emerging from the living room, but Livy on the brink–

And though she's standing, frozen, with her back to me, she's eclipsed by yet another image: a newspaper photograph. Bleached by the camera's flash, Livy's young skin is nearly as pale as the bandage on her cheek. Her eyes, in contrast, are eerily dark and I remember the dark stark headline too – *Daughter Prime Suspect in Fatal Stabbing.*

Then the flesh and blood Livy below me returns – and there's something glinting in her fist.

"No!"

I throw myself down the last four steps and slam into her, seizing her waist and yanking her backwards. Her hair whips into my face, filling my mouth, and my hands slip trying to hold onto her, but I don't let go. But she manages to squirm around to face me and for a moment, it's like we're dancing a freaky, freakily silent dance. Then I've somehow pushed her up against the wall opposite the living room, and she's looking down at me with those same black newspaper eyes, spit beading her curving lips.

And is she smiling? Surely she can't be smiling. My heart is banging furiously and I'm panting and sweating, the coat's fleecy lining sticking like dirty feathers to my skin, and though Livy is no longer struggling, I'm afraid to let her go.

I tighten my grip on her arms even as it dawns on me that she can't really have been fighting back – she's way taller and far stronger – but my grasp is clumsy and we overbalance. She falls against the door to Dad's therapy room, knocking the handle, and to my surprise, it gives. She's stumbling backwards.

"What the f–" I begin.

But *"Kitty!"* It's Mum. "Kitty-Cat!" She's shouting from her bed.

And as Livy regains her footing, her smile tightens – because yes, she's smiling, though it's an odd grim smile – and then she's running a hand through her tangled hair, her fingers jingling.

I stare at the keys she's clasping. She must have swiped Mum's set from my dressing table and my stomach lurches. Of course, she never had a knife–

"Kitty!" Mum yells again. "What's going on?"

I don't have time to think. Doing my best to avoid Livy's smile, I push her further back into the therapy room. The air spilling out is icy, but it doesn't stop me from slamming the door and shutting her in.

"Caitlin!" Mum's still calling.

And "Coming," I reply at last.

But the living room is as gloomy as ever. I move cautiously towards the bed.

"It's okay, Mum," I tell her. "You're still safe..."

But before I reach her, I hear her sigh. I think I see her shake her head.

"Christ, Kitty," she says. "Obviously I'm safe. There's no need for such a fuss. I'm perfectly fine. I had the strangest dream, that's all."

It takes me half an hour to return to the therapy room and though I'm standing outside in the exact spot where we scuffled, the fight's already another thing that feels unreal. Did I honestly grab Livy? *Did I shove her?*

So much that has happened seems impossible – the treehouse and bringing her back here and her body unfurling in my bed – and I've no idea what I've been doing either. After leaving Mum, I didn't rush back to Livy like I should have. I went upstairs to dress and then set about making Mum's breakfast.

Ignoring the puddles of melted snow, I faffed about brewing a pot of Earl Grey and when my thoughts turned to Livy – wondering how hungry she might be and just how she's survived – I shut them down and opened the fridge. After deciding to offer Mum a festive cheese plate, I dallied over her crockery and took my time digging out her favourite little antique knife. If I had known where the boiler was hidden, I might well have tried to sort out the heating too.

But when I eventually returned to the living room, Mum had fallen back to sleep and I was forced to abandon her breakfast tray along with my distraction techniques. My stalling had nothing to do with any sort of dissociative state, it was straight-up cowardice and I can't string things out any longer.

Trying to ignore the way my hands are shaking, I push open the door to the therapy room, but I feel like the floor's about to drop out from under me, sending me plummeting into the dark.

But I don't know why I was expecting darkness. With its high pale walls and massive windows, the therapy room was always filled with light and apart from one startling difference, it's exactly the same. Like stepping into a giant porcelain bowl.

So much of the room is white – the armchairs and the curtains and the sprawling sheepskin rugs – its small patches of colour seem apologetic. The couch's tawny leather is faded and the painting resting on the marble mantelpiece looks muted, though its patterns are intense.

The "artwork" is an unsuccessful O'Keefe rip-off, a crude melding of foliage with female flesh. Although this was my father's realm, Mum took charge of the décor and she probably thought the painting, along with the unrelenting pallor, provided an air of psychological gravitas.

But as wrong as the picture is, it's nothing beside the room's new addition. There's no ignoring the spirit cabinet – what the fuck is it doing in here?

I try to steady my breathing as I approach it. "Livy," I whisper, "please come out."

I'm sure she's inside – where else could she be? – but there's no answer and staring at the carvings on the cabinet's closed door, I remember how superstitious she used to be, those phases when she would toss salt over her shoulder and count magpies. Ranting on about veils and echoes and angels whenever she drank too much...

"Okay," I try. "Time's up! I've found you! Open Sesame."

But my attempt to sound playful falls flat and the cabinet's patterns are getting to me. Like the painting, the wood offers an impression of twisting vines and body parts, and before I can stop myself, I'm picturing it writhing into life. Nearby, Livy laughs.

"Please," I beg, hoping she won't insist I open the door. I don't want to touch that door. "Please, Livy, come out."

And suddenly, she's here, right here, sweeping towards me from behind the cabinet and not inside it, but that's not what makes me gasp. It's the fact that though she's smiling – the same weird taut smile she was wearing in the hallway – she's clearly been crying too and her tear-stained cheeks don't make any sense. My Livy never cried.

Then I'm taking in the rest of her – the nondescript greying jeans and sweater and the unfamiliar scar on her cheek – and it's like I don't know who she is at all.

But the thought is immediately followed by an avalanche of guilt. She looks so close to falling apart and "What's wrong?" I ask.

Livy laughs again. Of course she laughs, the question's so stupid, and yet I stupidly persist.

"Tell me, Livy, please."

She shakes her head. Her dark hair ripples, and "I..." I start, but she's turning away, leaving the air prickling between us.

"What *isn't* wrong?" She directs the question to the cabinet and then reaches out in a way I couldn't, trailing one hand across its door.

"I shouldn't be here," she says, and as her fingertips skim the handle, I want to snatch hold of her wrist – *don't open it* – though I don't know why I'm so afraid.

"It was a mistake coming back," she continues, and her tone is lighter, almost dreamy. "I thought you... but you... It isn't right. I don't belong."

And it's too late to stop her. She grips the handle and as the door swings open, my whole body tenses, terrified of whatever's about to come spilling out.

But there's just the rustle of the curtain inside and "It's *this*," I blurt, not really knowing what I'm saying. "Dad's cabinet. It's this that doesn't fit."

I can't tell if Livy's listening. She's leaning in and as she tugs at the curtain, I remember the escape hatch in the cabinet's back and wonder if she was hiding in there after all. Holed up like a magic trick.

"I don't know what Mum thought she was doing," I blunder on, "having this thing dragged down here. Maybe she's totally lost it–"

"Cat," Livy interrupts. "Don't be so dense."

Then she's turning to face me and I feel a flickering relief, and not just because she's pulled away from that thing but because of her impatience. This is the Livy I know.

"Your mother had nothing to do with it," she says. "Your dad moved it down here for our sessions."

"No," I begin automatically, trying to recall when it was before my most recent devastating visit that I last ventured into the tower room because wouldn't I have noticed that the cabinet was missing? But then the last time strikes me. It was the night I stole the Ouija board – the night Theresa died – and I'm incapable of remembering anything else.

And Livy's still talking. "He was trying it out as a therapy tool. You know what he was like."

"What?" I splutter.

But she's gone back to poking about inside and "He changed it," she tells me, "to fit his theories. Come and take a look."

Holding open the curtain, Livy steps aside, and "Don't!" I say, raising my hands instinctively. "I don't want to see–"

But it's too late to cover my eyes. There's no escape from the woman trapped inside the cabinet. She's staring back at me.

Chapter 22

Jill

6 August 2002, 11.26am

The woman in the glass was attractive, possibly striking. In the right light – and this wasn't bad – she might still be regarded as beautiful. She was certainly impeccably maintained.

With the phone cord looping her wrist, Jill leant closer to the hallway mirror, inspecting her face. Her hair was newly trimmed and styled. She gave her head a little shake.

"You don't understand!" the telephone squawked. "Something dreadful's bound to happen. The entire village is under threat."

Jill's reflection twitched, her mouth pursing, her blue eyes rolling. "Really, Helena." She smiled at herself. "How many coffees have you had this morning? I think you should calm down."

But Helena hadn't finished. "*I think*, Jilly, that you need to start taking this seriously. Don't imagine you're safe up there in those woods of yours. You know they've got a thing about the woods. It's just a matter of time until they hunt you out. Like I said, we're already overrun."

And though Helena had indeed said, it didn't stop her from circling back to the start of the call, intent on repeating every outrage, except in greater detail. Whenever she got worked up, her cut-glass accent sharpened towards a nails on a chalkboard screech and right now, she was bordering on hysterical. From her tone, you might think Underton had been invaded by a pack of marauding wolves rather than a small and probably temporary group of mildly disruptive travellers, and Jill's smile collapsed. Honestly, there were times when it felt like the whole world had gone crazy. She, alone, remained adrift in a sea of babbling idiots, the only sane swimmer left.

While Helena prattled discordantly on, describing the fires that stank of burning plastic and the rubbish spreading like graffiti onto private land, Jill held the receiver an inch further from her ear. Maybe she should just hang up?

The phone shouldn't have rung in the first place. When Richard was with a client, he was meant to unplug it, but it wasn't the first time he'd forgotten. Frankly, he was hopeless. *Perhaps the biggest idiot of them all.*

Jill's reflection gazed back at her sympathetically and though it was an effort to pull away, her new, neat hair swished reassuringly as she turned to stare across the hall.

The heavy door opposite the living room was firmly shut and even without Helena's screeching, she wouldn't have been able to hear whatever was going on inside. The therapy room's secrets were always rigorously contained and Jill wouldn't usually have lingered. Like a good respectful wife, she would have ended the conversation abruptly but politely, promising to call back soon.

But when the phone had started bleating, she was battling her way into the house with her shopping – as well as overdoing it at the butcher's, she had treated herself to a dozen red roses – and she'd answered without thinking, relieved to set down her straining bags. Then Helena had launched into her monologue and the mirror was obviously a distraction. In the salon, Jill never felt able to give her reflection the attention it deserved and several minutes must have passed before she'd remembered that Richard was working. Then, noticing the ratty black bag slung across the already overloaded coat hooks, she had realised who he was working with and decided to stay exactly where she was.

"It's getting dangerous," Helena was saying. "Completely out of hand."

If only you knew, Jill thought, her gaze shifting back to that bag – a cheap crushed velvet thing, with balding spots – and then down to the dirt tracked in across her parquet. *Just look what the cat dragged in...*

At least it would be the girl's last appointment. Jill had made that crystal clear.

"You're not to have anything to do with either one of them," she had told Richard. "Even I have my limits. Promise me no more."

And he stopped blustering to nod as if finally cowed. He had given her his word.

But knowing precisely what her husband's word was worth, Jill intended to keep a keen eye on the situation. She wasn't an idiot like the rest of the world. A casual observer might question the sanity of her choices, but she had taken control. If the marriage was to continue, it would be on her terms and the girl needed to be cut off as decisively as her mother. Richard could say whatever he liked about "professional responsibility", surely he wouldn't dare –

"Gullible," Helena was saying.

"What?" Jill snapped.

Helena laughed, a birdlike shriek. "I knew you weren't listening! Really, Jilly, I don't understand what's wrong with you lately. You need to wake up! You're as bad as those women at The Hunters. Even Maggie was wearing one of those hideous heather badges – can you imagine? Actually falling for that claptrap..."

"Claptrap?" Jill echoed, returning to the mirror and its singular sympathy, and ignoring the black bag, she leant back, allowing her head to rest against her family's coats and jackets. The folds of wool and tweed were comforting and as Helena continued, Jill felt the hallway's air gathering around her, just as soft and warm and close.

"It's worse than their opposition to the petition," Helena said. "All this talk about a curse coming to Underton, it's medieval, or simply evil. '*Darkness stirring through the light*' indeed! Obviously that crackpot farmer woman's behind it. She's always hated us, and now she's got herself a perfect little Gypsy army..."

With her spare hand, Jill rummaged absently among the coats, smoothing her palm along a satiny lining and fiddling with a leather button, and when her fidgeting happened to send the girl's bag slithering to the floor, she didn't pause to pick it up. As her fingers went on straightening sleeves and sliding in and out of pockets, the bag stayed where it belonged, dumped among the dirt.

"What a joke, Jilly – the idea that they're offering us protection! It's all part of their horrible battle plan. A blatant threat. Not even thinly veiled."

Inside Richard's blazer, Jill's hand closed into a fist. She thought she was pulling some old rubbish from his pocket, a flyer or a forgotten shopping list or parking ticket. Her husband rarely cleared up after himself, not in any way that mattered.

"Not a shred of consideration," Helena was saying. "They're out of control. Determined to ruin everything–"

Jill had had enough.

"Hel," she interrupted, fully aware of just how much her

213

friend hated the nickname. "Don't you think you should try to keep some perspective?"

"Jilly! You just don't get it..."

But Jill had given up any pretence of listening. Filled with a sudden wintry cold, she was staring down at the photograph clutched in her shaking hand.

No. It couldn't be. How could it be? How could he, after everything that he had promised?

When Jill found the other Polaroids, he had sworn to destroy them along with his foul "attachment". She wouldn't dignify the situation by calling it an affair – the slut wasn't worthy of that and nor was Richard – and Jill refused to believe this *attachment* was anything more than a nasty glitch in her life, another smear of dirt. She hadn't once doubted her ability to scour it from her home.

And of course, the photographs had only provided confirmation. Long before she'd gone rifling through Richard's supposedly untouchable study, she had suspected, and not just because of the things he had done in London. An intelligent woman always knows.

All those drinks parties with the neighbours. The way he would look at the slut, topping up her glass, and the Midsummer fête when he'd dared to set his hands on her shoulders, the pair of them gazing across the field at Caitlin and Livy as if they might all end up together one day. An obscene fake family. The sheer audacity of that.

And this outrageous last picture – what exactly did it mean? Was it something Jill's selfish stupid husband had overlooked, or some sort of vulgar farewell memento?

After she had sent him over to the slut's bungalow to put an end to it all, he'd returned within a couple of hours and seemed resigned, but what had he truly said and done? And what had he been thinking when Jill allowed him to roll her over in bed that night? *What had he been picturing?*

Whatever it meant, the photograph was vile. A sickening open wound.

The slut's skin was so flushed, it looked almost flayed, and they must have set up a timer because Richard was standing behind her, squeezing her fatty breasts, and her slutty red mouth was hanging open, laughing–

And no one laughed at Jill.

Within seconds, the cold running through her hands was replaced with a feverish heat and as it rushed to her head, Jill bent over her abandoned roses, still grasping the photo and the squealing phone. But the flowers' scent was no longer refreshing. It was cloying, *nauseating*, and for a moment, she visualised the bungalow's chaotic garden, Richard striding through the weeds.

"Are you even there?" Helena shrilled and then, as Jill plunged back to the hallway and the girl's pathetic fallen bag, "Well, don't say I didn't warn you–"

Jill let the receiver drop.

But though it clicked neatly into its cradle, the photo went on sticking to her sweaty palm and the mirror seemed suddenly untrustworthy. For a second, Jill was unable to face the glass, terrified of what she'd see.

Not a still-beautiful woman who knew her worth, but something else entirely.

"Come on, Jilly," she heard herself mutter. *Keep your chin up, keep swimming, keep staying sane,* and despite her wooziness, she could move again. She darted past the roses to snatch up the bag and then almost tore the tacky black fabric tugging open its tattered strings.

She didn't want to spend another minute dealing with that slut, but Jill wasn't the only one who would want to wipe the laughter from that slutty smirking face; how would the photo make her unhinged daughter feel? The girl was so volatile. And as Jill pushed the photo into the bag, her mind began to clear.

"There, now, Jilly," she soothed, retying the strings and hanging it carefully back up while her reflection nodded approvingly. In the mirror, her face was calm and totally her own, her eyes a cool, clean, knowing blue.

Chapter 23

Caitlin

26 December 2017

Livy's face appears beside mine and as she breaks into what looks like a genuine smile, I remember the way we used to mess about in the station's old photo booth – jostling in together, giggling and touching – and realise I've started grinning too.

There was never a woman in the cabinet. There's only us and the mirror that at some point, for some bizarre reason, Dad must have hung inside after nailing the escape hatch shut. All I saw was my own reflection and though my features are puffy with exhaustion, I can't explain the dumb horror of my reaction. How I didn't know myself.

Livy tilts her head, pressing her cheek to mine, and "Cat," she murmurs. Her dark hair curls across my blonde.

But despite the warmth in her voice, I'm aware of the house's chill and though the cabinet is empty, I don't like the way its shadows keep shifting, swilling around the mirror's frame. I take a step back, away from the cabinet and Livy. The photo-booth memories are already fading, sinking under cold grey waves.

"This thing," I say. "I don't get it. It's crazy."

When I was a kid, the cabinet was just another of Dad's

weird artefacts. It never bothered me, but finding it here is completely wrong. "What the fuck was my father thinking?"

Livy stares at me. "Oh, Cat," she says. "Your father..."

And though I can't work out her expression, I'm relieved that she's also turned away from that thing, but instead of reaching out to me, she folds her arms across her breasts.

"There's so much that I thought you knew, Cat. So much that I trusted."

It might be regret passing over her features, or disappointment, or maybe she's just trying not to shiver. She's hugging herself so tightly.

"*To unlock your truth,*" she says, "*you need to face your ghosts...* That's what your father used to tell me."

"But *this?*" I glance back at the cabinet's shadows. "What did he use it for? Some sort of crazy confession box?"

She shrugs, but "Something like that," she says. "He liked to experiment during our sessions, and he really loved his props."

She pauses to smile, that eerie version of her smile, and then "Honestly," she continues, "it surprised us both, the things that sometimes worked. But looking back, I'm not sure how ethical any of it was and his influence–"

"No. I don't understand. What exactly did he do? He didn't really make you get inside?" My mouth has filled with cold. "And what about the others? His other clients?"

For a second, I see them, Mr Brown or Mr Jones or whoever in their business suits and funny old Mrs S, with her facial tic. "I don't, I can't, believe this."

"Caitlin." Livy cuts through my rant. "What exactly do *you* believe?"

And now the way she's looking at me freezes me entirely. My outrage can't compete with the accusation in her gaze and I need to swallow before I can answer. "I... I don't know what you mean."

Without taking her eyes from mine, she reaches behind her to swing the cabinet's door shut and "You're weak," she says. "Too weak to admit what you're thinking, but I know your truth. You still believe their lies."

"I..." I try and fail again.

"You think that I killed Theresa."

Theresa, Theresa... The word echoes through my head and I'm briefly stupidly hung up on how Livy didn't choose to say "my mother" or "Mum". But she's already moving on.

"What did you want, Cat, when you came looking for me? What made you bring me back?"

"You were already here..." I'm fumbling. "I thought you needed... The treehouse was freezing–"

"Weren't you afraid that I'd attack you? You're clearly scared for Jill."

"Livy..."

But I don't know how to defend myself. When I grabbed her in the hallway, I was terrified. There's no denying it, and that fear's still not far away.

"It's you," she says, "who's killing me. You've been killing me for years."

Then she's storming past me towards the hall and I'm freed from her gaze. But something comes loose inside me.

"Wait. Livy, please wait."

Because I can't do this; I can't let her go, not after all the lonely years, and before she can escape, I fly after her and seize her shoulders, and as I feel her tense, more of last night returns.

I see her hair pooled across my pillow and the silky gleam of her skin and her softly parted mouth. I didn't dream her warmth or the way she unravelled when I touched her. And the way I gave myself up to her too, that sense of truly coming home.

But when she turns to me now, Livy's beautiful features are

219

blurred with tears, and the pain between us runs so deep. I can't stop the words that babble out of me.

"When you left, I knew nothing. I had *nothing* – and you confessed, Livy. You told them! And you'd left me all alone."

I lift my hands to my face and I'm crying like her. I blub into my palms.

"Caitlin," she says, and I feel her hands brushing mine. "I never thought that I would need to explain." She strokes her fingertips down to my wrists. "Not to you, my Cat."

Then her grip tightens. She tugs my hands away and there's no controlling my tears or anything else.

"Livy, I've got to know what really happened! You need to tell me about that night."

"Cat..."

She whispers my name as if exhaling a long sad breath and before she drops my wrists, I wonder if she can feel my hectic pulse. But she's looking past me to the cabinet, slowly licking her lips, and then her expression tightens.

"Whatever," she snaps. "Whatever makes you happy. Perhaps we should sit down?"

And even with my emotions all over the place, the irony isn't lost on me as we move over to my therapist-father's couch. Sinking into it is like re-enacting one of Livy's old games, or possibly one of his, but "Your mother," Livy says. "Maybe we should start with her–"

"What the fuck?" I jump in, and Livy's eyes flash darker. But then she carries on.

"Your mother was so angry that night. After all that stuff with Sam and Ali and the Ouija board, she completely lost it and there was no way she was going to let me stay. Your mother sent me home to mine."

I nod, but I'm gritting my teeth. Thinking back, I know what she's saying is true, but wasn't it also my fault? On any other occasion, I would have insisted on keeping her no matter what Mum said, or else I'd have sneaked her in again later. But that night – *that night* – it didn't seem worth it. I was already in a ton of trouble; Livy and I had sniggered about it while I washed the splintered glass from her palms.

"Your mum's face!" she'd said, and though I cracked up with her, I didn't do anything to stop her leaving, too afraid of Mum's next move after she returned from dropping Sam and Ali home.

"It was so strange," Livy says. "Heading away from your house and back through Underton. Maybe it was because of how stoned I was, or the Ouija board, but the woods felt bad that night. Cutting through them, they didn't seem safe like they normally did. The trees felt endless and I got it into my head that I wasn't alone. Like something was following me or waiting up ahead... I kept expecting to see it around the next pine, or bush, or turning, and the further I went, the worse that feeling got. It was terrible, like a part of me already knew... When I reached the high street, I stopped for a smoke, but I couldn't shake myself awake."

While Livy's been talking, I've shut my eyes. As if I'm the watching, waiting thing, I've been tracking her progress, imagining her frantic steps and the darkness crowding in.

But perhaps the moon was out? I don't honestly have a clue. While Livy was slipping through the woods and then past the empty shops, rummaging through her bag and shakily sparking up that one last joint, I would have been clearing my childish bedroom of dead candles and bottles and shattered glass, pointlessly trying to get rid of the evidence before my mother came back. Unless I was tucked up under my bedclothes, already lost to a drunken dreamless sleep.

"By the time I reached the cul-de-sac," Livy says, "the watching felt everywhere. I could feel it invading my body. I was scared shitless even before I stopped outside the bungalow and saw the door flung wide..."

I open my eyes. "Don't. You don't have to do this. I'm sorry. I never should have asked."

But she insists on going on, and as she does, I'm still right there. I'm following her along the overgrown path between the hushed black bushes although, just like her, I want to turn and run.

"At first," she says, "I didn't get it. The shadows looked wrong and the mat had slipped out across the front step. I kept staring at the mat."

She clears her throat, but she's far from finished, and I go on seeing what she's seeing. The mat and then the shape behind it blocking the hallway, and as she comes to a stop at the end of the path, I long to drag her back.

But there's no unseeing the rest of it now. The dripping walls and spattered ceiling, the pools already congealing around Theresa's sprawling legs.

"Her poor bare legs," Livy's saying, "and her kimono. She loved that kimono..."

But as she goes on to show me the torn sodden fabric and the torn sodden skin, none of it makes any sense. Where Theresa's breasts should be, there's only glistening meat, and when we take in her face–

"I dropped to my knees," Livy tells me, and the ground is crashing in around me too.

"My hands," she says, "went skidding through the blood and they found the knife. I don't know why I picked it up. I never should have touched it. It was wet and warm–"

"*Livy*," I override her. "Livy, please..." I'm sobbing hard now, desperate to escape.

But though I'm flooded with relief as the white walls return and the couch's leather creaks, it's clear Livy's still trapped in that place where she's been trapped for so many years. For her, that night won't ever be over.

"I knew it was hopeless," she says. "But after I threw the knife aside, I put my sticky hands on her. I tried to hold her." She sucks in a shallow breath. "But she wasn't like the knife. She was already turning cold."

"Livy..." I rub my eyes. "Oh, Livy..."

And though her face looks masked, I don't give up. I need to pull her back. "You're here with me now. I've got you."

Her shoulders are shuddering, and "It's okay," I tell her. "Just let it out."

But Livy isn't crying, she's laughing – a weird, thin, croaking laugh – and then she's mumbling darkly. "I bet you wish you'd never asked."

And though the laughter rapidly subsides, that bitterness remains.

"Are you satisfied yet? Do you believe me, Cat? Or do you have any further questions?"

"I'm sorry," I say. "I'm sorry."

I want to wrap my arms around her, to hug her tight, but she's so stiff sitting beside me, all stony bones, I can only blunder on. "At the time, I thought... and afterwards, there was so much other stuff... and you, Livy, you..."

I stop, aware of how hesitant I'm sounding, and as Livy finally meets my gaze, I know she's heard my uncertainty. If only she had let me touch her.

"Well?" she says. "What is it?" Her tone, like her gaze, is flat now, unnervingly restrained. "Is it the fact that I panicked and ran away? Is that what you're wondering about? Or is it the confession I don't even remember making, I was so messed up. Theresa had always protected me, and what had I ever done for her? Of course I felt guilty! And they all expected me to take the blame."

She turns to the windows, regarding their icy glow in the same measured way that she is studying me.

"They gave me so many drugs," she says, "like I wasn't lost enough... I should have kept running, but I felt so haunted, and I didn't imagine your dad would give up on me. I was so fucking alone."

"Sorry!" I explode. "I'm sorry!"

But though it's the only thing I seem capable of saying – I don't know what to do with my own guilt – there's still one question I can't bring up, terrified of her reaction.

But when she looks back, Livy's gaze has softened and as she rests a hand on my thigh, I find myself hoping that she'll somehow read my mind and I won't be forced to ask.

"I came back for you, Cat," she begins instead – and then the banging drowns her out.

The knocking's so loud the room seems to quake, and I realise I'm staring at the cabinet as if it's about to fly apart. But then the doorbell adds its chime and I leap to my feet and as the battering resumes, Livy's up beside me, grabbing my arm.

"Who is it?" she yells.

And in the confusion, it's like she's echoing my unspoken question. *Who was it, Livy, if it wasn't you? Who first picked up that knife?*

From the steps outside, I hear the rough caw of Bethany's voice. "Jill!" she's shouting. "Jilly!"

"Fuck," I say, shaking Livy off. "Stay here and stay quiet."

But as I push past her into the hall, the house falls still. I freeze with it, staring at the front door, but nothing happens and though I can't imagine that Mum's still sleeping, there's not a whisper from the living room. But would Bethany really give up that easily?

Fuck off, Bethany, I pray. *Please fuck off.*

But my prayers aren't answered. The banging is replaced

with the clinking of keys – I should have guessed that Mum would have given Bethany a set – and then by the door whining open and a blast of wintry air.

"For crying out loud!" Bethany wails.

She's huffing and bustling her way in, her cheeks slapped red with cold. But after wrestling free of her enormous beige faux-leather bag, she straightens her shoulders, challenging me with the full force of her glare.

"Caitlin, what the hell's going on? Where's Jilly? Why didn't you…"

She drifts to a stop, the colour draining away, and then "My God," she mutters. "For the love of God, what…"

And as Livy barges past me into the hall, Bethany raises her hands.

"What are you doing here?" she murmurs, her fingers grasping for the heather pinned to her coat collar.

"Well, what a surprise," Livy says, and as she carries smoothly on, I can tell from her tone that she's smiling.

"Bethany! It's been too long. It's so good to see your face."

Chapter 24

Richard

6 August 2002, 5pm

Feeling as lazy as the sunbathing cat he'd met outside, Richard had spent the last ten minutes trying not to fall asleep. Theresa's mattress was old but comfortably lumpy, and maybe he should just give in? It had already been an indulgent afternoon, far from the short sharp visit he'd been planning. When he arrived, he had expected to find Theresa alone, but he also caught her fresh from the shower and everything he meant to say evaporated.

Her face was flushed, her hair a wet enticing mess, and her cleavage beaded with water. Leading him through the bungalow, she left a twinkling trail of drops behind and she smelt so clean, all soap and flowers. She had been wearing nothing but her old kimono.

Within seconds, the kimono was another puddle on the floor and Richard was kissing her beautiful, damp, jewelled breasts, telling himself *for the final time* as if he'd never had that thought before.

But he couldn't bring himself to worry about his guilt or lack of it, not right now, with Theresa curled, less clean but warm beside him, bathed in golden light. The sun washed easily through her curtains, but even with the window wide open, there wasn't enough breeze to ruffle them and the air felt syrupy. But the heat, sticking Richard's body to the sheets, wasn't entirely unpleasant and giving up the fight, he closed his eyes. It was such a dozing kind of day.

The sounds from outside belonged wholly to the summer. The soft growl of a distant lawnmower and chirruping birds and every now and then, the brighter piping voice of a child playing in the cul-de-sac.

A little girl, Richard decided. She seemed to be alone, trilling away to herself, but he couldn't make out a single word and she kept interrupting her chatter with other noises. There was the light skitter of her footsteps and a series of scrapes and taps and rustlings, and he pictured her wielding a stick, poking through the bushes to annoy the bees. Except her jabbing seemed more aimless than angry. He realised she'd started to sing.

The song seemed to be genuinely wordless, a nonsensical half-hummed lullaby that drifted Richard back to his own childhood, to those nights when he'd sneaked into his mother's bed. He remembered the musty lavender scent of her pillows and her affectionate grumbling as she hauled him close. Her silly *kotenok*, too scared of the monsters in his wardrobe to stay in his room alone. *They can't get you, my kotenok. Settle down and go to sleep...*

And though Richard found himself obeying now, just as he had then, the little girl followed him into his dreams, and his old wardrobe was waiting too. He could hear the child knocking about inside it, clattering her stick against its worn oak doors, and he was holding a key. Apparently, he'd locked her in, but he couldn't recall what game they were supposed to be playing, and as the scraping sounds grew louder, he caught himself praying that the doors would hold. He hoped he had done enough.

When he dared to glance away, the chamber, or wherever they were, was solidly dark. There was no sign of any exit or anyone or anything to help him, and when he turned back, the wardrobe was shaking, rocking closer, and he could hear a voice among the other sounds. It was hard to tell if the girl was crying or laughing or singing at first, but then the scraping paused and her words grew clear:

"Daddy, my daddy, please come back."

Except the girl wasn't Caitlin. It couldn't be – Richard would never have trapped his daughter – and yet as he jerked awake, it was with the feeling that he'd made a terrible mistake.

But I can't let Livy out.

Livy. Obviously he had been dreaming of Livy. The wardrobe, the noises, even that *daddy*... It hardly took Richard's level of training to figure it out. But as undeniably strange as their latest sessions had been, he'd thought they had left him more exhilarated than disturbed.

When he first introduced the cabinet, he wondered if he was pushing his luck. The automatic writing and object work were practically standard and it wasn't only the Jungians who enjoyed their tarot cards, but the cabinet was an altogether riskier prop. But so far, the results had exceeded his expectations. Just this morning, Livy's attempts at channelling had been remarkable, the cabinet proving so much more effective than Gestalt's boring empty chair...

Richard rolled over and stretched, taking up most of the bed. Theresa must have slipped away while he was sleeping and although that was something his mother would never have done, he felt relieved. There was no need to explain jolting awake. It had been such a blatant anxiety dream.

It was probably down to the threat to his practice, the fact that his sessions would have to change. It was hardly ideal having to move out of the house and continue in secret, but there wasn't any arguing with Jill when she got like this and he'd simply have to make the best of the situation. There was no way he was about to give up his work with Livy, not after the progress that they'd made.

"Hi there, sleepyhead. Are you back in the land of the living?"

Theresa stood in the doorway, holding a glass of red wine. She was back in her kimono, but she had left its slippery belt untied and where the fabric gaped, he glimpsed the perfect curving shadows underlining her breasts and the honeyed skin of her stomach and a dusky patch of pubic hair. He wished he had the camera, wanting to capture her all over again, and when his gaze settled on the purplish marks blotting her rounded thighs – the small bruises that he'd left on her – he did nothing to hide his stare.

He knew she liked him looking, just as he knew she didn't mind him playing rough. Theresa was so easy-going, so open, and as he watched her raise the glass to her lips, he understood he wasn't ready to give her up either. Eventually he would have to concede to Jill, but not quite yet. *Just a few more final times...*

Theresa's mouth was always distracting and as she lowered the glass, it was looking even more bee-stung than usual. He'd kissed or bitten most of her lipstick off, but the wine had left a smudge at the corner of her smile like a tiny bloody thumbprint and Richard imagined pressing his own thumb there. If he wanted to, he could.

Instead, he returned her grin. "Get over here," he said.

She came bouncing across the room straight away, kicking through the clothes heaped across the floor, his discarded shirt and boxers among them. Her foot caught briefly in his belt, but she shook it free, climbing onto the bed, and as she crawled awkwardly towards him, trying not to spill the wine, the concentration in her frown was endearing. But then so much about Theresa was endearing. Her unbrushed bird's nest hair and the heavy sway of her breasts and the fact she was so eager. Already on her knees.

"Rich," she said when she reached him and before he could sit up properly, she pressed the glass to his mouth. Still smiling, he tipped back his head as if she was in charge. He had always loved their games.

But though the wine was good, it brought with it a ripple of unease. This was the second time Richard had bought a bottle on his way over, hoping it might help when it came to ending things, or telling himself that at least.

During his last visit, the wine had quickly unravelled his plans – it made Theresa's kisses taste like jam – and this afternoon, they hadn't even got round to digging out the corkscrew, and of course, a part of him had known that would happen. The part of him that hated Jill.

"Okay?" Theresa asked as he took the glass from her and then, as he downed it, "Wow, you're keen. Do you want some more?"

He shook his head, reaching for her through the kimono's folds, but though she laughed, she batted his hands away.

"Are you sure?" she said. "Perhaps I should fetch the bottle? You might want it... Rich, we need to talk."

"Oh God," he answered. "Really?"

For a few seconds, the face he pulled made her giggle again, but then her lovely swollen mouth snapped closed. She was hopping off the bed, away from him, and "Yes, really," she said. "I mean it. We can't go on like this."

"You sound like a soap opera." He was trying to maintain his teasing tone, but Theresa wasn't smiling now and he wasn't feeling too amused either. Whether she was honestly preparing to end their relationship or simply wanted reassurance, he didn't appreciate the sense of demand. He could feel the blood beating in his temples, and maybe it would be better if he just got up and left.

But she was standing next to the window and the shape of her framed in the sunlight was stunning, her figure such a contrast to his wife's. While Jill was all jutting hips and xylophone ribs – there was no escaping the bones – Theresa's body was so generous and giving, and "Come back," he blurted without thinking it through. He probably should have stopped himself.

Because if Theresa was intent on finishing things, then wasn't that for the best? After all, he couldn't keep putting it off indefinitely and wouldn't it be easier if she believed the decision was hers? But Richard couldn't get past the feeling that her body belonged to him.

And if he was being honest, it was about more than her looks, as luscious as they were. It was her kind nature, seeing him for the man he was and forgiving him as well as admiring him. It was her warmth and her willingness, the way she rarely said no.

But Theresa wasn't in any hurry to return to him now. She'd only moved to hang her head and *here come the tears*, he thought. A callous thought, which should have left him feeling guilty. Perhaps he was trying to protect himself?

But Theresa didn't start to cry; she wasn't falling apart. Instead, her quiet deepened and as Richard became freshly aware of the birds outside, he tried to refocus on their summery calls, but when their chirps gave way to a scraping sound, he sat up fast. But it was only Theresa fiddling with the ornaments on the windowsill. The little girl, with her stick, was gone.

"I can't keep pretending Jill doesn't exist," Theresa said, "and that she won't be hurt. And it's not just her. It's everyone.

All the damage we could cause... Rich, I know you understand. I'm sure you feel the same."

"Theresa," he said. "Please come here."

She stayed where she was, still fidgeting. "Jill's not stupid. She's bound to find out, and we both know you'll never leave her."

"Well," Richard began, but he couldn't go on. His head was suddenly crowded; Jill was screaming through his thoughts.

How dare you humiliate me like this? I won't have it, Richard, not again. You need to stop this thing immediately. Who do you think you are? You'd be nothing without me.

When Jill found the Polaroids, she had totally erupted, unleashing one of her rare full-blown witchy tantrums, but what was the use in reliving all that? His crying and the coldness that had consumed his wife the instant her screaming stopped.

For Christ's sake, Richard, what's wrong with you? You call yourself a man...

"I understand how tough it's going to be," Theresa was saying. "It won't be easy seeing you and not touching you, and it will be difficult avoiding each other round here. We'll need to set some rules..."

And as she went on talking, still averting her gaze, Richard changed his mind about her tears; it might have been better if she'd wept. There was a cool detachment to her voice reminiscent of Jill's and that felt incredibly wrong. Where was Theresa's usual generosity, her clumsy, helpless passion?

The first time Richard kissed her, Theresa had been weeping. She'd been distraught about Livy and so excessively grateful to him it had been impossible not to feel moved, and her vulnerability hadn't ever lost its appeal. The way she gazed up at him when he held her down...

But there was no sign of Theresa's neediness now. No gratitude. As she carried on dredging up clichés – "we have to stay strong, we mustn't give in" – Richard wondered if it was too late to reconsider her offer of the wine bottle. Getting drunk might be the best idea because she was right – they couldn't go on like *this*. It wasn't how they were supposed to be.

"There might be times when it seems impossible," Theresa said, "and it will be a struggle for Livy too–"

"Livy?"

Richard's bark surprised him and Theresa jumped, but at least she was looking over.

"Yes, Livy…" she said, but the uncertainty he knew so well had returned to her voice and her eyes were shining, growing wet at last.

He stared hard as her tears began to fall. "Theresa, what do you mean?"

"Well, Livy, she…" Theresa trailed off again. She was still holding a small dark wooden ornament, turning it over and over in her shaky hands.

"What about Livy?" he said, trying not to be distracted by her fingers, but then he recognised the thing she was clutching. He'd picked it up himself before.

It was one of the little animals that Theresa's dead ex had carved for Livy. An intricately whittled cat carrying a tiny mouse by its throat, he'd been impressed when he first saw it. Although Livy had told him about her father's gifts during their object work, Richard had expected something much more basic from this man whose brutal life and death had cast such a crudely weighted shadow. The level of craftsmanship put Richard's own amateur forays into carpentry to shame and ignited his curiosity. He'd even briefly regretted the fact that he would never have the chance to meet Steve McKinnell in the flesh.

But that had been before Livy started making such a concerted effort during their sessions, attempting to draw her father out. The occasions, like this morning, when the process left him astounded; *Transcendent*, he'd actually scribbled in his notes. Who would have imagined that what had begun as a playful experiment might offer such an effective shortcut to the subconscious? He could never have guessed its power.

"I don't think you should see Livy anymore," Theresa said. "The boundaries are already too messy. How healthy can it be?"

For a moment, Richard couldn't speak. All he could think about was his excitement, how the risks that he'd been taking were more than paying off.

"But we've come so far," he said. "She's doing so well."

"I know," Theresa answered quickly. "I know that and I'm so thankful. I can see the changes. You've helped so much. And I'm not talking about stopping her therapy altogether. There's no way I'd want that. But I was hoping you could recommend somebody else–"

"No," Richard interrupted. "There's no one else. The work we do... You've no idea what you're suggesting. You haven't got a clue."

"Rich, please." Theresa's tears were falling faster now. "Please can you stop shouting?"

And had he been shouting? He wasn't sure. He could feel the anger wedged in his throat, a dark dirty lump like charcoal, but though his mouth had filled with an acrid taste, he didn't think he'd let that bitterness out.

"I don't know," he said through gritted teeth, "how to make you understand. If you could only see what we've achieved."

But of course, that would be the last thing to convince her. Seeing her daughter in a trance state stepping so willingly into the cabinet... And if Theresa heard the things that he had heard once he'd shut the door...

Despite everything, this morning's exhilaration refused to fade. The way the voice from inside had deepened, it had felt almost like a genuine manifestation, and as Richard gazed at Theresa sobbing, its demands returned–

But Richard couldn't think about that now. He hastily shut his eyes.

But there was another door flickering behind his lids, a wardrobe door hanging open, and he was struck by the strange thought that the girl from his dream was always meant to escape. And while the child with her stick was nothing like Theresa, with every word that Theresa spoke – "I'm sorry, so sorry, I just want to make things right" – the little girl seemed to keep coming closer, slashing through the dark inside his head.

"*Theresa!*" Richard wasn't shouting now, he was roaring, and as his eyes snapped open, the wooden cat fell from her nervous hands.

"Theresa," he growled. "*Come here.*"

And to his surprise, Theresa obeyed. Although she went on weeping, she came stumbling towards him as if invisibly dragged and when she reached the bed, he pulled her shuddering body into his and held on tight. The voice from the cabinet had been astoundingly clear, and Richard would do whatever it took. He couldn't let Livy go.

Chapter 25

Caitlin

26 December 2017

In the dark, the attic doesn't feel much larger than a crawl space, which is fitting seeing as I'm down on my hands and knees, trying not to panic.

I don't think I've ever been up here before – the attic seems older and damper and somehow less stable than the rest of the house – but that's not why I'm so worked up, slick with sweat despite the chill. As I sweep the torchlight over the crumbling bricks and sloping boards, I can't stop thinking about Bethany – Bethany and Livy – and the way they cast me out.

"It'll be the pressure," Bethany had said.

The boiler hulks a few inches above my head, messily bandaged in fibrous padding. The control panel and taps are supposedly buried underneath, but all I can see is a confusion of cobwebbed wires and pipes, and when I shuffle closer, everything flickers. An icy drip hits the top of my head and slithers through my hair.

"I'm sure you can fix it," Livy had added, turning back to Bethany.

The three of us were in the kitchen by then, Bethany and I sitting at opposing ends of the table while Livy glided between us, rummaging through the cupboards and chattering as if she owned the place.

"You're looking so well, Bethany. Tea or coffee? Here, let me take your coat..."

With Mum's carer in the house, Livy had become a breezy carefree stranger. It had to be an act.

But though I was watching her closely, I couldn't work out what she was playing at and maybe Bethany didn't understand either, but she seemed more than willing to join in.

She claimed she'd come straight over after hearing about Mum's accident – of course she had heard already; there was no end to Underton's gossip – but as soon as Livy explained that my mother was going to be fine, Bethany set her worries aside. Agreeing "poor Jill must need her rest", she wasn't in any hurry to check on her and I probably shouldn't have been surprised. An old lady falling over in the snow could hardly compare with the excitement of Livy's reappearance. Such a thrilling reunion.

While Bethany and Livy plunged into their shared past, exchanging names and anecdotes, it gradually dawned on me who Bethany was, not one of the village's bus shelter bullies as I'd imagined, but a traveller child who had ended up staying. Except I wasn't altogether clear about that. There hadn't been any travellers in the village for years and I wasn't sure if Bethany had felt called back, like us, or if she'd been taken in by the Mary-woman they kept mentioning, who had apparently died around the same time as Dad.

But as Livy gushed with sympathy – she seemed genuinely saddened at the news – I was still trying to work out when she first met Bethany. It might have been during one of her regular trips to the traveller site to buy our weed, though they seemed to have bonded later while Livy was hiding out. I hadn't paid enough attention to Livy's explanation of her "missing" days; I had been too caught up in the shock of seeing her, the fact she'd come back just for me.

For me, I kept thinking it, pretending to sip my tea as they reminisced. *For me, for me,* though I could barely speak, not even when they sent me off to fix the boiler.

But though my dumb outrage followed me up here, swelling with every stair I climbed and each rickety rung of the pull-down ladder, perhaps I should be grateful? I've stopped fretting about Mum or Dad and Theresa and the night she died. I've been too busy sulking and I haven't felt like this in years.

Even during Phil's affair, I was angry rather than jealous and despite his pathetic attempts to shift his guilt onto me, I refused to blame myself. *You're the one who's been absent for most of this marriage,* he said. *You've never loved me like she does.*

But as I poke the torch about, it occurs to me that as cowardly as Phil's defence was, he might have been partially right. In the twelve long years we spent together, did I ever belong to him like I still belong to Livy? Perhaps the accusation could have gone both ways? *You never loved me like she does...*

Only there's no applying any kind of adult perspective to my childish resentment and to top off my frustration, the torch is caught in a particularly sticky nest of cobwebs. "Fuck it all," I mutter.

But while I'm shaking free the clinging strands, I'm rewarded with a sudden glimpse of dials and switches, the panel and the pressure taps materialising. But with each inch I burrow further under, the air grows danker. It smells like mouldering stone and when I manage to grasp the nearest tap, it's stiff and encrusted, but I can't give up now.

"Come on, Cat," I whisper and as I tighten my grip, I imagine returning downstairs, triumphant, to find not just the heating but the whole house restored. Bethany gone, and Livy–

Behind me, something slumps and scrapes across the boards.

I release the tap to peer over my shoulder, but the torch's beam goes zigzagging and the shadows swirl. They spill across the ladder's hatch and while I'm trying to pin them still, a different scent comes bowling over me. A blowsy tide like roses, summer cutting through the cold.

"Livy? Livy – is that you?"

I should have known that she wouldn't leave me here alone. *She came back just for me.*

But I'm still battling to steady the torch and as I wriggle out from under the boiler, my grip begins to slip.

"Hold on," I squeak, but it's too late. I've lost it.

The torch knocks against the floorboards, the attic turns black, and the new scent disappears along with everything else, engulfed once more by that stagnant smell.

I scrabble about, desperate to find my light before I'm found. Because it has struck me, with a terrible nightmare certainty, that Livy hasn't come up here but *something* has – and then the black turns white with pain.

I've cracked my scalp on the boiler's metal corner, but I don't stop searching blindly on. Through the ringing in my skull, I think I hear the sound again – and is the scraping louder? Is it closer? For a second, my head is filled with blades and claws and then my groping hands hit plastic and – *thank fuck* – I've found the torch.

Praying I haven't knocked the batteries out, I grapple for the switch and for once, my prayers are answered. And though the beam swings drunkenly across the sagging joists and floorboards, when it skims the hatch, it reveals just an ordinary empty square, and all I can hear is my thin moan of relief.

I'm definitely alone. Livy didn't come charging up here to get me, but nor did anything else. Nothing's scraping through the dark except my stupid panic. But when I turn the torchlight back towards the taps, I feel a second rush of fear.

Only this time, I don't give in to it. I force myself to breathe and to properly look until the small red pool next to the boiler starts to make sense. It's just where the pipes have been dripping. A rust-tinged puddle that really doesn't look like blood.

"Somebody's desperate," Bethany says. She's holding my phone and though it's silent, "It won't stop ringing," she tells me. "It might be an emergency."

In my absence, the house hasn't reverted. Everything is just the same, apart from the way Livy has joined Bethany at the table and I don't like how closely their chairs are tucked. Their thighs could be pressing together out of sight.

"Thanks," I say, but my phone looks trapped in Bethany's hand and I make no move to take it.

"Caitlin?" Livy says. "Don't you think you should check it out?"

I reply with a noncommittal "Um". I'm still struggling to speak and when Bethany stands and tosses the phone at me, I can't help flinching. And though I somehow manage to catch it, she isn't finished yet.

"The reception's so dodgy in here," she says. "You'd be better off outside."

Fuck you, I think, but even if I could find my voice, it wouldn't make any difference. I've been dismissed again. I turn around to leave.

But when I pass Livy's chair, she seizes my arm and for a second, as she pulls me close, I'm sure she's about to kiss me, but then she reaches up and plucks a cobweb from my hair.

"Dirty girl," she says, and Bethany laughs.

The laughter follows me into the hall, and while I spend far too long digging through the coats, searching for the warmest one, and dithering over Mum's pashmina scarves, neither one of them calls me back.

———

Despite being wrapped up tight, I'm not prepared for the cold. The wind has dropped and for now, it isn't snowing, but the air remains abrasive. It scours the breath from my lungs and the tears from my eyes, and it seems to have obliterated every scent. Even the heady aroma of the pine trees has been scrubbed away and there's something about that, combined with the quiet, that makes me feel self-conscious in a whole new way. I'm so small out here, and bumbling. I can't work out where to put my feet.

The snow blanketing the drive doesn't just look deep, it looks impenetrable. The tyre marks left by the ambulance must have filled in hours ago and apart from Bethany's practical tracks, the ground is unruffled and far brighter than the sky. The sun is low and moonlike, surrounded by dusty grey clouds that remind me of Dad's old jar of "ectoplasm" and I quickly turn away.

I don't want to think about Dad's things, about Dad at all. Forcing my tired boots into Bethany's footprints, I plunge out into the snow.

I keep going till I've passed the turning in the drive where the woods creep in. I don't want to check my phone with the house looking on, but by the time it has disappeared behind the frosted trees, my hands are numb. All that deliberating in the hall and I still forgot to grab any gloves. I'm not sure if my fingers will cooperate.

But maybe the phone doesn't matter? It seems quite possible

that Bethany made up the ringing just to get rid of me. But then the screen flashes into life and as Scarlet's face beams out at me, I cringe with guilt. There are ten missed calls in total.

My daughter rang four times yesterday, and six today, and there are countless texts and several voicemails.

"Fuck," I mutter, and then "Sorry, Scarlet. I'm so sorry."

My voice jars, too loud against the still, and I turn away from the drive and wade up the verge. But underneath the trees, the quiet is nearly as oppressive. I can't hear a single bird and there's nothing rustling through the snow-capped undergrowth. The only noise is a distant dripping coming from deeper in the woods, and though it isn't much to hang on to, I wander towards it while I listen to Scarlet's first message, left yesterday at noon.

"Merry Christmas, Mum! I hope you're having fun! Did you get any good presents? Dad's put a ton of money in my bank account... There's some fancy party going on in the bar, but I'll take my phone along..."

Clenching my jaw, I make myself press on, skipping over the voicemails until I reach the final one, left less than half an hour ago, after all those other unanswered calls and texts.

"Mummy," she begins, "are you okay?"

I turn the message off.

I can't remember the last time Scarlet called me Mummy. I've been Mum for years and the word, spoken with such unnerving calm, makes me want to cry. I stop walking and jab at the phone to call her back, like I should have right away.

But her phone just rings, a far off muffled trill, and "Please, Scarlet," I murmur, trying again. "Please pick up." And after the third attempt, I bypass my usual qualms and try Phil's number and though it sends me directly to his voicemail, I start to babble.

"Tell Scarlet I'm okay. I'm totally fine! And tell her I love her. Mummy loves her..."

But my words, echoing back at me, don't sound entirely sane and I hang up. Maybe banging my head has left me with a mild concussion? The dripping brings back the attic too and I look around, trying to work out what's making that sound, but there's no sign of anything thawing.

The trees hemming me in give nothing away. The canopy forms a rigid net overhead and between the snow-clumped branches, the sky's been reduced to small, tattered patches. A frail spattering of grubby confetti.

Preparing for dusk, the clouds have turned a sallow greyish pink and I know I ought to head back and phone Scarlet later when I'm calmer. Except I can't remember when I last felt calm, and my boots refuse to budge.

"Get it together, Cat," I mutter. "You're not trapped." But saying it aloud only draws my loneliness closer – and then my phone begins to bleat.

"Scarlet?" I blurt, nearly dropping it in my hurry to answer. "Scarlet, I'm sorry–"

"Really, Caitlin?" A grown woman's voice slurs into my ear. "You're still apologising? Whatever have you been up to now?"

"Who's this?" I begin, but then the woman laughs, and "Ali," I say. "Ali, is that you?"

"Alice," she corrects, sounding momentarily sober. "And Sam... I've got Sam here with me. We spent Christmas together, isn't that nice? Only now she's refusing to leave–"

She's interrupted by a drawling "Screw you, bitch," and I recognise Sam's laughter too.

"Please excuse my old friend," Ali resumes. "*Our* old friend. She never did learn any manners and she's been here since Christmas Eve. We're running out of supplies..."

And as she goes on to list everything that Sam's consumed – not just the wine and the whisky but the chocolate log and most of the stilton – I set off again. Maybe returning to the house will be easier if I'm not feeling quite so alone?

But the light is dimming fast and the view ahead won't settle. With the shadows crawling between the branches and bruising the snow, I remember what Livy said about the woods feeling bad and Ali's only making everything more surreal.

"Caviar," she's saying, "on toasted rye" – and why the fuck is she telling me about her canapés?

"Ali," I say, and then "*Alice*, what do you want?"

"Oh. Oh, right..."

But beyond the trees and bushes, the drive has reappeared, and it's an effort to concentrate as she drifts back.

"We heard about what happened with your mum. That she had a fall? We wanted to find out how she's doing and if things are okay? And Sam... Sam had this dream about you. It felt important to let you know."

Stumbling down the verge, I've no idea how to respond; maybe it's my turn to laugh? Shaking my head, "Who told you about Mum?" I ask.

"Jess, down at the garage," she says. "Apparently she's been seeing some paramedic guy – well, good for her. She's such a lard arse. She ought to enjoy it while it lasts..."

While Ali goes on digressing, I make it onto the drive, but though the shadows haven't taken over here yet, the snow is streaked the same dingy salmon colour as the sky and its troughs and ridges are hardening to ice. There are patches where it's glinting like shattered glass and as I follow the turning back to the house, I'm sure that every crunching step is about to send me skidding.

"Bloody hell!" Sam yells, and I realise she's grabbed Ali's phone. "How's Jill? And what about you? *How are you, Caitlin? What's going on up there?*"

For a moment, I can't reply. The house is back and in the

twilight, it seems more like something out of a fairy tale than ever. The snow layering the roof looks far softer than the snow on the ground. The chimneys are draped in pink-tinged velvet, the gutters stuffed with fur, and every window is glimmering rose-gold, and I don't know why I've come to a stop. There's no reason to feel afraid.

"Caitlin? Are you still there?"

"It's all going to be okay," I say, but even to me, my voice sounds distant. I can't break away from the house's glow.

"What do you mean?" Sam demands. "What's happening?"

And Ali pipes up in the background. "Sammy," she urges, "tell her about the dream."

"Jesus." Sam groans. "It doesn't matter."

But then, although she's sounding tired now, a wistful drunk, "I dreamt you were lost," she says. "Running up and down all these silver corridors..."

While she talks, I take a deep breath and push myself on, but the windows' gleam doesn't seem any friendlier.

"You couldn't get out," Sam says. "You couldn't find the right door–"

"Yes!" Ali interrupts. "Get to the door. Tell her what happened when she opened it."

And the front door, I realise, is opening, and at first, I'm not sure what's blocking the hallway's light and then Livy's silhouette emerges, her distinctive curves.

"There was something waiting for you," Sam says. "Something horrible."

For a moment, my thoughts threaten to drown her out. I imagine overriding her dumb drunken chatter to tell her everything. *You won't believe it! Guess who's back?* I could even lift my phone and snap a picture.

But shouldn't I know how dangerous photos can be by now, and I'm suddenly feeling paranoid. Did Sam and Ali really call to tell me about some stupid dream? I think about their Jess at the garage and about whatever gossip brought Bethany over, and perhaps the news of Livy's return has already started to spread – and what else might Sam and Ali and the rest of Underton suspect? About my mother and my father and Theresa...

It dawns on me that Livy isn't moving and I don't like the lopsided way that she's standing. She looks hung up wrong and as I close in, I see she's clutching her right arm. I start to run, or try to.

I stagger, messing up Bethany's sensible tracks, while in another world, Sam's still blathering.

"The room was worse than those corridors. The walls were smeared – and do you remember what the Ouija board said that night?"

I switch her off. I can't take any more and Livy is finally moving. But though she has lifted her head to gaze out at the drive, I don't feel seen until I've mounted the steps. Then she stiffens with a jerk, her eyes find mine, and "Thank God," she says, but she sounds so sad. "Where were you? I needed you."

And I realise why she's holding her arm so awkwardly. Her sleeve is torn and I can't stop staring at her fingers – they're covered in blood – and "Cat," she tells me. "Your mother wouldn't stop."

Chapter 26

Sam

6 August 2002, 10.40pm

Mrs Shaw's anger was another black hole, Sam thought. *A vortex.* It had already consumed their clumsy apologies and now it seemed to be sucking in their air. Shrunk into the shadows in the back of the car, Sam felt overly conscious of her breathing, and Ali, squashed in next to her, looked about to start freaking out. While Sam was trying to hold herself as small and steady as possible, Ali kept fidgeting, gnawing at her fingernails and the tips of her hair, her gaze darting between her lap and their bags in the footwell, looking anywhere but straight ahead.

Sam couldn't blame her. Mrs Shaw's driving was erratic and it had been bad enough when the trees and hedgerows came juddering close, but passing through the village was terrifying. There were too many looming streetlamps and sudden black windows – the whole night felt full of smashable glass – and each time she caught the silver flash of Mrs Shaw's eyes in the rear-view mirror, Sam wanted to disappear.

It wasn't like her to feel so cowed by a parent's disapproval, but this was no ordinary disapproval and no ordinary parent. Sam couldn't even give Ali a conspiratorial nudge, afraid the connection might set her off, bursting into tears rather than

247

giggles. Everything had got so twisted, Sam just wanted the night to end.

But despite their speed, the journey had never felt so endless and as they hurtled past the grey blurred block of the village hall, the car lurched with such violence that for a second Sam saw them spinning out of control. Ali grabbed her arm.

And though the car didn't leap or roll – they barely skimmed the kerb – as they swerved back to the centre of the road, Ali didn't let go. With her bitten nails digging into Sam's elbow, she craned her head to look out of the rear window, and "Shit," she muttered. "Did you see that? She almost got him. Sam, did you see who that was?"

But though Sam turned too, she didn't know what was more disturbing – the tall figure, suspended on the pavement next to the twitchel or the fact that Ali had dared to test the silence. Ali, who rarely disobeyed.

"Sam, that was Caitlin's dad." Ali kept her voice lowered, but as she went on, Sam wasn't sure if it was low enough.

"I thought she was going to run right into him. She must have seen him standing there–"

"Ali," Sam whispered, "please shut up," and just saying that much felt risky, but Mrs Shaw was bent over the wheel, ignoring them. Her shoulders were tensed in a way that made Sam think crazily of giant, bunched-up wings, and Ali didn't seem to care.

"What a night," she said and her eyes were glittering. More excited, Sam realised, than scared.

When Caitlin had unveiled the Ouija board – literally, it had been wrapped in a red silk cloth – all four of them were struck by a similar giddiness. Already drunk and high, Sam had felt the electricity bouncing between them when they reached out to touch the glass. Her friends were glowing in the candlelight.

She had even felt warm towards Livy. She usually resented

Livy taking charge, but this evening, Livy laughed at Sam's jokes and her teasing seemed light-hearted. For the first time in months, the group felt united. As if all four of them belonged.

Later, of course, that bond had changed. Up until tonight, Sam hadn't really believed in hysteria. She had thought it was a soap opera device for when a leading lady required a satisfying slap, or just another melodramatic symptom from one of Caitlin's lurid medical stories. Caitlin had a long list of tales about the evils of old-fashioned doctors, cadged from her dad, and more than once she'd described women having their wombs cut out, as if simply owning a female body was enough to drive you mad.

But it was difficult to tell how much Caitlin exaggerated. Mr Shaw was such an easy-going guy, Sam was pretty sure Caitlin made up the most shocking details. Many of her accounts – often involving experiments in sensory deprivation and isolation, as well as the operations – were about as convincing as Ali's claim that Mrs Shaw had tried to mow her husband down.

Although Caitlin's mum was seething, she wasn't a total psycho and besides, it hardly seemed likely the weird figure hanging about in the dark was Mr Shaw. If he had been heading back from The Hunters – and where else was there to go around here? – they would have seen him earlier along the road, not wandering this far into the village.

But while Ali had clearly been mistaken, Sam found herself thinking about how different the evening might have been if Mr Shaw had been at home. Surely he would have managed the situation better than Caitlin's mum, though perhaps he'd have sat them down for an excruciating discussion about their feelings, or perhaps he might have joined in? It still seemed crazy that the Ouija board belonged to him – unless psychiatrists were secretly the biggest nutters of all. Whatever.

He probably would have been powerless once the screams took hold.

Because it had truly been hysteria. It had bowled over them like a force of nature, a tidal wave or lava erupting, and even after Sam and Ali had broken free of the board, it wouldn't let them go.

It was like somebody else had taken over Sam's mouth and lungs and most of her mind, and that had been just as scary as the Ouija board's message. For several dark minutes, she had been terrified of losing her essential self. As if her Sam-ness was a precarious thing that could be easily cast aside.

"It wasn't just how the glass was moving," Ali said, tuning into Sam's thoughts the way she often did, only tonight Sam didn't like it. She shook free of Ali's grip, but Ali took no notice. Why wouldn't she shut up?

"It was more than the board and what it was telling us. It was the other thing – you did see the other thing?"

"See?" Sam murmured, baffled. "It was the sounds, the screaming..."

At the start, they had laughed when the glass began to move. As incredible as it seemed now, the idea that the board might honestly work had been exhilarating, and the first word the glass appeared to spell out only made their laughter worse. They had spent so much of the evening smoking and "herb" the board insisted on telling them again and again. *HERB, HERB, HERB...*

But then the message changed. Although it kept circling back, a gap appeared as the glass repeatedly forced their hands to pause, and then it started adding other letters, tentatively at first.

HER B...
HER BL...
HER BLOO...

By then, their giggles had dried up. The glass was moving

faster. It seemed more determined, and even before the panic took over, there was a sense of reality slipping. Sam stopped wondering which of her friends was cheating; it had become clear that no one was purposefully pushing the glass – that the glass was moving them.

HER BLOO...

HER BLOOD...

HER BLOOD – HER BLOOD–

It was impossible to tell who started screaming. It had come with the blood – *HER BLOOD* – and by the time the message expanded, both Sam and Ali had completely lost it.

With the next words the glass spelt out, they scrambled away from the board, but though they had broken the circle, they couldn't escape. While Caitlin and Livy kept going, they huddled on the bed with those sounds still pouring out of them. And even when Mrs Shaw came bursting through the shadows, neither the screams nor the glass would stop.

"Why couldn't we just stop?" Sam wondered aloud. "It didn't even make sense, the things that it said..."

But Ali was shaking her head. "That's not what I'm talking about. Yes, the board, the message, all of that was freaky, but it was that thing – *that thing in there with us* – that horrible shape. You can't have blocked it out."

"What?" Sam peered into Ali's eyes, but as Ali went on, she was gazing through Sam, seeing beyond her, and she didn't look excited anymore.

"The way it gathered behind Caitlin and Livy. Rising over them and opening like some kind of disgusting tree–"

"Ali," Sam snapped, "stop talking shit," and then, glancing at Caitlin's mother's rigid shoulders, she reined in her voice.

"We all went mad for a bit, but that's it. That's all. Nothing really happened. That message didn't mean anything and look at us now, we're fine... Whatever you thought you saw, Ali, it wasn't there. You were just frightened like the rest of us."

"No," Ali hissed, ignoring the jolt as they hit a pothole. "I didn't imagine it, Sam, and you know that I'd never lie, not to you."

Through the windows, in another universe, the village had fallen away. The car was surrounded by empty black fields. There weren't any sheep or cows or people, just a normal flood of normal shadows. No eager spreading shapes.

But though the idea was ludicrous, as Sam stared into the dark, something stirred inside her, a creeping nightmare-thing, and "None of it's real," she heard herself say. "Forget it, Ali. It's over." Then, forcing herself to sit up straighter, "And look, we're nearly home."

The road had forked and with the turning, Ali's sprawling farmhouse emerged ahead, its whitewashed walls floating like a cloud beyond its wide neat fence. Sam unclipped her seat belt, readying herself to run.

She had been praying that Mrs Shaw wouldn't insist on delivering her back to her own house. During the lecture Mrs Shaw had given them while herding them into her car, she had threatened to call their parents and when Sam left this afternoon, her mum was already in bed with a migraine. It was unlikely she'd wake up on her pain medication and with her dad sleeping over at the restaurant, Sam's house – a converted farm like Ali's, but with much more brutal boxy glass – would be surging with shadows. She'd never get to sleep.

But if she stayed at Ali's, they would top-to-tail under the expensive handmade patchwork quilts, talking and talking, and she could persuade Ali to give up her dumb ideas. They would retell the night until it became just another anecdote and Sam might finally feel safe. She didn't want to stay in the car a second longer than she had to. The thought of being trapped alone with Mrs Shaw was almost as scary as everything else.

As the fence parted and they rattled over the cattle grid, Ali leant forwards beside her and Sam thought she was just as eager to get away, but "Mrs Shaw," she said. "Watch out for the bunnies."

Sam gawped at her. Ali didn't appear at all intimidated and Sam hadn't a clue what was going on in her best friend's head. She didn't know if Ali had gone nuts, or if she had. The whole night was insane.

Mrs Shaw was definitely on the edge. When the security lights kicked on, she barely slowed, though Ali was right; the driveway was swarming with rabbits.

Like Watership fucking Down, Sam thought as they poured away from the car – countless little bobbing bodies illuminated in the bluish glare. She was still watching their escape, willing them on, when the car skidded to a stop, tyres crackling through the gravel.

Sam and Ali snatched up their bags, then grabbed for their doors, tumbling out together. The humidity made Sam instantly sticky – she hadn't realised how effective the car's aircon was – but as she drew in a gasping breath, even the baked manure odour from the black fields smelt good and when she slammed her door, its bang filled her with relief.

And Mrs Shaw made no attempt to call Sam back. She was sitting as still as a mannequin behind the wheel now, her face staring spookily ahead. But despite the urge to flee like the rabbits had fled, Sam didn't go running off towards the house and Ali didn't appear to be in any rush either. Having come to one of their unspoken mutual decisions, they stood side by side to watch Mrs Shaw reverse and then go careering off, raking giant claw marks through the drive.

But the rabbits were safe for now. They had melted

smoothly into the dark, and *good*, Sam thought and then *Good riddance, Mrs Shaw*, but just before the car passed through the last smoky beams of the security lights, its windows blurred. For a moment, Mrs Shaw's silhouette appeared to be joined by a larger blacker shape. A shadow figure that overtook the front passenger seat, and as Ali reached out to take Sam's hand, the shadow kept spreading, branching out.

Only that couldn't be happening – *could it?*

There was no way of telling. Within seconds, Mrs Shaw had driven out beyond the lights, and like the rabbits, the car and whatever was inside it was swallowed by the night.

Chapter 27

Caitlin

26 December 2017

Most of the cuts on Livy's arms aren't as deep as they look, just vicious little scratches, but I'm worried about her hand. Sitting beside me on the stairs, she's cupping it gingerly in her lap and I think it might need stitches. The blood is soaking into her cuff and trickling between her curled fingers and every now and then, another red penny lands between us on the step.

Drip, drip, drip... Like the woods and the boiler, except Livy's blood falls soundlessly. The house is unnaturally quiet.

After I shut the front door behind us, sealing us in, the silence felt sympathetic, but now I'm not so sure. In the few minutes that we've been sitting here, the air has grown taut and the walls seem to be straining towards us. As if the house is listening.

But I can't afford those kinds of thoughts. "Here, Livy," I say. "You need to let me see."

When she told me what happened, Livy kept her explanation succinct and mostly managed to stay calm, but as she lifts her hand, she's shaking and there's an animal alertness to her unblinking gaze. She's probably in shock.

Unless this is how Livy looks when she's frightened? I don't think I've ever seen her truly frightened. Even hunted down in those old newspaper pictures, she looked more pissed off than scared.

But those pictures never made much sense to me. They only confirmed how unreal the world had become, and as I peel back Livy's sodden cuff, I'm not certain I believe in this moment either. Because all this – her fear and her blood and the things she has told me – how can any of it be real?

"Your mother totally lost it," she said. "When Bethany went to see her, they both seemed fine. But maybe Bethany told her I was here. I thought I could trust her, but as soon as she left the house, Jill called me in. She used my name, Cat – but I shouldn't have gone to her, not without you. The minute I stepped through the door, Jill came at me." She paused to swallow. *"She was waiting with her knife."*

Across the hallway, where the air seems tightest, the living-room door isn't just shut, it's barricaded. Livy's pushed the old telephone table against it and though it's hard to separate her blood from the dark polish, there are red handprints smudging the door and the wall around it, and I don't want to imagine the effort it must have taken. The coat hooks are in disarray and the heavy blue glass bowl's lying on the floor, not shattered but cracked in two, and for too long, I find myself staring gormlessly at the nearest chunk. I need to get it together.

I know – or at least a part of me knows – that I have to face Mum whatever state she's in, but if I stay where I am for long enough, perhaps I'll wake up, or time will rewind. The table will creep back to where it's meant to be and the bowl will mend and right itself. Like magician's coins, Livy's blood will disappear.

But when I turn back to her hand, it's the same sorry mess. The worst cut runs diagonally across her palm and though the bleeding has started to slow, it opens like a toothless mouth when she spreads her fingers and then a fresh glut goes dribbling down her wrist.

"I was trying to protect my eyes," Livy says. "She was going for my face."

And I recall the newspapers again. Not just Livy's stare or her bandaged cheek, but how eagerly the reports lingered over Theresa's body, calculating and recounting every stab wound, meticulously mapping each one of them out, and a different penny blocks my throat. It tastes of tin and dirt and tears.

"Help – we need to get help," I say. "We should call someone."

But I don't reach for my phone, though it's right there where I dropped it, on the next step down, and Livy releases a strange soft laugh, following my gaze.

"Who?" she asks. "Who exactly are you thinking of calling? Do you honestly still believe someone out there's going to rescue you? Haven't you learnt by now that we can only save ourselves?"

"But look at your hand! Your poor hurt hand. It needs proper medical attention."

"Fine, Cat. Great idea. And just what do you think will happen if you call a doctor, or the hospital, or what – the police? They'll take me away again. Is that what you want? And not only me. What do you think they'll do about your mother?"

I let go of her wrist. "But Mum must be sick, really sick, to have done this and I don't know–"

"When we were young," Livy carries on, "we cleaned up our own messes. We never needed anyone else."

And she's right. She's always right. I remember washing the slivers of our broken Ouija glass from her palm and how I was more fascinated by her blood than frightened. We kept giggling and the air between us was rippling...

"We didn't believe that anything could hurt us," I say, and

Livy nods, smiling now like she was smiling then, and then she's reaching out, drawing me close, and her warmth is just the same.

"Invincible," she agrees, and as she kisses me, everything changes. My panic immediately transforms.

Forgetting about her cuts, I grab her back, greedy for the press of her breasts and the taste of her tongue because even now, in the middle of all this, I want her.

I want her touch and her skin and her irresistible mouth. I can feel the beat and rush of her body through our teasing clothes and in this moment, there is only us and our longing. The love that has never left me, filling my heart, my veins, my bones.

But then she pulls away – *please don't let me go* – and her blood is still spattering the hallway and Mum is still trapped in the living room and I can't put anything off any longer. I've been a coward for most of my life, but there's no hiding anymore.

"Okay then," I mutter, standing up.

My legs feel watery and the walls begin to wobble, but I reach out to grasp the banisters, determined to take control.

"Cat? What are you doing?"

I don't answer her directly. "Wrap your hand in your sweater. Keep it wrapped up tight. Keep holding on." And treading carefully to appease the dizziness, I step down into the hall.

But I stop in front of the table, staring past it at the living-room door. Perhaps I should call out to Mum to warn her or to reassure her. To let her know it's only me.

I cock my head, trying to listen, but I can't hear anything other than the hall's strange air heaving in and out of me – and then Livy breaks the spell.

"Wait," she says as if I'm blundering ahead. "Just take a minute. We ought to have a plan."

Her voice is a nervous whisper and glancing back at her, I do another double take. She seems so un-Livy-like huddled on the steps, and *please don't cry*, I pray. *Don't fall apart yet*. I need her strong and fearless, the way she used to be.

"Cat, we could just leave. We could get out of here, just you and me, like we should have years ago. If only we had left together that night. I thought I was protecting you, but what did I know? I was a stupid fucked-up kid, but it's different now. I've learnt so much... And don't you see, Cat? This could be our chance to be together, maybe our very last chance, and after all the life we've wasted, perhaps it's a kind of gift? We can finally set things right."

"Oh, Livy, my Livy..."

Her desperation, washing over me, is sadder than the sight of her blood. It's heartbreaking. I can't look at her wet eyes.

"You could sort Jill out later," she says, and her attempt to lighten her tone only makes my pity more painful. "After we're gone, you could call someone. If you really wanted to."

It's impossible to reply. Her need is huge and I can't begin to guess what she's imagining, the places we might go or how we'd live. She hasn't a clue what she's proposing. As well as the madness of leaving my sick mother behind, I doubt if Scarlet's even crossed her mind.

But she looks like such a vulnerable child herself, it feels cruel and pointless trying to explain, though as I turn back to the living room, I'm aware of the front door waiting too. For a moment, I picture the snow glittering through the dusk outside. The drive leading us away.

No, I tell myself, *no way, Cat*. I can't entertain Livy's madness for another second, and as I scroll back through the other things she said, "So, Bethany went in there?" I ask.

"What?" Livy sounds as surprised as I feel by my question. "I explained all that! Bethany dropped in on Jill and

259

everything seemed normal. They chatted for a while, then Bethany left."

I nod. "Okay..."

But I'm thinking about the frozen drive again and how quiet it was when I was out there, those dripping noises carrying easily through the trees. I suppose I might have missed Bethany slipping past when I strayed off into the woods, but I'd felt so completely alone – and could Livy be confused?

Confused, or deluded. Because what if Livy's version of events is warped by her shock? I glance down the hallway towards the kitchen. What if Bethany's still here?

Turning back to the living-room door, I'm acutely conscious of Livy's gaze, but now that I've started questioning her story, I can't stop. Is my frail elderly mother honestly capable of such a vicious attack? And the possibility hits me in a nauseating rush – what if Mum didn't do this? What if Livy hurt herself?

But to take a blade to your own flesh like that – surely Livy wouldn't go to such extremes however badly she might want to take me away with her–

Except what about the scar on Livy's cheek? I seize hold of the table. I need to see my mum.

But the table is heavier than it looks and as its clawed feet screech across the parquet, *"Don't,"* Livy says. "You don't understand, Cat! You can't go in."

"It's okay." Reaching for the door, I sound like a recording. I'm on repeat. "Everything's going to be okay." The handle is cold inside my fist.

"But, Cat, she's still got the knife. I couldn't take it off her."

The knife, I wonder, *who had the knife?* That eternal question – and I'm stuck again, staring at the door as if my gaze could burn right through it. But when I try to conjure up my mother, I don't see her in the living room but crumpled in the garden. Driven out into the snow.

"You don't trust me." Livy reads my thoughts. "Even now, after everything I've told you. Have you ever honestly loved me, Cat?"

My grip tightens on the handle, but I can't turn it. The cold is creeping up my arm and into my chest, and "How can you say that?" I blurt, craving her warmth. But Livy's voice is icy.

"It's hopeless, Cat. I should have known that you'd never be strong enough. The poison runs too deep."

Unable to face her, I keep focusing on the handle. The metal is sticky as well as cold, and as Livy goes on, I think about her dripping fingers and then about Sam's dream. *You couldn't find the right door... The walls were smeared...*

"It's not your fault, Cat. You were born with their poison in you. I should have got you out of here long before your dad started playing his games, but he got inside my head. He stirred everything up, and that fucking cabinet..."

I take a deep breath, but Livy hasn't finished.

"He wouldn't stop spreading his poison and Theresa was weak, even worse than you. There was no hope when it came to your father, and as for your mother – your fucking mother. I always knew she'd get what she deserved."

"Livy – *what?*" The words burst out of me. "What are you saying? *Livy, what have you done?*"

But I don't swing around to confront her. I push down hard on the handle and shove open the door. There have been altogether too many doors, and "Mum," I'm shouting, barging in. "Mum, are you okay?"

There's no reply. The dimmed room looks empty and I flash back to Christmas morning again, to the horror of finding her gone. But this evening the curtains are hanging open and though the windows have darkened, the snow offers a thin ethereal light that scuffs the edges of things. It glimmers around the bed and the coffee table and the unlit lamp standing next to Mum's chair. It outlines the hunched ridges of her shoulders.

I rush to the chair, blinking back tears, but Mum is sitting so stiff and still, and I have to switch on the lamp before I can touch her. I need to see her face.

"Look at me. Mum, please look."

Her hollowed cheeks are speckled red and there's more blood staining the bodice and sleeves of her nightgown and her hands folded in her lap.

"I'm here, Mum. Your Kitty's here." And when I reach out to her, she tilts her head – *thank fuck*. "Mum, show me where you're hurt."

But at my touch, she flinches and as her bloodied hands leap up, I see that she's clutching the antique cheese knife that I left in here. Such a harmless-looking thing.

"Mum..." My voice cracks and I sink to my knees in front of her. "You need to give that to me."

Close up, it's clear that the blood marking my mother's skin and dress doesn't belong to her, and "The knife," I try again. "Mum, give me the knife. It isn't safe."

"Safe?" she says, and her blue, blue gaze slides over me. "That's all I've ever wanted."

I lean towards her cautiously. No sudden moves. Her hands are bunched together again and though she won't open them to give up the knife, she lets me take hold of her slippery wrists and I keep my grip gentle for now, allowing her to speak.

"I always looked after you, Kitty, like I always looked after your father. Neither one of you understood the sacrifices I made. But I'm old now, Kitty-Cat, old and tired, and it's all been too much with her coming back..."

"I understand," I murmur, hardly aware of what I'm saying as I try to ease her knotted fingers apart.

"Why couldn't she have stayed where I put her?" my mother asks. "She was meant to be gone, and as for Bethany..."

"She left," I tell her, tightening my grasp by miniscule degrees, trying to work up the courage to make a grab for the knife.

"She's right here," Mum hisses, and I look up at the change in her tone. Underneath that fine red spray, her face is as pale as paper.

"She's over there," she says. "Just look."

I turn, following her gaze across the living room, and as Livy's shadow floods the doorway, "Keep back!" I shout, but it's too late.

"Bitch," my mother says. "It's all your fault. I worked so hard! Why couldn't you keep away from her? You've brought this on yourself."

Her hands slip, twisting out of mine, and as she jolts forward, the knife reappears. For a second, it's a small bright star rising between us, and then my mother's out of the chair and on top of me, knocking me back against the floor.

And there's no mistaking her intentions as she pins me down. The knife isn't falling but slicing through the air towards me, and I can't grab her arms or push her off. The best I can do is avert my face. The pain is dazzling.

Chapter 28

Jill

6 August 2002, 11.13pm

Don't think about the hurt or the anger. Just get through tonight.

Jill knew she ought to drive straight home. She had left that girl alone in the house with her daughter, and who knew what they were getting up to. Caitlin was clearly going through another rebellious phase and she couldn't see how vulnerable that made her. She had always been impressionable when it came to her friends, and that little McKinnell bitch was capable of anything. She had her mother's eyes.

Even with everything else simmering inside her, Jill kept coming back to the way that Livy had glared at her over the Ouija board. That look, almost as intense as the girls' screaming, had been packed with such hatred, but Jill would never have turned away if Caitlin hadn't distracted her. It wasn't like her to concede any battle, no matter how minor. The whole bloody night felt weighted against her.

She stepped down harder on the accelerator, trying to ignore the darkness rolling across the fields. The shadows invading the car were only making her angrier. Rubbing against her, making her sweat.

She reached out to jab at the aircon, but its acrid gusts didn't do much to ease the humidity and when she leant back, sighing at the blinking panel, the night felt closer than ever. For a few seconds, the air didn't just feel dense, it felt occupied, and though Jill managed to resist turning to double-check the back of the car where the girls had been, she found herself glancing at the passenger seat.

Of course, there was no one there. But as she tried to refocus and two more small furry bodies streaked across the road in front of her, her damp skin prickled. She couldn't shake the feeling that she was being watched.

Obviously, it was just her nerves – and the endless sodding rabbits. And after everything she'd had to put up with this evening, was it any wonder that she felt so strung out? Caitlin's friends' ridiculous theatrics, and Richard – *bloody Richard–*

All over again, she saw him emerging from the twitchel, his foolish face caught in the glare of her headlights. Another gormless rabbit, except he didn't even have the sense to run. He had just stood there on the pavement staring helplessly back at her, terrified because she knew.

Ha! She certainly knew. After nineteen years of marriage, surely such a renowned therapist as Richard Shaw couldn't still believe his wife was stupid. Even if Jill hadn't unearthed that last photograph, the fact that he'd gone AWOL tonight would have been enough to tell her everything, and had he honestly thought he could lie his way out of this one? For all his groundbreaking papers on projection and perception, Richard didn't have a clue.

Not just clueless, but a coward, Jill thought as the car crested the hill overlooking the main part of the village and the road ahead of her forked. She could see the high street's lights below her, a flickering trail that would lead her home, and the odd gold square of a cottage window, but most of Underton was safely tucked up, dreaming, the way Jill was meant to be.

The turning on the right was narrower, hedged in and as black as oil apart from the thin winking of its cat's eyes. Although it was a relatively recent construction, it was little more than a shoddy backroad, already buckled with cracks. It had clearly been flung together as carelessly as the cheap orange-brick estate that it led to. The estate where Jill's coward of a husband would have spent the evening, and where he had probably gone scurrying back to after seeing her on the high street. Returning to his slut.

Go home, Jilly, just go home, a part of her kept insisting. *You'll get through this.*

But she yanked at the wheel, snuffing out that reedy pleading voice as she turned decisively right.

The car lurched and started to judder immediately, but though Jill refused to allow the ruts to slow her down, the air went on thickening. With the hedgerows pressing in from both sides of the road, the shadows were stifling and she still couldn't entirely dismiss the sense that she might not be alone.

But for Christ's sake, what was she thinking? She was no better than her daughter and her gullible friends, conjuring up imaginary spirits. Jill was furious, that was all, and rightly so, her anger so enormous it felt solid.

Still, she knew what she was doing – she was taking charge – and while she tightened her grip on the wheel, the hedges began to retreat. They were replaced with low brick walls and the pale haze of more streetlamps, and with the next turning, she was surrounded by the ugly boxlike bungalows, an insult to their setting.

But despite the council's efforts to ruin the landscape, the countryside refused to be contained. When Jill swung the car into the lane that led to the second cul-de-sac, her headlights picked out a hawthorn half swallowing a street sign and a second later, another small frantic creature flitted blindly into the road. It seemed to throw itself directly at the car and it was too late to swerve or stop.

The bump was sickening, but softer than the jolts from the road's worst cracks and Jill didn't bother glancing back to see what she had hit. Surely, even down here, people knew better than to permit their pets to roam freely at night and so if that idiotic dashing thing had appeared more cat than rabbit-shaped then it was probably just a stray. And besides, she had arrived.

She pulled over in front of the McKinnells' bungalow and climbed straight out. She didn't stop to check her bumper for fur or blood and nor did she pause to pay her reflection any attention. She didn't need her usual rituals tonight. Her thoughts were coming hard and fast, but her mind felt sharp, and behind its tacky curtains, the bungalow was lit up like it had been waiting. As if it somehow knew.

Not that the dark would have kept Jill out. In fact, she mused, kicking open the pathetic little ornamental gate, she was deliberately bringing the darkness in.

As she marched into the garden, the anger churned through her like black water. She only slowed when the roses merged to block the path and she pushed impatiently on, shaking free of their hooking branches. The night air was even closer than she had imagined in the car and all the crowding rampant growth added an extra layer of stickiness. There were too many different unfurling leaves and straggling blossoms, too many clashing scents, and even the largest creamiest roses looked graceless. There was something greasy about the insistent glimmer of their fat pallid faces and quite frankly, it bewildered Jill how anyone could live among this mess.

But in a way, it fitted. The blowsy untamed sprawl was as gaudy and overblown as the woman who had nurtured it. The slut who, like her roses, needed cutting down to size.

At the door, Jill raised her fist and rapped twice. She waited less than thirty seconds before knocking again and then she turned to glance back past the garden's jungle to the rest of the cul-de-sac, wondering if she'd woken the neighbours. Not that she really cared.

None of the other windows were shining – every squat building looked shrouded, shut up tight – but that didn't necessarily mean the residents were sleeping; they might have been hiding. The council had originally offered the bungalows to the elderly, and it could hardly be the first time that the McKinnell household had disturbed them late at night. After everything those old people must have put up with, they probably wanted the McKinnells gone nearly as much as–

"Jill?"

She somehow managed not to jump, though she couldn't believe she'd allowed Theresa to sneak up on her. Through the gap where the door had inched open, Theresa was trying to unhook the chain and getting tangled in her dressing-gown cord, and from what Jill could see of her reddening face, her expression was just as clumsy.

But perhaps the bumbling was a performance? A means of distracting and delaying Jill while Richard made his getaway, probably escaping out the back. Jill had never expected her husband to show up at Theresa's side. As clueless as he was, he must know he was way beyond excuses by now and he'd never have the guts to give himself up. He would leave his slut to face the music by herself.

Having finally dragged the door fully open, Theresa was doing her best to smile, but her lips were trembling and Jill had always been irritated by her damp plump mouth. There was something queasily childlike about it, and it didn't help that Livy's pout was just the same.

"Jill," Theresa said again, and her husky rasp was equally annoying. "Hi, Jill. Is everything okay?"

"Okay?" Jill echoed, and her anger surged. But she kept it in check. *Not yet*, she thought.

"Is it Liv?" Theresa asked. "Is something wrong?"

Maybe she was about to give up pretending? That fake smile seemed to be unravelling and she was no longer making any effort to hold Jill's gaze, but looking past her, squinting out into the night. As she craned her plump neck, Jill continued to study her with a strange detachment and while it was true that Theresa and Livy's mouths were practically interchangeable, Jill realised she'd been wrong about their eyes.

Theresa's eyes were a more tepid brown than her daughters, lighter, and possibly wider. In fact, Theresa's face appeared generally looser. While there was a harsh kind of drama to Livy's looks, Theresa's vitality seemed muted as if something had been buried or drained away, leaving her with a vacuous type of little-girl prettiness despite her age. And wasn't that bizarre, like their roles had been reversed...

But as Theresa went on peering past Jill, she leant closer and confronted by her jiggling cleavage, Jill's detachment fell away.

Theresa's dressing gown was a cheap faux-silk oriental thing. Its scarlet fabric – of course it was scarlet – gaped on either side of its slithery belt, too flimsy to restrain the flesh inside.

All that lolling rolling flesh that Jill's husband knew so well. The hips and meaty rump that he'd clutched and the shameless extravagance of those monstrous breasts, which he would have squeezed and stroked and sucked–

Jill clamped her mouth shut against the vomit rising in her throat, but as Theresa straightened, her body blazed for a second as if caught in a camera's flash, and "Is that Liv in the car?" she was asking, daring to talk. "Did she do something? Did you have to bring her home?"

Jill turned to stare into the cul-de-sac too, but her car went on sitting silently between the garden and the dead-looking bungalows opposite. She had left the driver's door open in her hurry, but there was nothing inside except more darkness, its shadows leaking out to mingle with the night.

"Jill, where's Liv?"

Absurdly, this still seemed to be Theresa's main concern and inside Jill, the black water roiled, eager for release.

"I thought Liv was staying at yours tonight. Where is she?"

Christ, she was like a dog with a bone – *a bitch in heat* – and "That's the wrong question," Jill said. She'd had enough. "The right one, as I'm sure you're aware, is where is Richard? I know he spent the evening with you and I'm pretty certain he came running back here – but perhaps he's abandoned you again?"

"Richard?" Theresa's tone was more scratchy than husky now and her insipid brown eyes were blinking fast.

"Yes, Richard," Jill said, and as she continued, she did nothing to disguise her contempt. "My *husband*."

"Jill, I," Theresa started. "I..." She stopped. She was still blinking, her slutty face trembling, but she was also stepping surreptitiously backwards, reaching slyly for the door.

Jill placed one foot against the jamb – *oh no you don't* – and though the hallway behind Theresa appeared deserted, she took her time studying the ragtag heap of dumped coats and jackets, and while she didn't recognise anything of Richard's, she glimpsed something hard and bright among the clutter.

The knife didn't make any sense. It didn't belong there and maybe Jill should have worried, but it was glinting back at her with the silvery promise of a Christmas gift and "My husband," she repeated, and as she slipped across the threshold, she sounded composed once more.

"The man, Theresa, who you've been fucking for months. Who you won't be fucking anymore."

Chapter 29

Caitlin

26th December 2017

Together, we grapple for the knife. My shaking hands, and hers, so aged and roped with veins but still so strong – *so fucking strong* – and where did she get this strength? She's on top of me, pinning me down and I can't keep hold of her slippery wrists. Each time the blade wrenches free, she comes at me again, her aim clumsy but determined.

I've somehow managed to protect my face and throat, but it's impossible to evade every furious jab. Though the knife's small, it's sharp and she's quick, and where she first caught my shoulder, the pain's a wet, blistering heat.

"Please," I beg between my gasps, "don't, Mum, please," and then my voice is overwhelmed, ripped apart by Livy's screams.

"Bitch!" she screams as she pounces, or it might be "*witch*", and as the pressure on my breasts and stomach lifts, my mother's face floats over mine, a glaring mask. Then Livy is hauling her higher and as they stagger backwards, my mother's small grey feet escape her rucked nightgown to tread the air like water. She isn't giving up.

But Livy keeps backing away. She turns, swinging – hurling – my mother aside, and there's no more kicking, no more fighting, just a hollow crack as my mother strikes the door frame and something inside her snaps. Maybe everything snaps. Her body looks emptied, slumping to the floor, and the shadows leap and then go reeling after her, the lamp falling in her wake.

But though it crashes with far more force than her rag doll landing, the lamp refuses to die. The bulb hisses and putters behind its crumpled shade, casting strange shapes across the room and Livy, who is stumbling back to me. The light flutters teasingly over my mother so that it's hard to tell if she's lying still.

If I wanted to, I could go to her; I could touch her. But I don't want to touch her. I can no longer pretend she was simply sick or confused. I don't know what she is. In the lamp's flickering, she's barely a person, just a flimsy sack of bones.

I sit up, wincing, while Livy sinks to her knees in front of me. She cups my jaw, steadying my gaze, but her eyes, staring into mine, seem to hold no shine and their flat darkness makes me shudder.

But "Hang in there," she murmurs, and then in a reversal of our roles, "Cat, I need to see."

And as her wounded hand moves tentatively across my tender skin, her black gaze softens and I feel how close we are. After all these years, she's still my blood-pact sister and so much more. Her touch is everything.

But though she's careful helping me to my feet, the cuts on my shoulder blaze when I straighten. I can't tell how badly they're bleeding and I can't stop trembling.

"Don't worry," Livy says. "They're not too deep."

"*Don't worry?*" I rattle out a stranger's laugh. "Did you just say 'Don't worry'?"

"We'll get you cleaned up. You're going to be fine–"

"But is Mum? Is that even my mum?" I shake my head, aware I'm hardly making sense, yet somehow Livy understands.

"I'm not sure if you have ever really known who your mother is, Cat. All the different versions inside her. All the things that she's let them do."

As she speaks, the pain flares across my collarbone and I half raise one hand, but I'm too afraid to inspect the nicks and scratches cross-hatching my knuckles let alone the deepest cuts. I'm fucking terrified–

"Theresa?" I hear myself ask. "Did Mum..."

Livy glances towards the windows as if entranced by the snow-lit dusk, but when she turns back, she's nodding. Of course she's nodding, and I resist the urge to shut my eyes, though I want to disappear.

"How long have you known?"

"Oh, Cat..." Livy starts, then shrugs, and in that shrug, I see the teenager she used to be. My most protective friend, with her hard-girl shell, and as she continues, I also see what she rarely revealed to anyone else. The weight of the hurt that she carries. How wronged she has always been.

"There was something off, something cold, about Jill from the beginning," she says. "The way you could feel her hatred, it was like my dad when he was building up to one of his rages, except his temper was hot and Jill was all ice. When she made sure I saw that photograph, I should have guessed she was only getting started, that it wouldn't be enough..."

Between my cuts, my skin has stiffened into goosebumps, but I refuse to allow my gaze to settle on the rumpled shape lying next to the door while Livy murmurs on.

"I don't know which one of us she hated more, Theresa or me, but either way, she got what she wanted. She destroyed us both and she got to hold on to your father, and to you. Her precious family–"

"But, Livy," I blurt, and though I'm aware of the protest in my voice, I'm unprepared for the words that come tumbling out. "I thought you came back just for me."

Livy's features jump in surprise or confusion, but then she flashes a bemused smile and "Cat!" she says. "My poor little Cat." She reaches out with her good hand. "It's always been about you. Nobody else."

Then she's grabbing my arm and yanking me with her towards the hall and though my shoulder rebels, I let her, and I don't look down. I can't look down. I might trip over my mother, but *I can't look*. I feel too sick to think.

And somehow Livy pulls me past my mother's body and "She's gone," she says. "They're all gone, Cat. We're finally free. Can you see that yet? Do you understand? They can't stop us now. We can do what we want, go wherever we want..."

And this time, I think, I need to speak up and bring her back to earth. Remind her of my life, of Scarlet, and about everything that we'll need to deal with here first.

Except I can't imagine dealing with any of it. My mother coming at me with a knife and the truth about her. The way she's still lying crumpled on the floor behind us... The future feels as bewildering as the past and the present is impossible. For a brief but terrible moment, I can't even recall my daughter's face.

"I love you," Livy says, trying to drag me on, but as I take in the hall where the table's out of place and the walls are smeared and the stairs still scattered with red pennies, my feet grow heavy.

"I've only ever loved you, Cat."

My boot knocks aside a chunk of blue-glass bowl, but I gaze past it, distracted by the coat hooks – by the big beige bag that I hadn't noticed earlier among the tangled scarves and hoods and sleeves.

"Livy, that's Bethany's bag! I didn't think she'd left!"

Releasing my hand, Livy strides over to look.

"No," she says. "It can't be – she can't be here. I was upstairs when she went, but I heard her go. She's definitely gone. I heard her slam the door."

She gestures at the front door, with its loose hanging chain and undrawn bolts, but I'm already turning towards the kitchen, wondering again if that's where Bethany's hiding. But as I stare down the hall, it's the therapy room that draws me over. I move towards it in a daze.

"She's forgotten it, Cat, that's all, or maybe she left it on purpose. Perhaps she borrowed it..."

There's more blood marking the therapy room's door, the handprints much clearer than on the opposite wall, and never mind the bag, I don't know how I could have missed them. When I was cowering on the staircase with Livy, I was concentrated on the living room, but still, shouldn't I have learnt to open my eyes by now? The panels are streaked a sticky red and the handle looks coated. But I wouldn't have to touch the handle to open the door. All I would need to do is push.

The door is standing ajar and I've no idea how long it might have been that way either. I'm certain I shut it after Bethany arrived, while trailing behind her to the kitchen, but I'm no longer imagining Bethany hiding in the kitchen. I lean towards the bloody wood.

"Fuck, Cat," Livy says.

She's suddenly behind me, with both hands on my shoulders, and as she gabbles on – "What if she's coming back for it? We need to get out of here" – she squeezes, forgetting about my cuts. But ignoring the spiking pain, I tap on the door, just a quick light tap, but enough to send it creaking open. I peer into the dim.

"What are you doing, Cat? We've got to go."

"Wait." I reach inside, patting the wall till I've found the switch – but when the lights flare on, nothing makes sense. Livy's hands drop away and then she starts to scream.

The room seems to rise with the sound, a cone of spiralling fear, and through it, I glimpse the dark stretching mouth of the cabinet – its door wedged open by the thing inside – and I blink away. But it takes me a second to remember that the rugs are meant to be white. Everything is swirling and swimming – there's so much blood – and I hang on to the door frame, praying my knees will hold, as I force my gaze back to the cabinet.

"Bethany?" I whisper.

Her left arm is lolling free of the wood and for another moment, I'm stuck, freezing on that. Like the rugs, Bethany's sleeve is soaked crimson, but it's easier to focus on her leaking arm than the horrible angle of her head or the things that have happened to her face and neck.

She's sitting up inside the cabinet, or else been propped that way. Her hair is clumped dark, obscuring one eye. The other eye is smeared shut and so is her mouth. Her lips look smudged with jam, and Bethany's throat–

Her throat is gaping open.

The cut is a wide wet ragged noose, deep enough to slip your fingers inside. Bethany's chin juts to one side above it and below it, her torso is drenched. As if she's swapped her Christmas jumper for a polo-neck, the dumb thought strikes me. A polo-neck made of blood.

And like Livy, I'm backing away, newly stunned by my mother's strength. Bethany's throat looks sawed almost all the way through, and to have attacked her so ferociously and with that paring knife – unless she didn't use the knife?

Bethany's lap isn't only gleaming with blood. There are jagged slices of glass glued to her thighs and more glass caught in the curtain wadded to the wood behind her. The cabinet's mirror is nothing but an empty frame and maybe my mother used the broken shards after bundling Bethany inside. Or perhaps Bethany climbed in herself, trying to escape, and my mother refused to let her go...

But why? Why Bethany? I thought my mother loved her–

And you? Another voice overwhelms my thoughts. *What about you? Wasn't she meant to love her Kitty-Cat more than anyone – and look at how she came for you. You'll never understand what possessed her –* and I realise that I'm screaming too.

But though the whole house feels like its screaming, when I turn around Livy's making a different sound, an animal growl, and I don't understand what she's doing. Arms flailing, she seems to be bobbing on the spot outside the living room and then she's falling, dropping faster than my mother sagged. When she hits the floor, the parquet shakes, and *her head*, I think, *please, not her head –* and then *no, Mum, please, no–*

Because Livy isn't alone down there. My mother's on her hands and knees, hunched over Livy's sprawling legs, and what did she do? Scuttle up behind Livy to snatch her ankles out from under her, or did she stab her – has Livy been stabbed again? *Why didn't we take the knife?*

It's too late to wonder. Though Livy's been stilled – she's lying on her back, with her eyes shut, her expression scarily blank – my mother is moving fast. With one clawlike hand, she grasps hold of Livy's jeans and crawls her way onto Livy's thighs. Then her bony shoulders heave and though she slows down as she straddles Livy's hips, she doesn't turn or pause despite my screams. She keeps going, keeps crawling over Livy, her head swaying like it's strangely weighted. And the knife's right there, still glinting in her reaching hand, and the screaming needs to stop.

"*Just fucking stop,*" I yell, kicking past the halved bowl as I fly towards them, but my mother won't let Livy go and even now, as she raises the knife, I'm too scared to touch her. She's a nightmare-thing; I can't push her or grab her. I can't touch her skin. But I turn and snatch up the hunk of blue glass, and though it's heavier than I expected and my shoulder cries out, maybe I've inherited some of my mother's strength? I keep a firm grip on the bowl as I turn back around and swing it hard into her face.

For a moment, she wobbles, her blue eyes gazing up at me, her nose and mouth broken open. Between her split lips, a thick red bubble expands like a sigh, but then her pupils widen, darkening the blue, and as she falls away from Livy, collapsing onto the floor, I smell the darkness inside her too. It's the sweetly sickening scent of dying roses, but it's also iron and dust, the soaked sawdust stink of a butcher's shop, and *lie still,* I pray. *Lie still...*

But though the screaming has stopped – everything's stopped – it's a struggle just to set down the bowl. It's cracked and dripping, and I still can't bring myself to put my hands on my mother to check if she's truly gone, but then "Cat?" Livy whispers, and I've never heard her sound so small.

And I can't pretend I'm the little helpless one anymore. As I turn to her, I don't like the way that her chest is hitching, but when I reach down for her hand, she lets me pull her up and as soon as she's standing, I pull her closer. As far as I can tell, Livy's knocked head isn't bleeding, but that doesn't mean she's not concussed. She's weaving on her feet.

She buries her face in my hair and begins to cry and for a while, we stay like that, with her quaking in my arms, leaning against me, and when she cries harder, I hold her tighter, offering her my warmth. I'm afraid to let her go, sure she'll slump back to the floor without me.

But then "My best girl," she says, "are you ready now?" and she sounds almost like herself.

I don't answer, or maybe I do. I slide an arm around her waist, taking the brunt of her weight while we shuffle towards the front door. I don't glance back until Livy reluctantly releases me, fumbling for the latch.

But though my mother is lying still, completely still, behind us, as the door whines open, I imagine her twitching and wonder what will happen to her body after we have left. Will it lift its broken face and start to crawl again? With the house stirring around it, will it creep up the stairs and along the landing, and what will it find if it reaches my room? Four teenage girls, who are just as trapped, reading the same message again and again – *her blood, her blood–*

Her blood on your hands.

I open my fingers and stare at my palms. The skin is flowered red.

But "Cat," Livy says. "Come on, Cat, my best of all girls. I'm still here..."

And when I turn back to her, the door is wide open and though the dark has closed in, the snowy drive is keeping the deepest shadows at bay and Livy is right; she's here. We are both still here, and whatever happens next, with Scarlet and the rest of my life, we'll keep holding onto each other. We will somehow make things right.

"I'll never stop loving you," I tell her, lacing my sticky fingers through hers, and then I'm leading her down the steps to that shimmering path. Together, we walk out into the night.

Chapter Thirty

6th August 2002, 11.57pm

I had raced through the dark to return to you, but when I saw you opening the door, the sense of urgency faded. I slipped off the path and into the bushes, happy to keep watching for a little while longer.

As soon as you appeared, I felt a kind of peace. I knew why I'd come back and I could afford to take my time.

But unlike me, you couldn't relax. I could see the worry in your posture and in the way you kept to the light. You didn't want to be standing there, peering out into the night again. It had already been quite the evening for visitors, but at least you still had the knife and the cul-de-sac seemed quiet.

The car was gone. There were no headlights waiting slyly at the curve of the road and the bungalows opposite seemed to be sleeping. The shadows were as soft as silk and as I gathered them around me, I could feel you longing to trust in this place. You used to believe that you'd be safe here and I understood how badly you needed that illusion back, just as I could see how brave you were, coming out to look for me when, more than anything else, you wanted this night to end.

But the night had never frightened me the way it frightened

280

you. I could slink through it as silently as a fox and I had always been far stronger than you. I rarely felt alone.

Hovering on the step, you looked so lonely and weak and vulnerable. You looked exactly like what you were.

Your hair a mess and scantily dressed, you had laid yourself bare, exposing too much flesh as usual. Your skin was gleaming nearly as brightly as your searching eyes – and just what did you think you were going to do with that shiny knife? Maybe you had waved it about earlier, attempting to ward off your unwanted guests, and perhaps you thought you'd succeeded? Perhaps you finally found your voice, telling them "You have to go." Telling yourself you weren't afraid.

But even through the bushes, I could see how the knife was trembling and it made me angry. No matter what you imagined you'd achieved, you were broken inside, too desperate for love, and I couldn't watch you anymore.

Still, I paused to stretch and then cleared my throat as I wandered over. You were already scared enough.

But though I brought the scent of your beloved roses with me, your whole body stiffened when you turned. Confusion replaced the worry on your face and maybe you thought you were dreaming? The last few hours had undoubtedly felt like a nightmare. That pounding on your door...

But you once told me that your roses smelt of hope, and as I drew closer, your expression changed. Your mouth leapt into a grin and "Thank God," you said. "It's you."

Then your grin loosened, becoming a rushing laugh, but as you opened your arms, you had clearly forgotten what you were holding and how embarrassed you looked when I stopped to stare at the blade. But while I scolded you, I smiled.

"Theresa," I said, as if we were playing that game where I was the mother. "You should be more careful. You'll only hurt yourself."

You nodded. "I don't know what I'm doing," you admitted and despite your best efforts, you couldn't hide the crack in your voice. "I'm sorry," you said. "I'm sorry."

And for a moment, I almost felt sorry too, but then "You're right," you went on, "I can't be trusted, Liv," and you placed the knife into my hands.

THE END

Acknowledgements

Firstly, a giant thank you to Giselle Leeb, excellent writer and great friend, for her keen eye and her advice while going through an entire early draft, and for generally sharing all the writerly ups and downs, among so many other things. And thank you to the other writers and good friends who have taken the time to offer kindness and feedback on extracts along the way, especially Roberta Dewa, Josie Barrett, Ian Collinson and Nicholas Royle.

For further writing encouragement and so much more, huge thanks to Anstey Harris and all my wonderful Halloween friends and to the joyful, essential Moniack Maniacs – can't wait to see you all again soon! And thank you to Nottingham's writing community for the ongoing support, to Ross Bradshaw at fabulous Five Leaves Bookshop, Rory Waterman, Alex Davis and to so many others.

I'm enormously grateful to Betsy Reavley for taking a chance on this novel and to Tara Lyons and the rest of the dedicated team at Bloodhound Books for treating it with such care. Particular thanks to Ian Skewis for his enthusiasm as well as his attention; the editing process has been a pleasure.

All in all, there are too many lovely people to thank, but a special last shout out goes to Film Club for the cinema trips and pizza, but mostly for the chats, and to my partner in cocktail crime, Paula Rawsthorne.

And of course, massive thanks to Catherine, Mel and Lola – love you with all my heart.

About the Author

Megan Taylor is the author of four dark novels, How We Were Lost, The Dawning, The Lives of Ghosts, and We Wait. Her short stories have appeared in numerous publications as well as in her collection, The Woman Under the Ground. She is currently working on a second collection alongside writing her next twisted novel.

Megan lives in Nottingham, where she has been running fiction workshops and courses for over ten years. For more information, please visit www.megantaylor.info or find her on Twitter @meganjstaylor and Instagram @megantaylorauthor.

A note from the publisher

Thank you for reading this book. If you enjoyed it please do consider leaving a review on Amazon to help others find it too.

We hate typos. All of our books have been rigorously edited and proofread, but sometimes mistakes do slip through. If you have spotted a typo, please do let us know and we can get it amended within hours.

info@bloodhoundbooks.com

Milton Keynes UK
Ingram Content Group UK Ltd.
UKHW021509160824
447011UK00004B/71